WILD VIOLETS

MOUNTAIN WIVES SERIES

BOOK 3

J.R.BIERY

Cover created with Gimp 2, using a background of a free commercial use licensed image from Bing and altered small images from Wikipedia and Pixabay.

ABOUT THIS BOOK

Charlotte Stewart is the daughter of the president of Newton Seminary College in Boston. Although her mother wants her to learn the graces and skills needed to be a housewife and hostess, Charlotte wants to learn everything that the young men do at her father's school. She has only one burning desire, to teach others and be an old maid. Finally, she convinces them both to give her a chance.

William Delmar Monroe has graduated with honors and passed the bar exam. As his father promised, he now wants time off to pursue his love for music. Heir to a famous political dynasty, Delmar's freedom is hard won and he turns to his Great Uncle William for lessons in fiddling and making instruments.

Both Charlotte and Delmar find themselves in the small mountain community of Kyles Ford, Charlotte as the new schoolmarm and Delmar searching for the big hardwoods he needs to make his own special instruments. It takes being thrown together repeatedly for the stubborn, unfriendly couple to find true love.

DISCLAIMER

This book is a work of fiction. Names, characters, and incidents are products of the author's imagination. Any reference to actual events or persons, living or dead, as portrayed herein are either the product of the author's imagination or are used fictionally.

DEDICATION

Dedicated to Jerry, my darling husband for forty-eight years. Also, to Cookeville Creative Writers' Association members who helped me aim for publication. Special thanks to those few dear souls who have loved my other work and encouraged me to write closer to my home and heart, especially JoAnn for requesting an Appalachian series. Thrilled at the helpful contributions of my Beta readers, JoAnn B., Cindy N., Jenette G., Judy E., and Dolly M, Linda L.. Thank you ladies for your contribution to this book.

CHAPTER ONE

Charlotte Stewart – Boston, 1848

Charlotte sat upright in horror, the pages full of neatly penned prose dropping like leaves around her. At the noise from the kitchen of her sister's squabbling, she stared at the sun spilling through the lace curtains around her. Rubbing her eyes, she scrambled up and dressed quickly, barely taking time to brush back her heavy black hair to tie with a purple ribbon.

She squatted and searched until she had all ten sheets of paper, neatly ordered and secured with a brass fastener at the top corner. She was dead. Dead.

Elizabeth screamed her name. Charlotte raced down the steps, shoving the papers in her draw-string bag as she sailed past them all. Mama nabbed her beside the back door. "Halt, let me look at you."

Charlotte tugged the top band of her blouse over the dark skirt and tried to breathe instead of scream. "I'd look better if my new clothes would ever arrive. I'm too old to be walking around with the ruffles on my pantaloons showing."

"Any day now," Mama said. "Alright, but you need to wait on your sisters to walk with you to Miss Lynn's. Sit down and eat." Mama lifted a small metal container and rolled her eyes. "That man."

Grabbing the lunch pail, Charlotte kissed her mother's cheek. "I have to run by Newton. Papa forgot his papers, too."

"Charlotte, did you steal Papa's speech again," but Mama was talking to empty air. Angrily, she closed the door on the cool morning air. The three girls at the table all began to complain about Charlotte again.

Charlotte stood outside the imposing four story brick front of the Newton Seminary College, trying to catch her breath and let her color return to normal after the mile long run to the campus. With any luck, she was on time, and could slip up the stairs to Papa's office to return his notes to his briefcase.

Charles Newcomb whistled as he walked up the walkway to stop beside her. Leaning over, he made her face flame red again as he whispered, "It's snowing down south."

Trying to be discreet, she tugged at the loose waist of the pantaloons and made sure the blouse covered where she had rolled them up. As she slipped past him, her steps hurried but short, she whispered, "Thanks, brother Charles."

He chuckled and she wished she were close enough to give him an elbow in the ribs. If the young man were really her brother, she would have knocked him silly. Instead, he was one of Papa's pet students. Papa liked to have them over for Sunday dinners to continue to ask more questions about the lectures of the previous week. Her sisters hated the young men, calling them 'chowder heads,' but Charlotte liked them. She always managed to hang around the study, occasionally slipping in to hear and learn more. She knew how they felt, always hungry to hear Papa talk.

Charlotte was glad when Charles still stood at the door, holding it open for her. She looked up the wide marble stairs to her right, but Charles shook his head at her. "The Reverend just went in there."

Charlotte stood frozen, taking a deep breath to calm her fears. Charles released the door and moved her over to the side, where she stood on tiptoe peering into the huge auditorium. Over his shoulder she saw and heard Papa at the podium and guiltily slipped inside, past the shocked ministry students and up to the podium beside him.

"Here, Papa, you forgot your lunch and your speech notes."

He glared at her and pointed sternly to the chair behind the lectern. Charlotte stared wistfully at the door, now packed with students jostling each other to enter and be seated before the bell.

"Sit down, Charlotte. I'll talk with you later."

Charlotte sat on her hands, her feet still swaying back and forth below the seat with her restlessness. Last night, she had waited until she heard Papa go up to bed, before slipping down to take his notes from the library. Confident she could have them back in place before he woke, she had enjoyed reading them, but she had never been so fascinated by one of his lectures before.

Papa banged the podium and she heard the noisy boys shuffle into total silence. In minutes, she was lost in his resonant voice and back into the story of the rebellious Martin Luther. She had almost fallen back asleep when he pounded the podium and raised his voice. "Martin, didn't deliver the Ninety-Five Theses, he nailed them to the door of All Saints Church in Wittenberg, Germany."

Charlotte sat upright. She could see the young men were as focused as she was by the subject. Of course, they couldn't see the many footnotes he had added to each page. She knew it didn't hurt Martin that his friend, a printer, had published the German translation of his thesis and it had become the most popular and debated book of its time.

Actually as she thought of it, it was because of Martin Luther that priests in the Lutheran church could marry. All the Protestant churches had followed his example. Smiling, she wondered if Papa realized she wouldn't exist if Martin hadn't taken his stand.

Papa's thundering voice was quoting Martin Luther at his trial at the Edict of Worms. "Here I stand. I can do no other. " Charlotte put her feet on the floor at the front of the chair, ready to sprint away as the boys exited, now that the lecture was almost over. She silently mouthed the words as he reached the conclusion. "Luther refused to recant his thesis. Because of his brave stand, resting on principles he saw as true, the Protestant churches were formed."

He stood there, his black robe still smooth, like some commanding black bird. Charlotte wasn't fooled, she could smell the starch, had watched Mama iron it last night. She watched as he reared backward, his chin raised and she leaned around to watch the boys that were as spring loaded as she was.

"Dismissed," he said.

The lads all pounded for the door as Charlotte shot out of her chair. In horror, she felt Papa's big hand grab the collar of her over-blouse and hold tight.

As she stood teetering on the edge of the stage, Charles Newcomb turned and waved goodbye with a cheeky grin. She hated men.

◇◇◇

Charlotte kept arguing with Papa, even as he scolded her for taking his papers. Clearly unafraid, she reached up and kissed him, offering a rather insincere apology. "Yes, Papa, but I want to study here. I want to learn all I can." He wanted to continue, but she smiled at him. "It was marvelous, this lecture. I can only imagine what I will learn at the next one. Can I listen to the other professors?"

"Of course not, women are not allowed at Newton."

"But you are the president. What if I come in disguise? If you don't say anything, the others probably won't even notice."

At this he laughed. At sixteen, his daughter was as beautiful as her Mama, and made his other three girls look drab in comparison. They were already beginning to complain that Charlotte wasn't even trying to find a husband.

"No, you can't come in disguise, it would never work. From now on, you will arrive as today, with my papers or lunch. I can let you stay at the back of the room to listen, even to take notes. But you won't be enrolled in classes and you will not be eligible to graduate. I can't afford the tuition, so you won't receive any credit. That is, if we can convince Mama."

When he laughed, Charlotte knew she had won. Now all she had to do was convince Mama. "You're right, she won't be easy. But Papa, if I have to hear Miss Lynn tell us again how to offer a gentleman tea and serve cake, I will scream. I know how to dance, and I'm never going to be any good at embroidery. I want to learn history, mathematics, and literature, not little French phrases and another lesson on the pianoforte. Oh Papa, help me please. Try to imagine if you were forced to take lessons on how to curtsey and use your fan." Charlotte pretended to bow gracefully and flutter a pretend fan while giving him a coy look. "It's disgusting."

CHAPTER TWO

William Delmar Monroe

William stood, added his new shirt, and the letter that had arrived today to his travel bag. It wasn't going to be easy, but after he bearded the lion in his den, then he would be on his way. He had already sent Asa to saddle the horse.

As he put his bag on the floor beside the front door, William reminded himself he was not going to use William on his sojourn. William belonged to his great uncle who he was named after. He was going to be Delmar Monroe from now on. He looked around and felt relieved no one else was up. He knew the women, his mother and two sisters were still abed. He didn't want to go through the choked throat, teary eyed conversations they had shared last night. Debra and Ellen had whined, asking him to please, please stay.

After being away the last four years at school, he knew it was mainly to make him feel missed. As soon as he walked through the door, they would return to their regular routine without him. But Mother, that had been different. When she held up the shirt she had made him, to measure if it would fit his wide shoulders, they had ended up hugging and trying not to cry.

"Well, are you coming in or not?" his father barked impatiently.

Delmar stepped through the door, admired his still fit and handsome father. "I didn't want to end things the way they stood between us. You look fit this morning."

His father harrumphed for an answer, but stared at his youngest son as he shook his head. "And you look like a vagabond. Don't you have anything more suitable for meeting your Great-Uncle William?"

"I dare say, I will be the better dressed of the two of us." Delmar smiled, shook his head at his father and held his arms wide instead of arguing. A lifetime of being reminded that he was a relative of a president was enough. At twenty-three, he wanted to forget it for a year or two. His love was music, and his father knew it.

His father embraced him, pounded his back as he let him go. "It makes no sense to me. You've passed the law exam with marks higher than me or your brother. I have offered you a place in my firm. There is Eleanor, and the prospect of a good marriage at hand. What sense does it make to leave all that, and for what, to learn from that old scoundrel how to carve a fiddle? It's absurd."

Delmar growled and turned toward the door. His father sighed and moved from behind his desk to pursue him. "You packed food for lunch. You know there are only a few slaves on that derelict plantation, and probably none of the food will be fit to eat."

"I have. Mother and the girls packed enough to keep me fed for a month."

"Good, when it's all gone, then you'll come back to us. I have great need for another junior partner, now that I'm running for state office."

"Stop asking. I finished at William and Mary, as you ordered. I have the law degree you wanted, and now I've passed the bar for you. You promised me a year for my music. I've waited long enough." Delmar had raised his hands and his voice, he stopped and sighed. His father stared him directly in the eye.

Delmar laughed, picked up the bundle and the saddlebags packed with food and everything else old Henry had thought the young man would need. "You have James, we both know he is the best lawyer in Richmond, if not the whole state of Virginia. I know as you do, that you have been told the office of Senator is yours if you'll run."

Delmar handed his gear to Asa and watched as his friend and valet expertly secured them on Brick, his favorite horse. The big red gelding moved in place, eager to be on the road. His father caught his hand, turned him back toward him as Delmar was ready to mount.

"Promise, you'll remember you're a Monroe. You can be anything that you want, a wandering fiddler or the next President. I know every young man must sow his wild oats. It's normal, when you've been so long constrained by school, and your duty to your name. But, please take care. Eleanor is a real beauty, and she won't wait forever. The Turner fortune would make you set for life."

"Point her at James then, if you want her in the family so much. I'm not marrying for money, or wealth. I'm going to do just what I like, and if I like it enough, it may be all I ever do." He shortened the reins on the prancing horse. "Tell me you'll love me, still call me your favorite youngest son."

"Bah, be off with you," his father said with disgust, slapping the rump of the thoroughbred horse.

Delmar looked back over his shoulder as the horse's hooves rang out along the paved drive, and smiled when he saw his father still standing there. He was proudly looking after his son, with a smile on his face. Delmar waved and his father waved back.

It was late as he rode down the fall line onto the coastal plain. He clucked to his horse, thumped his sides to urge him into a gallop. Here in the tidewater, it was still easy to get lost in the swampy terrain and his father had given him specific warnings about how to reach Sparrow Walk before sundown. He rode the lathered horse into the yard of the dilapidated plantation, surprised when one of the blacks still on the property ran out to take his horse, lantern raised.

As he dismounted to free his traps from the horse, the boy told him, "You best go on in, I got these things. Master's waiting dinner for you."

Delmar thanked him, then turned to race up the high steps to the wide veranda. In the ghostly hour of twilight, he could see that the place was as big and grand as he remembered. He hadn't been here since he was a boy of ten, but he had never forgotten the gay music his great uncle had played. He remembered the beautiful ladies who smiled at his father and mother, and welcomed them to dance in a brightly lit ballroom.

Since then, like the other Monroes, his Great-Uncle William had freed all his slaves. A few, like the boy outside, had stayed out of loyalty. They continued to tend the fields and run the house to take care of the man who had always provided for them and had given them the gift of their freedom. Still, over a hundred had disappeared, most to the cities, many into the swamps and Piedmont to build their own homes.

◇◇◇

Delmar followed the tall man who emerged from the shadows, as dark and scary as the shadowed halls through which they walked. He noticed the stained glass panel doors leading into the ballroom were open. He was surprised by the familiar scent of sawdust that drifted from inside. The man opened the door to a closet sized room beside it. "In case you'd like to wash up, Sir."

Minutes later, Delmar was glad when the dark man halted and opened the solid doors at the end of the hall. He announced in a booming voice. "Master Monroe has arrived."

He moved inside, reassured to find the old man, his Great-Uncle William dressed for dinner. Even the candles on the candelabra were all lit. The butler pulled out a chair to the right of his great-uncle while the two embraced, then Delmar sat down. He noticed the girl who carried in a soup tureen gave him a resentful gaze before setting it down. "Fetch the bread and butter, girl." The butler scolded her and the girl rushed away while the man served.

"My, my, but you do favor your father, William. I trust I won't offend when I say I see a little more of the Scot about you than in him. How fares the rascal and the rest of your family."

"Fine, fine sir.' Delmar noticed there was steam rising from the soup and grinned hungrily at him. "I'm sorry, sir, to make you wait for dinner. I did lay into my horse Brick when I saw the sun was falling. I'd forgotten how quickly night fell in the Tidewater."

"I imagine so, you were only a sprout when you came last. I've worried you'd forgotten your request, or would wait too late to return."

Delmar waited, wondered if the man would want a prayer before breaking bread. Instead, his great-uncle motioned to the scowling butler who poured a dark wine, while the resentful girl returned with a basket of warm bread and a china plate with curled pats of butter.

"Hope you like our chowder, not as white as it is up North."

"Looks just like the kind Mother serves." He took a deep spoonful, smiled, then reached for the glass of wine. He blew out a breath. The butler grinned at him as he poured a glass of cold water for him. "Delicious," Delmar said, surprised smoke didn't leak out around the rim of the water glass.

"Thad, you can tell Matilda, a little less fire and a few more clams, next time."

The butler nodded and bowed himself out. Delmar saw the man's wide grin as he pushed past into the kitchen. For a minute, they ate in silence. Then, with his Great-uncle's encouragement, he talked about home. He finished with the argument he'd had with Father, before leaving.

"Trust James to draw a blister on a plaster saint. Did he not think I would be a good example for you?"

Delmar nodded, swallowed the bite of buttered roll he had bitten. "My, goodness no, he warned me you'd be exactly the opposite."

With the loud laugh of the merry older man, Delmar relaxed completely and dug in. The Butler shook his head as though suffering some personal misery.

If there was anything lacking in the big house, he didn't mention it. Delmar decided to wait until tomorrow to ask his great-uncle why there were no women present, especially when the butler brought out a battered case and the old man's eyes lit up.

Delmar watched in awe as his Great-Uncle William took out the shiny violin, with the front plate scratched and well worn. He watched him tune it up, and allowed the maid to remove everything but his wine glass, which she refilled.

The music was as he remembered, slow, high and beautiful. As they drank more, the music changed, speeding up. The maid returned with her tambourine and the butler raised his banjo. Delmar stared at it in awe, then delighted in the music. At the end of the second song, the old man held out his violin. Hands shaking, Delmar accepted the well-loved instrument. He stood, raising it to his shoulder, and played "Believe Me If All Those Endearing Young Charms."

When he finished, they all laughed and clapped and he realized he had found his new home.

The two talked until the butler hissed at him, and Delmar realized the older man was asleep.

"I'm sorry," Delmar whispered, "is he ill?"

"Too much wine," the butler snorted and called the maid to lead the young master to the best guest room. The house and room smelled musty, but the bedding was clean.

As he fell asleep, Delmar tried to remember Eleanor's face and wondered if he'd made the right decision or not. When he couldn't recall a single feature, he relaxed and slept.

CHAPTER THREE

Charlotte Stewart - 1851

Nineteen-year-old Charlotte, threw down her latest sampler in disgust. Her Mama was frantically chasing after her housekeeper and her sisters were angry and complaining because they wanted to roll up the drawing room rugs. Papa had invited all the men from the graduating class to the soiree. Mama reminded Charlotte she still hadn't had her last fitting and she must try this time.

"Why do we have to move the rugs? The men are only coming to talk one last time about their plans. The only music will be the string quartet from the school's music academy, two violins, a viola, and a cello. We've heard them a hundred times. There won't be dancing and there won't be singing. Cook's only preparing cakes and pies, no shrimp or oysters, nothing celebratory. There's only tea and coffee, nothing to drink," Charlotte said.

As the girls erupted into a storm of screeching and squawking, Mama who was looking frazzled, actually screamed at her. "Get out of that chair Charlotte Grace Stewart, or I am going to turn you over my knee. Do you have any idea how much work and expense goes into entertaining? No, of course you don't. You of all people should be excited by this opportunity. Really, one would think you have no interest in finding a husband."

"I don't," Charlotte said. She let her little sister Dottie take the blasted needlework and stood as Rebecca pulled away her chair. Elizabeth and the housekeeper began to roll the rug determinedly. Charlotte at least had the courtesy to step off the rug as her younger sister took hold of Mama and helped her into the chair. Rebecca carried off the rug.

At her Mama's tears and hand wringing, Charlotte bowed her neck and sighed. "All right, I'm going up now."

"The pink satin, the one with the daring décolletage." Mama turned to whisper to the girl holding her right hand. "Hurry Rebecca, go up and help tighten her corset, make sure she wears her best crinoline, and please, please have Susie help with her hair."

"But Mama, you know how she is. And your maid won't want to go through what we had to at the Christmas party."

"Now," Mama snapped, she sagged back into her wounded warrior position. "What is a mother to do with such a willful child? And to think I named her after dear Aunt Lottie."

Upstairs, Charlotte didn't even try to resist. She knew she only had minutes before they would descend on her, to 'help her'. If she refused, Mama would come. She opened her copy of the letter she had taken from Papa's desk last night. It was from a Reverend Watkin in some place called Kyles Ford, Tennessee. The town needed a young schoolmaster who could control children, had an outstanding scholarly background, and would work for room, board, and $100 for the school term. Charlotte held the letter to her chest, her hands shaking so badly the paper rattled.

She could hear Rebecca yelling for Dot, and quickly folded and tucking the letter away. She should have left it, now she would have to slip into Papa's office later to return it. She prayed that he didn't discover it was missing in the meantime.

She reviewed the young men in the graduating class in her mind, while she opened her closet, quickly moving through all the dresses inside. There wasn't a single worthy candidate in the lot. Mama was a fashion follower and she wanted her daughters to be the same. Really, if Mama hadn't wanted Charlotte to be the opposite, she should never have named her for her younger sister.

Aunt Charlotte was now thirty, a definite old maid by anyone's definition. All Aunt Lottie wanted to do was write her plays, which was precisely what she did. It hadn't stopped Mama from holding the woman up as both a bad and a good example, depending on her mood at the moment. She would have to ask Aunt Lottie how she had managed to elude all the match-making efforts of Grandmamma and Mama on her behalf.

Rebecca sailed into the room and removed the pink satin Charlotte had been sent up to try on. "Mama says this is the one you're to wear tonight."

Charlotte tilted her head at her closest sister and shook her head. 'I tried it on. It's too tight in the bust and the waist, and the color makes me look naked up here." She raised her hands to indicate her bodice, suitably shielded in the voluminous gown she wore.

Rebecca put her hands on her hips. "Mama said to get you in it, and to lace your corset. She's sending her maid to do your hair, so you better hurry."

"Or," Charlotte quirked her lips in a smirk.

"Elizabeth, Dorothea, I need help, right now."

Charlotte shook her head as her taller sister held the corset raised, ready for her to pull over her head. "No …,"

Rebecca nodded, "Yes, or I'm calling Mama."

The drawing room was warm and packed with too many bodies, dressed in boiled and starched shirts and dark wool coats. Charlotte felt like she would faint. At least the wide basket of her crinoline kept the men from getting close enough to steal all the air. Despite what Mama had warned, Charlotte had worn the blushing pink gown, with her favorite red scarf tucked around her neck and into the bodice. Really, the pale satin was almost skin colored, and against Charlotte's pale skin seemed invisible. It did nothing for her. She needed rich colors with her jet black hair, and violet-blue eyes. Charlotte had wanted to wear her green plaid taffeta, but it had disappeared from her closet.

Charlotte nodded when Charles Newcomb held up a glass of punch and elbowed his way across to hand it to her. With her Mama staring at her, Charlotte leaned forward and took a deep draught. When Charles reached for the glass, she held onto it and gulped the rest. Handing him the empty glass, she rolled her eyes toward the big case windows at the end of the room.

Charlotte bent after pointing to the closed latch. On tiptoe, Charles managed to flip it and Charlotte gave the window a big push upward. "Can you pull down the top panel?"

"Of course," His face was red as he tugged at the heavy, resistant window, but the moment it moved, Charlotte clapped her hands as the soft night air swept into the room. To her left she saw Davis and the Jewish boy, Malcolm, working on their window. She nodded as she and Charles moved to the right while two other young men rushed forward to repeat the process on the last of the four enormous windows. In the room, there was a great yell, and collective sigh. Mama was standing beside Papa, biting on her lower lip in rage. She had told Charlotte when she first begged to have the windows open that everyone knew night air was dangerous.

The first young men who had struggled with their instruments clapped the loudest. Charlotte stepped to the back of the room and swung open the doors to the cool, unlit hallway. She sent the first men who had helped out to the darkened dining room to carry in some of the chairs.

Papa was busy calming Mama, but her younger sisters, 15-year-old Elizabeth and 13-year-old Dorothea rushed to hug her. Rebecca, a perfect copy of Mama, stood beside her parents, chin raised and eyes disapproving.

Now the big room was full of commotion and then silence as the musicians tuned up. Charlotte insisted the boys put all furniture against the walls so that those who wanted to continue to stand and talk could. When the musicians began to play Beethoven, the lilting music drifted out the windows.

Other than the young men standing stiffly around, talking to her father, there was little motion in the room. Charlotte didn't dare to look over toward her mother. Tugging Charles behind her, she approached the quartet and whispered, "Strauss, at least two waltzes. Ready, and a one, two, three." As they began to play the Viennese waltz, she raised her hands to Charles. He was shaking his head, but she moved into position and tapped her foot impatiently.

As though by magic, Papa and Mama took a seat. Her younger sisters looked so hopefully at the nearest young men that the boys shyly moved toward them. Awkwardly each pair joined the couple dancing around the floor.

CHAPTER FOUR

When the guests were gone, Mama and Rebecca walked upstairs, leaving the girls to help the housekeeper restore order. Papa motioned Charlotte over to his room. She had actually enjoyed the evening and dreaded following him, but knew he would be easier on her than Mama.

"Well," he said.

"Papa, I'm sorry, but I couldn't breathe and your poor students looked like they were melting."

He waved a hand, motioned to the chair in front of him. Charlotte walked over and plopped down, sighing, waiting for the onslaught of words. She knew from Papa there would be no yelling or scolding, no fake sighs. But his disapproval could be devastating.

"I am not going to criticize your behavior; I believe Mama will have plenty to say to you in the morning. I thought you had made a promise to me, the day you brought my speech notes to class."

Charlotte stood and raised her skirt enough to remove the letter from her stocking where she had stored it, ready to sneak into his office. Her hand shook as she handed it to him. He was staring at her like the liar and thief she was. Rather than look away or fall apart, Charlotte raised her face to his and said. "Papa, I want that job. This is my calling, to be a teacher."

Later, she lay in bed, staring at the ceiling. Through the thin walls, she could hear loud voices, only catching a word once in a while. Papa had not been surprised to learn she wanted to teach. In all the better schools around Boston, women were being accepted into the classrooms to teach the younger children. She had told Papa with his recommendation, she knew they would hire her. This was where God wanted her to go, into the wilderness to teach the ignorant and needy. In Boston, everyone had an opportunity to learn. However, in the wild, primitive mountain community of Kyles Ford she could change lives.

She wasn't discouraged, it would take time and effort, but she knew she could change her parents' minds. If she were to be happy, she had to.

A month later, Charlotte was disgusted. Mama had protested that she could not travel unescorted. Papa was afraid he might lose control of the university, if he took off over a month to escort her to Tennessee. The solution came from a neighbor, whose maid had an older child who had proved impossible to train. The woman wanted to send the girl to her sister, who lived in Sneedville, Tennessee. She had offered to pay the girl's passage and contribute twenty dollars toward Charlotte's expenses.

Her sisters had been shocked to learn, that she was willing to use the money that would have been her dowry to make such a trip. The salary would barely replace it, and she would have to work the entire year for the small amount. Charlotte was willing in a heartbeat, reminding everyone that she was determined to teach, not marry.

For the better part of two weeks, with Cicely, the untrainable maid, in tow she had been traveling by train and carriage. Thanks to her father's standing, she had been able to find lodging when necessary in the homes of good Baptists, many of whom were his former students.

When she arrived in Lynchburg, Virginia, it was by carriage. Once again, she had been promised that a respectable family would be there to meet her. There, sitting in a carriage, were the nicest looking couple yet. The man hurried up to greet her. Charlotte was delighted to meet Pastor Fortner and his charming wife.

Although they were both solicitous, she could tell they were a little concerned. The pastor was an exuberant talker. "Mandy has already prepared a delicious supper and we hope you will be comfortable."

"I'm sorry, but some of my family arrived yesterday. We really don't have a bed, and the nearest Inn, well, I wouldn't want to stay there if I were a young woman traveling alone," his wife said.

Cicely rolled her eyes at Charlotte as the woman continued. "There is plenty of room in the nursery for a bedroll, and if you don't mind, I think it could work for the night." Her husband told her to hush.

"My aunt and her family are driving back to New London tomorrow, but my parents are staying on. I had planned to travel with you onto Bedford. But Mandy's uncle says there is a short-line train," he said. "It's a logging train into the mountains that ends just above Harrogate, at the Cumberland Gap."

"Is that close to Kyles Ford?" Charlotte asked.

"No, and it would take about ten days to travel by foot, but the most miraculous thing happened. The son of a friend of ours came through, expecting hospitality yesterday, but as we told you, it is impossible this week. Anyway, he went on through town and pitched camp beside the river. You know how it is for young men, restless. Well, he is heading in the same direction as you. I think if you wait a day and travel back with my aunt's family in their carriage, you can catch the train." At Charlotte's confused look, he continued.

"You see, then you can get on the logging train. It may not be very comfortable,"

His wife interrupted, "Compared to the passenger trains you've been traveling on."

The pastor scowled at the woman who sat back quietly as he continued. "It will save you days of traveling by carriage, on horseback, or on foot. And in two days, when you reach the end of the track, there is another spur that switches down to a tiny little village called Blackwater."

"Yes, this young man, a most respectable young man, will be at the end of the track in Blackwater, and together you will only have a single day's travel to reach your new post at Kyles Ford," the wife said.

"Not to mention saving all the expense of staying in inns and hiring carriages. The Lord works in mysterious ways, doesn't he?" the young pastor asked.

"Yes, he certainly does. This would work well if I were headed to Blackwater, Virginia."

"Why Scott County, Virginia is just a holler away from Hancock County, Tennessee."

"A holler?" Charlotte asked.

"A big yell down the valley to the next town. Yes, ma'am, you're practically there. And, it is only the middle of August. You should have plenty of time to get settled in before school starts."

Charlotte was exhausted already. The so comfortable passenger trains were anything but, with their open carriages and the enormous black plumes of smoke constantly blowing back, sometimes into the cars themselves. Each day she was anxious to get off the jouncing cars and ever fearful that no one would be at the station to meet her. Papa had volunteered to take a short sabbatical to accompany her, but she refused to let him risk his position for her. Papa had been writing colleagues since he won the argument on her behalf, and had convinced Mama to let her go. With a confidence and bravado, she did not feel, she had assured him she would be fine. If one couldn't trust the clergy, well then who could one trust?

Her sisters pretended to be shocked and furious, but Charlotte knew they were relieved that she was going, especially Rebecca. Her sister had her cap set for Charles Newcomb. Charles was a steady, reliable young man, but far too dull and serious for Charlotte's taste. Still, he had been her steady beau all through her studies at the seminary and she had looked upon him as her back up plan.

Four days later, Charlotte rose with relief from inside the tiny caboose. If she didn't have her crinolines underneath her tasteful travel suit, the maneuver would have been less challenging. With the long flatbed cars and their ribbon of emptiness between the caboose and the engine, the only thing to see was the brawny man in a pair of striped coveralls, bobbing in and out of the engine cab to get shovel after shovel of coal.

She had asked the old man in the end car, what the flatbeds were for. He was either deaf, or deemed women unworthy to listen to. Finally, she had figured out they were for the tall trees the train would be carrying home. Cicely showed no interest in watching or helping. Charlotte realized, she would be glad to send her on her way to Sneedville.

As the last pastor had promised, the train stopped at a stripped mountain side. After watching the beautiful blue green mountains pass, Charlotte actually felt shocked by the devastation. Cicely finally seemed to sit up and come alive as she stared at the many men in the railyard. Charlotte looked around for the next pastor and carriage, but saw no one.

CHAPTER FIVE

At Blackwater, she waited at the end of the train line with all her baggage and a complaining Cicely. Charlotte swatted a noisy mosquito, lifted her hand away to see a dark smear. "Blood thirsty devils, aren't they?"

Cicely rolled her eyes and mumbled. "They don't give me no trouble, Mizz Stewart."

Charlotte sat on her small trunk, while the slim black woman sat in a squatting position beside the large wardrobe. Charlotte had the large portmanteau beside her, and the small carpetbag resting under her feet.

"How's I's sposed to get to Sneedville, if you's goin' to Kyles Ford?"

Charlotte slapped another insect, then rose impatiently. "I explained to you on the train. All I know is some friend of the Reverend Fortner," she stopped talking as a mosquito flew into her open mouth. Charlotte coughed and spit, certain if she had eaten anything at breakfast, she would be hurling it onto the ground.

Instead of a well-sprung buggy and high stepping horse, she saw a huge cart with a single ox headed their way. An unusually tall and disreputable looking man was leading the slow, lumbering beast. Her worst fears were realized when the man stepped forward, bowed and said.

"Miss Charlotte Stewart?" He removed his hat and swept her a most graceful bow.

Charlotte stopped spitting and pulled her handkerchief from her sash to wipe her mouth. The man continued as though she had acknowledged him.

"Delmar Monroe at your service. My father, James, received a letter from the Reverend Benjamin Stewart, your father I presume. I explained to Pasteur Fortner that I could not wait so long for your arrival. However, as you can see, we were able to connect in a timely fashion, after all."

Charlotte's mouth opened, ready to dispute his assertion when another whining insect made her snap her lips together.

"We's mighty grateful that you's here, Master Monroe," Cicely said with a rough curtsey. "Is there somewhere around here that's serving food?"

Charlotte snapped her handkerchief at the insect, then pointed to her trunk. "Do you think this will fit in your cart?"

Delmar was tempted to answer, "Hell no," just to see what the exalted college dean's daughter might say, but he removed his hat and scratched his head. "Guess it will have to, now won't it."

Charlotte gave him a grim smile, and moved over beside Cicely. This time it was she who rolled her eyes.

The dark girl's stomach growled loudly and she stared at Charlotte. "I's not used to skippin' meals."

Delmar grunted, as he removed his own possessions. The old violin his great-uncle gave him, the new mandolin they had built together, all his precious tools, and the new boards he had harvested at the logging camp. Noticing the impatient stares of the girls, he began to load the baggage. When he had it all inside, he only had room for one of his instruments.

Grunting, he started again. Resenting having to fit her two trunks into the crowded space, even angrier when she continued to stare at him in annoyance.

Setting the largest trunk on its side, he made certain nothing inside would shift before he raised the gate. He started to lift his discarded jacket from the side of the cart to cover his sweat stained shirt.

Charlotte spoke, "Where do I sit?"

Delmar turned, his beard shaking in disbelief as he clenched his jaws.

He jammed the raw planed boards in as a temporary seat, supported by the edge of the big trunk at the back, the smaller trunk and his tool case on either side. Delmar prayed the precious curly maple wouldn't split or be damaged.

As Charlotte stepped up, the cart shifted and she sank in shock as the seat hit her bottom. Her eyes widened and Delmar tried not to laugh as he prodded the big animal into motion. The dark girl seemed delighted to get to walk on the other side of the animal.

"Almost there," Charlotte muttered through gritted teeth. The irritating man ignored her, but tried to talk to Cicely. The foolish girl giggled.

Why the pastor in the last town thought this young man would be suitable, was beyond her. Determined to be pleasant, as any Christian should be at his help, she smiled and spoke directly to the young man. "We are grateful for your assistance. I would hate to imagine spending the night here. Are there even other people around?"

"Not the kind you ladies need to meet. The loggers who cut all the lumber that's being loaded onto the train have a big camp nearby, down this road. There's also a saw mill a little farther on, that's where I've been the last couple of days."

"Do they have food there?" Cicely asked.

Charlotte started to shush her, but then her own stomach growled embarrassingly. Delmar smiled at her and the act transformed him. For the first time, Charlotte realized without the beard and the rough clothes, the man might be more than presentable. His smile changed into a lazy, hungry grin as though he could read her thoughts. She blushed and looked straight ahead.

This time he laughed and Cicely laughed with him while Charlotte's cheeks burned.

◇◇◇

Delmar refused to rush or to walk as slowly as the little black girl wanted to go. But when he started to camp after three hours, Charlotte complained. "I thought we were going to be able to get there tonight."

Later, when they had traveled from noon until past suppertime, the sun began to set. Charlotte couldn't stand being in the cart a minute longer.

She complained, "You can't expect us to travel all night. Are you sure we're going the right way? I thought you said it was less than ten miles."

When there was no answer, she continued, "We can't see the trail, and neither can the ox. What if those rough loggers decide to follow us?"

Cicely started whining in fear. "We'll be eaten by wild cats or bears, or set on by those sawmill men. How you goin' to protect both of us?"

"See what you've done, you've frightened the girl." Charlotte shouted at him, surprised her own voice didn't quaver or break. "If you don't mind, can you let me out of this small cage. Cicely and I will need to find a place for privacy."

Irritated, he reached in over the tailgate and helped the annoying woman off the makeshift bench and down onto the ground. Charlotte was so surprised and stiff, her legs nearly folded beneath her. Ashamed of his anger, Delmar held the woman until she could straighten to a standing position.

He took a deep breath and inhaled her flowery scent, suddenly reluctant to release her.

Cicely was now jumping from foot to foot. "I's got to go too, Mizz Stewart."

Delmar growled and stepped back, fumbling in his pocket for his flint and striker. "Give me a minute, I'll get you a light and examine the bushes first. You're more at risk from rattlers and copperheads, then you are from cougars or bears."

When the black girl moved over beside her, Charlotte raised an arm and folded her in beside her. She was surprised to find they were nearly the same height, but she hoped she didn't smell as sweaty from the trail as Cicely. Shivering, they watched the tall man moving through the brush beside the road, the burning brand held high illuminating his face. When they heard a hissing sound, Charlotte's eyes widened, but Cicely sniggered and Charlotte realized what the noise was. This time, she was glad for the shadows that hid her face from either of them.

Delmar emerged quickly and handed Charlotte the burning branch. Carefully, she held it aloft while Cicely clung to the sleeve of her other arm, as they worked themselves off the road and out of sight.

When they emerged later, Delmar had managed to locate his own pack.

Charlotte was relieved to see him open the backpack, and pull out a bedroll, then a pan, a small pot, a spoon, tin cup, and plate. It looked like they wouldn't starve to death after all. When he shoved all the cookware back in the tote, she sighed.

"It's your own fault, if you'd listened to me, we'd have made camp an hour ago, we could have found a better spot, near a stream. Here," he held out his hand, and Charlotte hesitated. Cicely didn't, but reached out to take the strip of jerky and hard tack biscuit he was offering. Charlotte could see little but his pale eyes in the dim light. When he extended his arm and grunted again, she didn't hesitate to reach out, fumbling to touch his closed fist, stroking it with her other hand until he opened it and let her take her own meager dinner.

She waited until he'd removed his own food and gracelessly folded into a seat on the ground, her legs folded Indian style under her voluminous skirt. "Shall we pray?"

She heard Cicely guiltily stop eating, saw the man across from her watching and waiting. Softly she began, "Dear Heavenly Father, thank you for escorting us safely through the valley of shadows. Thank you for the blessing of this strong young man to shield us from the terrors of the journey, and for the precious food that he has shared. In the name of the Father, Son, and Holy Ghost, Amen."

The other two echoed with amens. They ate beside the small fire, coughing on the dry crumbs of the bread. Delmar wiped the top of his open canteen before passing it to Charlotte first. "There's not much, just a swallow each."

At least this time, he didn't point out it was her fault for her arguing about stopping when they were on the low ground. Charlotte took a swallow, feeling much thirstier as soon as she released the canteen to Cicely. She stared at the man, surprised that he hadn't taken his water next.

Apparently he had no trouble drinking after the black girl. Well, that was another point in his favor. He growled, as Cicely tilted the canteen higher and took it, swallowing the precious few drops that were left. If the girl felt guilty, she didn't apologize.

CHAPTER SIX

The next morning, as soon as the last crumb was gone, Delmar rose and held his hand out to help Charlotte to her feet. Cicely scrambled to her feet on her own.

All three followed the thirsty ox down the trail toward a narrow little creek. As the big animal pulled toward the side of the creek, Delmar moved ahead and quickly filled the empty canteen. He saw Charlotte lean down beside him to dampen her handkerchief. When the big animal moved beside her, she let out a squeal and reached out to steady herself, placing her hand on his thigh.

Delmar remained, half crouched, staring up at her. He couldn't help but wonder if her smooth white skin was as soft as it looked. He extended his arm to brace her and keep her from falling forward. She leaned into him, swaying against his arm before gaining her balance and raising her hand to grip his shoulder before stepping back.

He stared up at her, noticing that she was clearly unaware of the effect she'd had on him. Rising carefully, to conceal his excitement from the girls, he barked harshly. "Let's get moving, if you don't want to be caught on this trail after dark."

They were on their way, the path down into Tennessee clearly marked by the many who had walked this way before. Charlotte had chosen to walk with the other two for a short while.

Two hours later, a pair of hounds came bounding out of the brush lining the road. Cicely squealed, and the dogs turned and plunged back out of sight.

Charlotte looked toward Delmar but he was staring straight ahead where a pair of tall young men were striding toward them. Both men had rifles raised. Without hesitation, Delmar swept Charlotte up and onto her seat in the cart as she looked like she would faint. He reached in to grab his own rifle as he released her.

The two boys stopped, grinning at them, as they lowered their guns. "Sorry to spook you. We're huntin' a killer bar, dogs trailed him up this way."

Delmar extended a hand, realizing he was facing a pair of boys, no matter how tall or big footed they looked. "Thankfully we haven't seen any bear. I'm escorting Miss Stewart, the new school teacher, down to Kyles Ford."

The boys were staring in confusion at Cicely. "Didn't know they was goin' to be no darkie schoolmarm, or is she a Melungeon?"

Delmar shook his head in confusion. "No, not Cicely. She is just along to chaperone Miss Stewart. I'm not sure what a Melungeon is?"

"Mixed race, something lower than a white person. Ain't you got none where you're from?" Ned asked.

"I see, yes we have a few. I just wasn't familiar with the term. Cicely, she is escorting Miss Stewart, then heading on to Sneedville," Delmar answered.

The boys were walking around toward her as Delmar had pointed her out, when one of the hounds howled in pain. Both boys turned to fire into the woods. Delmar looked at where they were shooting in alarm, surprised that they had been telling the truth.

A black shadow broke from the shadowy cover of trees. Charlotte screamed and quickly raised both legs over the tail gate to leap from her little perch. As she started to fall, Delmar caught her, barely holding the gun ready as her momentum carried them to the ground. He noticed her skirt was belled up again. By the look of the two men, he knew what they were staring at. He wrapped one long leg around her, forcing the skirt down to cover her.

In horror, Charlotte sputtered beside him and pointed. He made what he hoped was a comforting hushing sound. At a roar behind him, he turned to stare. On top of the bench where she had sat moments ago, an angry black bear roared at him, raising its formidable front legs, with the pale heavy claws visible. He pushed her away as she screamed, and he raised his gun enough to fire.

Delmar fired, aiming for the center of its chest. He yelled for the boys, who were too busy staring at the bear beside them to focus on reloading. Both began frantically to ready their rifles, but it was clear that the animal was dead.

It was a minute before the boys rushed over to give the tangled couple a hand up.

Charlotte didn't want to, but she clung to the arm of the slim man beside her as she struggled down the overgrown trail beside the cart with its load of bear. The alternative of the hike was to ride with the dead animal and the thought made her shudder.

The hounds were following the loaded cart, occasionally barking, although the loud sounds couldn't hide the fear in their voices. Cicely walked in the lead with the noisy young men leading the light colored ox. Charlotte slipped and wrapped her other hand around Delmar's strong arm, grateful for his support.

When the glow of a lantern appeared up ahead, they both sighed in relief and increased the distance between them.

"Who's there?" a loud voice called.

"Us Pa," Ned hollered. "We found the new schoolmarm."

"We got the killer bar," Eb shouted even louder.

There was a string of curses, then the loud voice hollered, "Get out here now, Ivey." There was a pause, then the voice whispered in a loud gravelly voice. "Put your clothes on first, woman."

It was a strange house to Charlotte, larger than a small cabin yet primitive looking. Even with its two stories and a big front porch, it looked unfinished.

Delmar extended a hand to the big bearded man who had yelled. "Delmar Monroe and this is Miss Charlotte Stewart and Cicely."

"Davis Daniel," the man said, extended a thumb toward the bear hunters, "Reckon you done met Ned and Eb, my boys."

The bear hunters invited them all in, although the men seemed to eye both women speculatively. They offered Charlotte a chair and she gratefully accepted it, not surprised when Cicely crept behind her to squat on the floor. Charlotte almost expected the girl to raise her skirt and crawl underneath to hide, the way the mountain men were staring at her.

Ivey Boggs appeared from a back room and offered the late comers food. Charlotte tried not to stare at the woman's bright red hair, wondering if it was dyed. She must have failed, for the woman asked them curtly to follow her. They sat at a long dining table where she pointed.

Delmar turned to the men, "What about the bear?"

"Girls, help yourself," the woman said as she followed the men outside.

Charlotte was glad to be left alone with Cicely as everyone disappeared to gut and move the bear to the spring house. There was a large roast of some kind on the table, a cold half-circle of cornbread, and a simmering pot of beans sitting on a folded towel in the center of the table. Charlotte knew good manners required that she wait for the others to return, but her growling stomach wouldn't let her.

Cicely started to break off some bread, and Charlotte stood, looking for a knife. Carefully she cut the big half circle into eight wedges and put one slice on each of their plates. She repeated the process to slice a sliver of meat for each of them. Cicely reached over to spoon a huge pile of beans over both things on her plate and sat back down.

Charlotte scowled at her, but added a big spoonful onto her own plate. After she poured water into the chipped cups, she began to eat. Conscious of the girl noisily eating beside her, she cut tiny bites of meat to eat with dainty bites of beans and cornbread. She almost moaned over the first mouthful. She was amazed at how good everything was. She looked around as she finished, noticing the dark space behind a wall that must be the kitchen.

Charlotte guessed the first room crowded with wood, a stove and a half-dozen chairs, must be the parlor. There was an upper floor, but as she sniffed, she wasn't anxious to explore any of it. The whole place smelled like dog and unwashed feet.

Cicely voiced her own needs before Charlotte had finished the small amount on her plate. The dark girl had been sitting restlessly, waiting for her to finish. Charlotte nodded at her, and as soon as the girl darted outside through the door, Charlotte scraped the last of the food into a huge mouthful to swallow.

Curious, she stacked their dirty plates and carried them to peek into the kitchen. There was a large dishpan full of water on a high narrow board and she added theirs to those already soaking.

As in need as Cicely to empty her own bladder, she followed her instincts and walked out of the house and to the back where a large, well-built outhouse was in use. "Wait on me, please," Charlotte whispered, grateful for the shadows that kept her from seeing the impudent girl's face.

Inside was even darker, but the high moon cut-out let in a little light. Finished, she emerged to find the girl nowhere in sight. "Cicely," she called as she walked toward the house, frightened when she heard the threatening growl of the hounds. She rushed around and back into the house, almost running into the girl inside the door.

"I would have waited, Mizz Stewart, but them hounds done been trained to fight bears and they don't like my kind either."

Charlotte grinned at her, leaning against the frightened girl to reassure her. "They don't seem to like strangers, do they?"

Cicely blew out a loud puff of air, but followed her back into the parlor. The room had one oil lamp, wick turned down. This time Cicely selected the rocker near the lamp, curiously looking around for something to read. Disappointed, she took out her small prayer book from her drawstring bag and began to read. Cicely made a noisy, humming sound in her corner that was not unpleasant. Both women were nodding sleepily by the time the others returned.

Charlotte startled awake when the others returned, catching snatches of conversation.

"Told you there tain't no need to unload that critter. Tain't goin' to hurt nothin' having it and the cart both setting in the spring house. Good to move things around in there, chase out some of the rats and snakes," he said with a laugh. Charlotte could picture the fierce, red-bearded man who had first greeted them.

The men devoured the rest of the food. Davis Daniel got out his jug. When the men entered the shabby parlor, Delmar looked a little sheepish as he explained.

"They're hanging lanterns and want us to join them. I kind of promised to fiddle a few tunes for our supper. I mean, it's too late to make it down the mountain to town tonight. They promised to walk us down in the morning and offered us beds for the night."

Charlotte was already exhausted, but the thought of sleeping here made her skin crawl. If it weren't for the hounds outside, she would have argued that they could sleep in the cart. Then she remembered the bear still inside it and nodded. "Why are they hanging lanterns, couldn't you play in here?"

They heard the hounds baying in complaint. Charlotte raised her brows as Delmar rubbed his chins. "They're penning up the dogs."

He waited until the boys hollered that they were ready. "Sorry, but they like to dance," Delmar said.

CHAPTER SEVEN

Charlotte sighed and looked up at Delmar in amazement. "It's bedtime. Don't they go to bed like normal people?"

She heard someone clear their throat and looked up to see the red-headed woman smirking at her. "Davis is on the school board. He said he wanted to see what kind of a schoolmarm they'd spent their money on. You might want to rethink telling him goodnight and stomping off to bed."

Charlotte blushed, nodded warily, and reached up a hand to the grinning fiddler standing over her.

"I told him it had been a long day, and I only promised three tunes, figure it's just a dance with each one. Then you can plead your excuses. Right, Ivey?" He looked from the grumpy girl to the woman watching the exchange.

Charlotte watched the woman shrug her shoulders noncommittally. Stiffening her spine, Charlotte turned and walked out onto the wide porch to see the yard transformed by the lanterns hung from the eaves and a couple of tree branches.

When the father stepped forward and nodded at Delmar, the man raised his fiddle, and idling only a few seconds tuning it up. Cicely had been chased out by Ivey as well, but the young girl faded into the shadows.

Davis Daniel stared up at her and then bowed and held out his hand as the fiddler ran through a few bars of music.

"Turkey in the Straw," the big man announced as Charlotte was lifted from the porch and onto the bare dirt of the yard. She was grateful that she couldn't see what they were dancing on, remembering the dogs had only been locked up.

Each of the younger men stepped forward, copying their father and taking first Ivey, then Cicely off the porch to dance around the yard. They moved on big stomping feet, and Charlotte quickly began to pay closer attention to spare her toes as they wove in and out of the narrow pools of light.

Charlotte wondered if it would have been any worse, having to dance with the black bear. Davis seemed to expect her to be having as much fun as he was, as he spoke to her about her home in Boston and her journey here.

Charlotte gritted her teeth, wondering how long Delmar could play. The song ended only when the Daniels were all huffing.

"Eb, reckon you being the oldest, it's your turn to dance with Mizz Stewart. Mind her toes and be respectful. No pawing her, mind you," Pa said, with a growl.

Charlotte wondered what might have been her fate if the older man hadn't been so firm. Eb leaned over to bow to her, then pulled her into a tight embrace, hollering over her ear, "'Off to California,' fiddle man."

Delmar seemed used to shouted demands, as he struck into a tune of joyful enthusiasm. Charlotte was unfamiliar with the song, but it was like the wild reel he'd just finished. She found herself flying over the ground as the young man half-lifted and kept her feet above the ground as they swirled.

It reminded her of dancing with her fashion doll at home, spinning so fast, with the little legs bouncing in the air and the shiny heels clacking as she twirled. Suddenly, the tune changed to a slow, sad part. She was surprised that the ox man could play the high sad notes. All the dancers slowed to listen, but then the tune shifted quickly into the frantic gallop they had been dancing.

She saw Cicely swirl by under the lamplight and saw the girl pushing with all her might against the big man who had claimed her. For a minute, Charlotte wanted to close her eyes so she could endure the so-called dancing in her sleep. At least Eb wasn't a talker.

No sooner was she released, then the last man, Ned, appeared. He released a huffing Ivey to grab Charlotte's hand. "Bonaparte's Parade," he shouted.

Delmar hesitated, raised his instrument up in the air. "You mean the march, "'Bonaparte Crossing the Rhine'?"

"Tain't never heard that one, give it a play, and I'll set you straight if it tain't the right one," Ned said.

Faster than the last, at least the man seemed satisfied that the tune was right. This time, the youngest man managed to step on first one foot, then the other, before the music stopped. Charlotte hobbled out of reach, wondering if she smelled as strongly as the three Daniels. She caught

Cicely's hand as she passed and half dragged the girl up onto the porch. She glared at Delmar, and pointed toward the house.

"Goodnight, ladies," he said, holding the door open. She disappeared inside, quickly followed by the girl.

"Grateful for the chance to sleep under your roof. Believe the ladies are tired, I know I am," Delmar said, apologizing to the Daniels for Charlotte's abrupt departure. The loud men started to protest.

"Sure that fiddle ain't got one more tune?" the woman asked.

When Delmar shook his head, Ivey fluttered her skirts as she stepped away from the other arguing men. "Come on then, I'll get you folks settled."

Charlotte and her shadow moved aside as the woman walked past them holding her lantern up and talking over her shoulder. "You got a real fine man there. Course I thought Davis said they hired a maidenly Yankee to replace Mizz Dovie."

Charlotte cleared her throat before answering. "Yes, well, I certainly am the one who has traveled south from Boston. Mr. Monroe is merely escorting us from the train line at Blackwater, since he was heading to Kyles Ford."

"Both of you coming to Kyles Ford. What on earth for?"

"Well, I can only speak for myself. For me, I just received my teaching certificate from the Newton Seminary College in Boston. I am answering my calling." When Ivey just stared at her, Charlotte continued. "To help those who would not have an opportunity for a good education in the wilderness areas of our great country."

Ivey opened her mouth and laughed. "I've heard it all now." When she stopped laughing, she asked, "But what about the darkie?"

Before, Charlotte had only to explain that Cicely was a free person, and everywhere they had been able to stay together. She somehow doubted that such an explanation would carry any weight with this crude woman.

Ivey stopped at the top of the stairs with a hand on one of the doors. "We ain't never had none of her kind in the house before. Figured your girl would probably sleep in the barn with the animals."

Charlotte was aware the woman had raised the lantern higher, looking at one then the other, studying their faces as she made the last comment. Charlotte felt a hand clutch at the back of her skirt, remembering the frantic face of the girl as she'd grappled with the men dragging her around in what they had called dancing.

"I need Cicely with me to help me get ready for bed and to prepare my clothes and bath in the morning. She usually sleeps on a rug on the floor. If you don't have a rug, perhaps we could borrow a blanket for that purpose."

Ivey barked a laugh this time. "Well, la-de-da. Got you your own ladies' maid traveling with you, have you. You might find Kyles Ford is a bit more of a primitive wilderness than you thought. We don't hold no slaves in these parts."

"Really, I knew Massachusetts was a free state, didn't realize Tennessee was too."

Ivey swung the door open, showing two full-sized beds already made up. "Ain't no one slept here since Corinne's wedding, the youngest of Davis's three girls. Oldest one, Alma, made the room up before she took off with her

Melungeon. Reckon it should be clean enough, even for a refined lady like you."

She pointed at Cicely. "You plannin' to fetch the water girl, better hop to it now. Boys will be turnin' them hounds loose now the dancin' is over. Don't think they've ever seen or smelled a nigger before. They'll liable to snap you up."

Cicely rolled her eyes, but shot past to grab the pitcher on the small table between the beds. She managed to squeeze behind Charlotte's voluminous skirt on the way out as she scurried out the door and down the stairs.

The orange haired woman sprang past Charlotte to holler down after the frightened girl. "Pumps outside at the right end of the house. Better worry about if Eb and Ned catch you too. Heard them talking about trying a little dark meat." Ivey laughed as Cicely squealed. "Careful, 'fore you break that pitcher. Davis might hide you, if'n you do."

Delmar heard the raucous laughter and opened the door to hear the rest. He held out an arm to catch the terrified girl, made a face at her as he held her still. "Excuse me Davis. I'm powerful thirsty. Where did you say that pump was?"

"Thirsty, well why didn't you say. Got plenty of shine left in my jug."

Delmar grinned, rubbing his head as he released the girl and walked toward the edge of the porch. "No thanks. Think my head might burst if I drink anymore of that liquid lightening." He walked slowly as the girl kept pace in his shadow until he reached the pump, the Davis Daniel following along.

Davis pointed to the well and Delmar took the pitcher as Cicely released the handle to wait on the bucket to hit the bottom. In minutes, she had the full bucket wound back to the top and perched on the lip of the well. Delmar held the pitcher behind him and leaned forward. Cicely obediently held the gourd dipper of cold water out for him.

Delmar drank it, then motioned for another. Only after he'd swallowed it did he hand her the old clay pitcher to fill. He stood there in the moonlight, watching her step quickly, onto the porch and head back inside

"Want to thank you for your hospitality, Mr. Daniel. Understood from the lumberjacks that Kyles Ford was about a day's walk away. We must have taken a wrong turn. Of course, it could be because of the loaded ox cart and all the luggage Miss Stewart needed to move," Delmar said.

"Meeting that bar might have slowed you some. Fine music. We're glad to have you anytime. Sure you don't have another tune in that arm."

Delmar shook his head, rolled his shoulder as they walked back to the front of the house where he had laid down his fiddle. Quietly he snapped it into its case. "I can sleep in the barn or unroll my bed on the floor."

"Parlor then. I'll have Ivey bring you down a blanket and pillow."

After the goodnights and the couple had disappeared into the back room, Delmar settled into his make-shift bed. When he heard footsteps and giggles on the porch, he sat up, wishing he had his gun as he heard the screen door creak.

"Who goes there?" he called out.

Laughing, the two drunken young men ran back off the porch into the shadows. Grumbling, Delmar rose and drug his bed over in front of the door before settling down again.

CHAPTER EIGHT

They made a late start, the Daniels all wanting to take part in the parade. Since the bear still rode in a place of honor on top of her things, Charlotte had to walk like the rest of them.

She was already irritated. Cicely had been grateful enough to not have to sleep in the barn. Charlotte knew she was afraid of the young men who had pawed her when dancing. She wondered what it must be like to be considered so inferior that a man would presume anything he wanted with your person. She shook her head, unable to fathom how horrible that would be.

Last night, by the time the girl had returned with the water, Charlotte had already removed and shaken out her traveling suit, certain it would never come clean. The space was so narrow, she had remained at the foot of the bed, hopeful that the dust she shook out wouldn't coat the covers.

Luckily she had her handbag and was able to retrieve her brush and mirror. Before brushing out her hair to braid, she removed the annoying stiff petticoat, and tugged at her own laces to remove her corset.

When Cicely tapped at the door, she called for her to enter. While the girl poured water in the basin, Charlotte sat wearily to remove the tight little leather shoes, and pull off her dirty hose. Wishing she could have a real bath, she sighed as she rubbed the bottom of her aching feet and stared at her red toes.

Cicely hadn't spoken and Charlotte looked up at the girl. "Can you see any bruises yet?"

Cicely shook her head. "Did they all stomp on 'em?"

Charlotte shook her head as she stood and walked to the basin, astonished at how cold the water was at first. She managed to soap the cloth beside the basin and ewer to wash her face, neck, arms, legs and feet. Cicely was staring at her, or she would have removed the rest of her clothes and made a more thorough job of it. She rinsed out the cloth and repeated the process until she had removed the last of the visible soap and dirt.

She looked around the room. "Do you see a window to open?"

Cicely looked around then walked to the chair at the end of the bed, raising the seat to reveal the bowl below. "I can empty it in here."

Charlotte made sure to rinse the cloth as well as possible. "If you don't mind, after you finish, can you wash out my hose for tomorrow?"

The girl made a face, but then nodded. Ivey hadn't returned with a blanket and there was no rug on the floor.

While Cicely took her own bath, Charlotte made use of the chair, sitting and wiggling her sore toes. "They didn't all step on them, just the last. I think his name was Ned, and at least he was the lightest of the three."

Cicely didn't answer. Charlotte stared at her, noticing the dark mark of fingers on her bare arms, afraid to ask where else she had bruises.

When she pulled back the covers on the bed, she was relieved to see Ivey had told the truth. The sheets looked and smelled clean. She sat, brushing out her hair and braiding it quickly before climbing inside. Cicely walked down to use the chair herself, whispering.

"If I get up early enough, I can get this emptied and bring back some fresh water in the morning, 'fore any of them men wake up."

Charlotte yawned, looked up to see the girl beside her looking down at her. They both listened, but heard no one stirring. "Go on, just sleep on top of the sheets but under the cover. I'll help you wake up in time."

The girl was shaking and Charlotte surprised herself as she rose and went to move the chair carefully so that it was braced against the door. When she returned, the girl had crawled into the other bed. It was Charlotte's turn to smile down at her. She blew out the lamp and climbed back into her bed, asleep almost as soon as she stretched out.

Whatever else was waiting for them, she intended to enjoy sleeping in a real bed tonight. Closing her eyes, she saw the man with the strange little beard fiddling away on the porch. The rapid music throbbed through her head and down to her aching toes. She was still tapping her feet under the covers as she drifted into sleep.

◇◇◇

All the way down the mountain, Charlotte heard the Daniels' loud voices, only occasionally interrupted by the brash woman or the drawling voice of the music man.

"So what brings a man with your talent to Kyles Ford?" Davis asked.

"I'm on a trek for my Great-Uncle William. He taught me how to play, and also how to make instruments. I promised to collect some special wood for him and to learn about the local instruments here. He heard there were people playing something called a dulcimer, here in the Smoky Mountains."

"Dovie Watkin plays one, sometimes plays a mandolin too," one of the boys said. "Plays the dulcimer real good."

"Yeah, maybe Edward Goins, from up the mountain a piece," Davis said.

"What kind of special wood?" one of the boys interrupted.

"Well, my great uncle figured the trees might be bigger here, in uncut areas. Any hardwood will work, big leaf maple, black walnut, maybe chestnut for the solid backs. cedar or spruce to form the tops."

"Never heard of nobody making their own. Most folks get them when old folks die. Reckon they were made in the old country. Never even been anywhere folks were making them," Davis said.

"Oh, you travel a lot?" Delmar asked the big man.

Davis answered, "Site more than most. Have to travel to get the best price for my spring water."

Charlotte almost interrupted to ask how he could sell water, but remembered how harshly he had reminded Ivey that women were good for a few things, but not for talking.

As though he'd said nothing to her, the woman interrupted. "Promised to take me along the next trip. I hadn't been out of these hills since I married Harley Boggs."

"You're married?" Charlotte asked.

"Widowed," the woman said with a grin, staring meaningfully at Davis, "happily."

This time the big man laughed at her interruption. Charlotte pushed the hair back from her face, caught a sapling that lashed at her and repositioned her hat before taking another step down the steep trail.

"I thought Kyles Ford was in the mountains?" she said.

"It is, foothill of the Smokies anyway. Though we live up on a ridge and the town is kind of in the low place between us and the next ridge."

"Thought it was where you could cross the river, Pa?" one of the boys said with a whine.

"It is, but that sure ain't going to be on top of a mountain or ridge, now is it?" He looked to Charlotte for reinforcement.

"You hear that Mizz Stewart. Boys plumb ignorant. You're coming to this town just in time."

Charlotte nodded, lost in her own thoughts when they emerged from the trail into an area that looked inhabited. Suddenly her pulse began to beat rapidly. When Delmar looked at her, she could see approval in his eyes, and wished her face weren't flushed. Even though she knew her pale skin always bloomed with color when she was heated or excited. She needed to look her best, but thanks to the delay, she was wearing yesterday's dress. It was already coated in dust, her hair wasn't styled, just caught up in loose curls. The only hat she could reach in the cart this morning kept wanting to fall off.

Behind them trailed the loud Daniels' trio, along with the flame-haired woman. Charlotte was aware of all the people coming out of their houses and filling the road to stare at this noisy group.

As frightened as she was, Cicely kept almost stepping on her heels as she tried to remain invisible. Charlotte looked around, but saw no other black faces and understood why the girl was scared. On the other side of the cart, the tall young man looked anything but frustrated. His fine light brown hair was so long it skirted his collar but it was well combed, as was the silly, trimmed little blonde beard on his chin.

On the porch of what looked to be the local store, a tiny woman stood, dark eyes wide as she stared at them. Charlotte smiled in spite of herself as a giant of a well-dressed man stepped up behind her and the frightened woman almost shrank into him. When the little woman's mouth opened, ready to scream, Charlotte turned to look at what had frightened her.

The large pale ox with his long horns was intimidating. Perhaps it was the strange cart, which was a walled box with its sides leaning out at angles. It was piled high with boxes and crates in a jumble. When Delmar moved the ox up the street the little woman had let out a scream. Charlotte walked back to the Daniels and stared at the bear. Sitting with his legs and arms spread wide, the carcass was slit open down the front where it had been gutted, but the meat had not been skinned out.

As though they were a troupe of entertainers, the tall young man reached into the cart to open a case and pull out his fiddle. In a bright cheerful voice, he sang an introduction for each member of their party. Sweeping a low bow in each direction, he waved his hand at Charlotte.

"I present your new school teacher, the lovely Charlotte Stewart, all the way from Boston."

Charlotte blushed even darker and reached out to tug Cicely into view so she could curtsey to those in the crowd who were clapping. She wondered what her parents would think of her noisy arrival at her new job, and raised her head up a little higher.

"I am the fiddler, Delmar Monroe, though I can play anything with strings. I've come to fell trees for wood to make my own instruments."

There was more applause as he ran a little tune as proof. He bowed again and pointed at the flashy woman who stood with the three tall men. "You know the lovely Widow Boggs, her notorious past forsworn for the love of an honest man."

Charlotte was surprised to see the woman blush nearly as red as her hair and heard a scattering of catcalls from the small crowd. It suddenly seemed obvious what the woman had been famous for in the past.

"Davis Daniel, whose spring water will put the shine of the moon in an empty sky. And, Ned and Eb, his fine sons and the slayers of the biggest, meanest bear in these parts."

The little chorus of music must have been magical. She noticed the woman on the porch above them was shifting from foot to foot, as though ready to dance.

Annoyed at all the nonsense, Charlotte rolled her eyes at the song, and stood brushing her dress as he continued to sing.

Women rushed forward to greet the new school teacher. Mizz Dovie was first, quickly escorting her toward the new schoolhouse and the small cabin behind it.

The children and men milled about the cart to admire the big carcass of the bear. The Daniels and Widow Boggs stepped inside the store. Charlotte was relieved to be seeing the last of them as the dyed hair woman stood, smiling after her in a gloating way.

CHAPTER NINE

Delmar finished the first tune, enjoying watching the children dancing to the music. From inside the store, he could hear snatches of the loud conversation.

"Twas the fiddle man did it. That pretty woman come swarming out of that cart and he wrestled her to the ground by throwing a leg over her. That hoop skirt was fair to giving us a view if he hadn't," Ned said with a snicker.

"But he kept his rifle in hand, Pa, and good thing. 'Cause that bar had done tore through the hounds and had leaped up into the cart. It's a miracle that teacher seen him coming in time to jump out of there."

"Twas a miracle the fiddle man had a loaded rifle. The bear just stood there. His arms spread out like he was set for wrestling whoever or whatever was coming his way," Ned added, spreading his big arms wide in demonstration.

"Fired, and done hit it plumb center," Eb concluded.

"You kill it this morning?" Jasper asked.

Delmar ignored the rest, could tell by the storekeeper's angry voice that he was protesting the way they had handled the bear carcass.

"Why yeah. Sides, that teacher wasn't interested in seeing our skin him at all," Ned shouted.

Delmar was glad the conceited woman had already been taken away. He knew she would be irritated to be talked about in a public place, even if it wasn't a saloon.

"You put them up at your place?" The man called Sykes seemed shocked by something.

"Proud to, when I heard what the man had done, then saw he could make music. You know I'm partial to good music. Figured we had enough for a party. Ivey served up supper while we got the bar situated and shared a jug. After dinner, he played while we all took a circle 'round the yard with the pretty ladies."

"Teacher wasn't keen on that, either," Eb said.

Ivey had drifted away from the loud men. Delmar smiled when she stopped watching the children dancing around him, to give him a wink. In minutes, she was dancing in a whirl, dust flying and her red petticoat appearing and disappearing, encouraging him to play faster and faster.

He caught glimpses of the tiny woman in the shadows of the store, watching wistfully, and Davis glaring angrily at them. Ivey laughed out loud, happy for everyone to see and hear. A skinny old couple stood looking disapprovingly at her as their little girl clapped and tried to copy her wild dance.

Davis Daniel moved past her and out into the street. "That's enough of this damn nonsense. Get in there and find what you said you had to come to town to find."

He had grabbed the woman's wrist, jerked her arm, then gave her a loud slap on the rump as he pointed her to the store.

Delmar tried to keep his face blank at the rough way the man handled the woman as he stopped playing and put away his instrument. No one else seemed to object. In minutes, after the music stopped, the crowd evaporated.

The grim store owner stepped down from the porch, extending a rough hand toward Delmar. "I'm the store owner, Jasper Sykes. How'd you come to be moving our school teacher, Mizz Stewart?"

"Delmar Monroe. Pleased to meet you. I was traveling to the mountains. Heard there were some giant chestnuts and other hardwoods around these parts. Planning to collect some wood to make my own instruments."

The man stared at him blankly, and Delmar wondered if he'd understood a word he'd said. His eyes were intelligent, but his face seemed impassive.

"Can you help us get this animal around back to butcher?" the store owner said, as loudly as though he were shouting.

Delmar laughed. "Happy to have the ox pull him around back for you, but I've no desire to try and hoist him out of there." The joke seemed wasted on the man. Delmar wondered if he were hard of hearing.

The ox seemed eager to move from the bare street to the lush grass behind the store. All three Daniel's men followed them around. Delmar noticed it was the store owner who thought to carry a bucket of water to the animal.

"It'd be easy enough to skin him where he's sitting," the store owner said, "but probably would mess up your cart and trappings."

"No thanks, I wouldn't like it, and I'm sure Miss Stewart would take umbrage," Delmar said.

"Take what?" Davis asked, but all three of the others looked confused.

"Get upset," Delmar said. "She seems to be pretty fussy about her things."

He was remembering how the thin black girl almost dumped the night soil on him as she rushed down the steps and jumped in fright at seeing him on the floor in front of the door. Cicely had apologized, explained how she had to hurry to empty the slops and get Mizz Charlotte more water and some clean clothes, "'fore them wild men wakes up."

He had escaped unharmed, even gallantly escorted the frightened girl on her errands. He had been unable to budge the smelly bear and they had settled for the small carpet-bag. "She said if'n I couldn't get nothing else, I must be sure to get her tote with her clean underthings in it."

"Do you want me to check to see if they are in there?" he'd teased. The girl's eyes had turned white as she rolled them at him in shock. She snatched the tote, struggling to manage it, the clean chamber pot, and pitcher of water. She refused his help. He'd grinned as he watched her struggle inside and up the stairs.

The grunting men called him back to the present as he leaned in to help the others unload the bear. With all four helping, the store owner managed to skin and butcher it into quarters quickly. Delmar left them to it, walked up the hill to watch the women fussing over and escorting the troublesome woman into the school. He was about to climb down and move the oxcart out of the way, when he saw Charlotte step out of the school and take a deep breath. He watched her close her eyes and raise her hands as in prayer. Even from here, he could see all the tension in her body.

He tried not to notice, but when she arched her back like that and raised her head, well any man would notice a figure like that. Not to mention those disturbing eyes of hers. When he'd rescued her from the bear, they had deepened from cornflower blue to a shade that was almost purple. Then there was her perfect skin and those dainty features.

He shook his head. He hadn't decided if he even liked the woman. There was more than looks to consider. She was too prickly for his taste. Always anxious to make her schedule, too stiff to enjoy what was going on around her. The beautiful world passed by unnoticed, because she was too busy with her nose stuck in a book. From the faces she made earlier, he wasn't even sure she liked music, especially his kind.

Last night, instead of dancing and laughing like Ivey Boggs, she had looked as though every step was torture. And poor Cicely, she was the one manhandled and scared witless by the moonshiners, not Charlotte.

What kind of woman would demand her servant rush out so early to take care of her needs? The woman had two good limbs and could have made her own trips to the necessary. Instead, she'd expected that woman to risk being assaulted by one of the Daniels to serve her.

He turned away from the teacher to watch the men struggling with the hide. The bear skin was stretched and left leaning against the back of the store, the skinned head and paws tacked in a menacing pose against the wall.

He watched the noisy men trek through the back door of the store as he started down the path. He stopped, almost hidden from view by the roof of the outhouse. The tiny

woman he had seen earlier was sitting beside the grisly
trophy. He noticed when she covered her shoulder she was
holding something in her lap. A few minutes later, as she
buttoned her blouse he saw she held a tiny baby in her arms.

She had looked plain and sad when he saw her before,
then wistful as she peeked out of the store's door to watch
Ivey dance. Now as she talked to the infant in her arms, she
had one of the sweetest smiles on her face he had ever seen.
He wished he were an artist, he would have drawn them,
sitting there beside the black shadow of the fierce slain
beast.

He heard the store owner shout at her, "In or out, move
it." Delmar felt a slow anger. Did none of these men know
how to treat a lady?

"Don't worry about Widow Mouse. She's fallen into a
feather bed." A chirpy voice startled him and he turned to
see Ivey Boggs at his elbow. "I've got something to show
you."

The backyard seemed empty as he followed her back up
the hill. Suddenly, two voices yelled at him from below
where the carcass still dripped its dark red blood on the
grass. "Hey, Mister Monroe. We thought we'd better take

the schoolmarm's things over to her, now she's been shown her cabin."

"Guess I'd better come down and point them out to you," he said.

"Don't bother," Ivey said in her throaty voice. "I have an empty cabin, would be perfect for you, now the mice are gone."

She used the loud voice he remembered to holler down. "Hey boys, lead that ox along. Leave off the schoolmarm's stuff at her cabin, bring the cart and the rest on up to my old place," Ivey called.

One of the boys grabbed a horn of the grazing animal and led him and the overloaded cart around the store. Instead of protesting, Delmar shrugged. "Lead on, Madam."

The woman shook her astonishing hair and looked up at him with laughter and more in her eyes. She took his arm as they continued up the hill along a well-worn path.

Far below, he saw people rushing to and from the store. Occasionally, a few would walk around back to stare at the enormous hide and whisper about it.

CHAPTER TEN

Charlotte couldn't believe the rush of people coming at her. She laughed at her own nonsense. There probably weren't two hundred people living in this small town, maybe only half that number.

An older woman, with light colored hair and a big grin on her face reached out to touch her hand. "Why, you are so much prettier than we expected. Welcome, welcome to Kyles Ford, Mizz Stewart. We are so proud to have you join us. I'm Mizz Watkin and this is Reverend Watkin."

Charlotte curtsied, blushed at the flattering, warm greeting. "Mizz Watkin, you are too kind."

"Just call me Mizz Dovie, everyone does." The older woman tugged her up and Charlotte was surprised by her strength as the woman extended her arm to fold her closer in to an embrace. Such a motherly gesture astonished her. She would have to write Mama and let her know how kind everyone had been and describe this warm welcome.

"Don't worry, we'll come back for your things. I've got a delightful luncheon planned for you."

Cicely moved from the shadow of the cart and Charlotte reached out to take the timid girl's hand.

"Is this your girl? Don't worry, we'll get her something to eat as well," Mizz Dovie said.

Cicely made the same face she usually did when she didn't like what someone said. Charlotte didn't want to begin by explaining her relationship to her two companions. That could come later. For now, she let the woman and her two friends, and the two men who were clearly husbands, tow her along from the embarrassing commotion at the store.

The inside of the parsonage was crowded with the parlor chairs added to the dining table to accommodate all the guests. True to her word, Mizz Dovie welcomed Cicely, setting the girl in the kitchen to wait on the guests and to eat her own meal. Charlotte knew the free woman didn't like it, but also knew the girl would be happy to eat, as was she. For a moment she worried about Delmar, then shook her head at the idiotic notion. The man had reassured the Daniels that he was going this way anyway, and the pastor her father had arranged to escort her on the last leg of her journey, had vouched for him.

Really, he had not gone a step out of his way to assist her. She remembered the last two nights, sleeping in the ox cart first with Cicely, or last night, sleeping in the beds of those wild strangers. Instead, he seemed to delight in making inappropriate and embarrassing comments, and man-handling her in general like she was just another trunk to be loaded and unloaded.

Mizz Dovie was staring at her, clearly vexed. Charlotte apologized for her distraction. Thanking her hostess after she repeated the instructions, Charlotte settled on the chair across from her as commanded.

The food was good, cold ham, dressed eggs, potato salad, and cold iced tea, loaded with sugar. The best part of the meal was the light biscuits and sweet jam that were served warm by Cicely. Charlotte smiled when she saw the peeved looking girl with flour dust on her smooth, dark skin. She raised her napkin and took a moment to wipe Cicely's cheek as the girl served her. Charlotte thanked her and went on with eating. Mizz Dovie raised critical brows at her while one of the other ladies tutted.

"You address your darkie so familiarly. Is that the way folks do it in Boston?" The young woman who had arrived bearing the egg dish asked.

"Cicely is not my slave, or servant. She is traveling to Sneedville to live with an uncle there. My mother arranged with a friend for her fare so that I did not have to travel here unescorted. She was born a free Negro and has always been free. As soon as her uncle arrives here, she will be traveling on to the next town with him."

"We have colored people living in Vardy. They are Melungeons, people of mixed blood. But they look like this girl," the woman added.

Her husband interrupted her. "Not all do, some look like Indians or whites, only a little darker – like some Europeans."

Reverend Watkin had to respond. "The girl is lucky she is staying in East Tennessee. Don't know any slave holders in these parts, maybe a few who have house servants in Knoxville. Course, there are plenty if she travels farther south and west. I believe there are more near Nashville. People can't raise cotton without them it seems, so of course the western part of Tennessee would be dangerous. Does she have any papers?"

Charlotte stared down the end of the table to where the man sat. She was aware that Cicely no longer had her sulky face on, but she was staring at the reverend as she held a pitcher of tea in her shaking hand. The woman who had started the conversation held up her glass, and said, "Here, girl, mind what you're doing."

Cicely refilled the glass but moved to stand behind Charlotte, her eyes focused on the reverend. "Well, I'm sure the girl's uncle will know how to deal with the situation." he said.

Charlotte was glad when the topic was dropped and the meal seemed over. Mizz Dovie had the girl clear the table, refill their glasses, and bring in the desert plates. Everyone was served a sliver of cake. Charlotte had to admire Cicely as the girl served the desert without flaw.

Mizz Dovie addressed Charlotte directly. "We know you are well-trained. Your father spoke highly of your achievements. I was the teacher here before last year. I retired, at my husband's insistence, after I began to have trouble with my feet."

"It was Providence that brought you here," the reverend said. "In my church letter, there was mention of a special mission funding teachers in rural areas. There were a lot of conditions. The community had to raise a free-standing building solely for the school, provide accommodation for the teacher, and have a Protestant religious affiliation. The school had to be open and free to all interested students. All pastors were being urged to participate, either by collecting donations, or by accepting a teacher."

"You've no idea how difficult this was to convince the rest of the community. They would have been happy with Mizz Dovie teaching in the church during the week, for free, forever," the reverend added.

"Really, I couldn't, I just couldn't. I've developed an ache in my heels from standing all these years. The pain is intolerable if I'm on my feet all day. No, I'm permanently retired."

"And no one else was educated enough to take over learnin' the children," the egg woman said.

"Teaching is a demanding profession," Charlotte agreed, making the correction without additional comment.

The young husband was the first to say. "Guess you can see why we wanted a chance to meet with you like this. To explain our expectations."

"Share the school rules," Mizz Dovie said.

The reverend removed a tiny piece of paper from his vest pocket and sat unrolling it until it was a foot-sized sheet. "This is your copy. I'll pass it your way when I finish here."

"Your duties as the teacher are to arrive early and stay late to neaten up the school area. Of course we expect you to do these chores, every day before school or after. Wash the chalkboard, fill lamps, carry in fresh water, empty ashes, bring in new firewood, keep the room warm and clean," he read aloud and everyone at the table nodded at how obvious these things were.

Charlotte tried not to look shocked or nervous. She wondered what they would say or do if she announced she had never done any of these chores before. Mama and the maid had taken care of them, but there was no chance to protest as he was still reading.

"Start school at nine each morning by ringing the bell. Teach and keep all students quiet and engaged in work at all times. Release students at two each afternoon by ringing the bell, and after school, sweep the floor and wash student slates."

Charlotte considered giving a dramatic sigh, now that he had finished, but didn't dare. Besides, he was the one to take a deep breath and continue.

"We are most concerned about the morals of our young people, and aware that being a northerner, your sensibilities may not match our southern ones, so we've spelled out some moral guidelines for you," the reverend said.

Dovie added, "Being a minister's daughter, I argued that you'd have no need for this sort of list."

"We wanted to be certain you understood our expectations for the woman who is a role model for our children," the egg lady added.

The reverend cleared his throat loudly and everyone turned to him. "Teachers will use their time to read the Bible or other good books. Women teachers will not keep company with men. A teacher who marries or engages in unseemly conduct may be dismissed. Teachers will save part of their earnings to provide for their own keep in the off part of the year. Teachers will not smoke, use liquor, or waste time in gossip or idleness. A teacher who works faithfully and without fault may be retained as teacher for the next year, dependent on the Board of Education's approval."

Charlotte had grown numb as the list continued to grow. For the kingly fee of $100 a year, she would be little more than an indentured servant. As Mizz Dovie smiled at her reassuringly, Charlotte tried to sit up straighter and remember to breathe.

All the way toward the small cabin above the school, Charlotte listened to the school board members brag about what the small town had accomplished. They were so proud of building a new school and cabin for their educated teacher.

Dovie continued to prattle. Reassuring Charlotte that she would be on hand each day to provide guidance and suggestions, lest she might wonder if some of her actions would be considered inappropriate. She had taught the mountain children for over ten years, and she would be the first to admit, that some could be a bit wild and unruly, but if Charlotte would remember never to smile at them, and to keep her paddle handy, she should have no trouble at all.

When the reverend opened the door to the tiny cabin, Charlotte had to step back at the strong smell of new wood. As the egg lady pointed out all the modern conveniences, Charlotte felt a little dizzy. Part of the reason was the incredibly tight and crowded space.

A simple bed, made from stripped poles with a hung mattress was against one wall, a small stove with two eyes and a small oven beside its wood box could be used to cook on and heat the small space. She had been given a real window, the glass coming down from Louisville. The deep metal sink and pump would allow her to wash her dishes and clothes inside, whatever the weather.

The egg lady pulled the panel of plain cloth along the sink front to reveal a shelf for storage and her husband pointed out a second shelf from the window to the door. The young husband pointed out the two drawers under the bed for storage, while the preacher seemed especially proud of the double hooks by the door, that could hold her cloak and bonnet when she came home.

It was Dovie who pointed out, how to raise the hanging board on the wall at the end of the bed. It would make a table for dining on or grading papers in the evening, allowing her to sit on the end of the bed or in the single, ladder-back chair they had provided. Best of all, when it wasn't in use, she moved the drop leg and let the board bang against the wall. It would allow room to walk around the end of the bed, for changing linens or whatever.

As soon as they left, Charlotte sank onto the edge of the bed in despair.

CHAPTER ELEVEN

Delmar strode along, trying to move fast enough to prevent the woman from leaning into him again. "I had figured to build a lean-to, at least until colder weather. Unless this place is very small, or the rent is miniscule, I probably can't afford the place."

"You staying the full year?" she asked.

Delmar recalled the loud argument with his father. He had exactly one year to prove he could make a go at his music, then he had promised to return and join the firm with his brother and father.

"Ten months, maybe longer," he said.

She grinned up at him. "Foolish to consider any other place. Unless I move back, the place will stand empty and just be a worry for me. If I had a responsible young man like you looking after things, I would feel better."

She moved her hand along his forearm and Delmar felt the muscles jump. "How much rent?"

"Here we are," she said instead of answering his question. "Two large rooms. A clean drawing wood stove, has a nice cook top." She twirled, a bright flash of yellow in the dark room." Delmar remained beside the door, nudging it farther open to let the light illuminate the space.

"Come on in, it comes fully furnished." She pointed to a crudely made table with a bench on either side. "It's not much in here, but the bed is wonderful, and I have a cedar wardrobe."

"It's nice," he said, cautiously stepping inside with the bold woman.

She winked at him, beckoned with a raised hand and crooked her finger as she disappeared into the room that was a step-down from the one they were in. It was probably the steep hill, but someone had to be pretty good to figure out how to set the posts and get the place to sit so level.

Inside the next room, the floors felt a little rough under his feet, but there was no missing the prominent bed, with its bright red figured quilt on top. As he'd feared, Ivey leaped with a squeal and landed in the center of the mattress, her skirt flying up to reveal a shapely leg. He was surprised to see her bounce up a little. "Come on, I had it 'specially made. The straps are leather harness, gives it a little extra snap if you get it going."

Delmar blushed, stepped back up a step into the other room. "It looks mighty tempting, but I'm not sure I can afford a place this fancy."

"Hey, anybody home," a loud voice called from the doorway and Delmar turned to smile at his unlikely savior.

"Hey, Eb, just looking around. Mizz Boggs thought I might be interested in renting this cabin."

From the corner of his eye, he saw Ivey bounce off the bed as quickly as she had flounced onto it. She shook her skirt, straightened her blouse and even reached behind her to smooth the covers.

He walked toward the open door, looked around outside. Ned stood beside the still loaded cart. "I thought you boys were okay in delivering the luggage to the teacher?"

"We wasn't sure which things were hers, there's so much piled in here. We'd have asked her, but her little cabin was closed up tight and she never answered our knockin'. If'n you're renting this place, you might want us to unload your'n first?"

Delmar wasn't surprised to see Davis thundering up the hill toward Ivey's cabin. Fortunately, the woman appeared at the cabin door, looking innocent enough.

"You didn't tell me what the rent was?" Delmar called.

"You have ready money?" she asked.

Delmar shrugged, "A little."

"Twenty for now, we'll work out something else for the last half's payment. Renters aren't that common in Kyles Ford."

Delmar sent the gold piece flying through the air and was rewarded by seeing the laughing woman pocket the coin and shove it into the top edge of her thin blouse.

Davis was hollering already and Delmar swatted the oxen to make him move faster.

Eb and Ned were walking backward, slapping at each other as Ivey waited, smiling at their Pa. He left them behind, staring at the arguing couple, wondered if they'd get to see the pair fight or make-up.

As soon as he'd brought the animal to a halt outside the tiny cabin, he rushed to knock on the door. Then, without waiting for an answer, he turned back to remove the plank bench he'd made from the tiger-eye maple boards. Both looked no worse the wear from having the two women sleep on them. With the wood out of the way, he unloaded his violin and guitar cases next. Finally, he reached the massive trunk and hauled it up to the edge of the cart and then over the tailgate to land with a thump on the ground.

He set the hat-boxes on top, then slung the carpet-bag and a smaller bag on the ground beside it. He had climbed over the tailgate to look around inside, desperate to be rid of all women and their possessions for at least a little while, when the door to the cabin flew open. Delmar straightened in the cart, making it shift forward a little. Like a child on a see-saw, he tilted to regain his balance.

"You, what are you doing to my things now?"

Delmar's jaw dropped. He swore a moment, then caught his tongue and vaulted over the tail of the cart to stand face to face with the impossible woman.

"And please, watch your language!" she demanded. At his red face, she took a breath and pointed behind them to the hill where the Daniels were all involved in another argument. "People are watching and may hear you," she whispered.

"Oh, and we care about that, do we?" He glared at her until she dropped her hands from her hips. He noticed her dejected stance, and rumpled look. The silly little hat had been discarded, and her dark, thick hair had escaped all her careful pinning. Best of all, she seemed to have discarded her blasted bell-shaped petticoat that had made her seem so untouchable. For a moment, he was tempted to move closer and raise those pouty lips enough to kiss, wondering if he did, if it would make her eyes darken to purple.

Cicely rushed up, saying. "That church lady was about ready to fetch the chains for me. I did what she said and washed up after all you folks, but then she wanted me to sweep out everything and start her supper cooking. I would have argued, but she gave me such a fierce look.

"Finally, I just had to say something. I told her I was afraid you needed my help and would be worried about me. Sides, I didn't know where they had taken you. She walked me to the door and pointed out the schoolhouse and your little cabin. It sure is a cute place."

Delmar took a step back to make room for the chattering black girl. Charlotte raised her hand to her head and Cicely hushed. "Oh no, don't tell me youse got a headache, Mizz Charlotte. I can fetch some water and let you lay down with a cool cloth on your head. That always helped my Mammy when she got the blind head."

"The blind head?" Delmar asked.

Almost as rapidly, but a little softer, Cicely explained. "Her head would hurt so bad sometimes, she couldn't even see. Told me once it was from Master hitting her too hard once when she sassed him."

Charlotte groaned, and Delmar raised a finger to his lips and motioned for Cicely to look inside for a bucket. The girl flew through the door and in a minute back out. "I'se don't have to fetch a pail full, this cabin's got its own pump. Come look see."

Delmar gently placed an arm around Charlotte's shoulder and escorted her back inside. It was a small, tight space, but he could quickly see that everything had been provided. The bed was wider than a single bunk, and placed against the wall to maximize space. Cicely was working the pump, giggling as a stream of cold water appeared. She reached up to take down a cup from the shelf above the sink, filled it, and turned around to hand it to Delmar as he urged Charlotte to sit on the edge of the bed.

Both watched Charlotte take a sip, then clutch Delmar's hand to swallow it all. This time when she groaned, he guided her to lay back against the pillow, carefully placing his arm under her legs to lift them onto the bed. Cicely moved down to unbuckle the little leather shoes.

Delmar leaned against the counter, trying not to stare. There was no way to not make an inventory of the slender ankles, the pale skin marked with red welts where the socks and the top of the boots had pressed on the tiny feet.

Cicely moved to unbutton the tight little traveling jacket and worried one arm, then the other out of its snug confines. The linen blouse underneath was expensive and thin. Cicely cast a look of warning at him over her shoulder. Delmar nodded as he walked out the door, but continued to stare inside. He swallowed as he saw the rise of the large, perfect breasts barely constrained by the tight corset and chemise underneath the white blouse.

Outside, he wasn't surprised to see Eb and Ned headed his way as he paced. When he looked up the hill, he saw that the quarreling couple had disappeared. "You boys headed back home?"

"Pa and Ivey left. We got to go to the store, see if Sykes kept some of that bar meat like he promised," Eb said.

Ned jumped in immediately, "They were about to fight, did you see that."

Delmar grinned, "Guess your Pa is jealous, since Ivey's so friendly."

Ned elbowed Eb, waiting for him to answer. The older boy hesitated, "He was worried she might have been offering you a little extra, if you know what I mean?"

Delmar looked embarrassed, surprised the two seemed to know what had almost happened. "She was just apologizing that the place wasn't clean enough or might smell. It seemed good enough to me. She gave me a good price, so I've rented it. There's room enough for me to sit and work on my instruments inside. Won't have to worry about the weather warping the wood."

The boys didn't look convinced, but whatever they had to say, was interrupted by Cicely appearing at the door. "That Mizz Dovie woman done invited you to join her and walk Mizz Charlotte and me down when it's time for supper."

"Is she all right?" he asked.

Cicely nodded. "Yeah, all she needs is to sleep. Her head should be fine when I wakes her up. My Mammy's always was." She glowered past him at the big men behind him, who were eyeing her speculatively. "I guess I'll try to get her things inside and some of them put away while she sleeps."

"Here, I'll carry them in for you. See you boys."

"Yeah, we'll probably see you every day. Now we're thinking of going to school again. You want us to pull your cart back up the hill and unload it for you."

"No, I've got it. Thanks fellows."

Cicely wasn't the only one to warily watch the boys still standing there, trying to peer into the cabin as they worked.

As Delmar handed the girl the last two cases, he turned on the boys.

"You need something else?"

Eb held out a silver buckle, and Ned pulled out his own. "We wondered what you thought these were. We found them in the yard this morning."

Delmar accepted the dirty objects, sniffed in disgust. "They smell like…" the boy's laughter covered the word.

"That's where we found them, in the dog turds this morning. Figure they passed them from the bar innards they ate. What do you think it means?"

He handed them back to Eb. "Think it means your bear ate someone. Better ask the store owner. He probably knows everyone in town and if someone is missing."

They were already running down the path. Delmar loaded his things and headed back up to the cabin he'd rented. It was hard not to run after the excited boys, but in a place this size, he'd learn soon enough who the victim was.

CHAPTER TWELVE

With a roaring headache, all Charlotte knew was she wanted the annoying musician to leave, and leave now. Instead, he was slinging her belongings out of that terrible cart, probably expecting her to rush out and grab them.

When she did, it was Delmar who acted outraged, as though she were the one without manners or a sense of gratitude. Rage swept through her, making her shake. If he were Charles, or one of her sisters, she would call him an impossible, arrogant fool, but he was a stranger, like everyone else around her now.

For a moment, Charlotte knew his argument might have merit. He had rescued her more than once on this trip, but he had also subjected her to too many indignities for her to ever forgive him. When he stepped closer to her, she saw his light eyes sparking with anger.

The noisy girl appeared in time to save him from the lashing she was prepared to deliver. That, and the fact that Charlotte felt ghastly, as though her head were going to explode if she had to talk louder than the bearded monkey scolding her.

At least Cicely now had someone to chatter at besides her. When the two helped her to lie down on the bed, her opinion of them quickly changed. Cicely was working hard to make her more comfortable and for the second time today, Charlotte knew she was going to miss the girl.

Delmar presumed to lift her onto the bed, smoothing her dress beneath and over her legs. She didn't bother protesting, but succumbed to the moment of peace before Cicely started giggling as she pumped water.

Charlotte stood in the cool night air, surprised at how sweet the air smelled, how quiet the small town seemed. In the dark, she could make out Delmar walking down to greet them, his shirt glowing white in the dark. He bowed to them as soon as he was near enough, then held both arms akimbo to say, "Ladies."

Cicely giggled as Charlotte accepted his offered elbow on one side. The silly girl moved to his other side, barely touching his arm as they walked back down the hill toward the parsonage.

"It's nice of the Watkins to feed us twice today," Charlotte said.

Delmar's stomach growled in answer, and he apologized before adding, "I wasn't so lucky."

They were almost to the house when Cicely released his arm to stand behind them as Charlotte reached out to the door. Reverend Watkin swung it open before her hand touched it.

"Welcome, welcome," he said as he turned to yell over his shoulder. "They're here, better put it on the table."

During dinner, Charlotte described how helpful Cicely had been in helping her put her things away. She knew enough to remark how wonderfully designed the new cabin was. If even Delmar was impressed by it, then she had realized her error in not gushing about it with more gratitude this afternoon. She pleaded for forgiveness, describing her terrible headache.

Dovie Watkin rose immediately. "You must drink some of my herb tea, it contains Feverfew blooms. It is the best cure for that particular malady."

By the time they escaped the zealous reverend and his wife, Charlotte was certain her head would soon be aching again. The night air had grown chill, despite the heat of the day.

"Do you ladies have wood for your fire?"

Cicely nodded, her teeth chattering. An animal cried in the dark and the girls both stopped. He urged them forward, opening the door to the cabin for them. They just stood there and he entered while they huddled outside. He lit the lamp first, opened the small oven, and lit the neatly piled wood that someone had thoughtfully arranged there.

While he squatted, waiting for the fire to catch, he looked around at the chaos, noting Charlotte's discarded clothing. The huge trunk was forced into the space at the end of the bed, jammed so tightly that the fold-down table couldn't be raised. He looked up at the ceiling, noted all the space in the arched ceiling. Once the oven door was closed, he made sure the damper was open and walked out to allow them access to the room.

"Soon as I cut and haul another tree, I'll try to bring some boards and make you a little loft to store your empty bags."

Charlotte stared at him as Cicely squeezed between them. Swallowing, Charlotte dropped him a curtsy, surprising them both. "You are too kind sir. I won't be able to pay you."

He waved a hand dismissingly, as though insulted. "Goodnight, ladies."

He heard the black girl giggling behind him as he heard the woman inside drop the bar over the door.

Charlotte looked around at the tight space and knew she should have been embarrassed to have the man see the clutter. Surprisingly, she wasn't.

Cicely stood by the fire, pumped and put a kettle on to boil. "That bossy Mizz Watkin done sent home some of her feverfew tea. Maybe you should have another cup while I figure's out where I'se going to sleep.

Charlotte unbuttoned her blouse and then her clean skirt, carefully draping them over the trunk so they would be wearable in the morning. "Don't be silly. There's room enough in the bed if you don't wiggle around too much."

Cicely rolled her eyes and pointed to the door. "What if that nosey woman comes by to see how we settled? You done told her I sleep on a rug on the floor, like a pet dog."

"I told her what she wanted to hear. Trust me, she's not going to come out in the dark to see. We only need to wake early, before she runs to the outhouse. You know, she'll come over to look in on us then."

Charlotte looked about, finally noticed the two hat boxes stacked precariously on the shelf beside her single set of kitchenware. She couldn't even see her satchel and carpet bag. "Did you unpack everything?"

Cicely looked around guiltily. "No, ma'am. I put the things from the little bags under the bed. Most all your clothes are still inside the trunk." She shrank back into the corner beside the sink and Charlotte smiled.

"You did fine, thank you."

Later, as she stretched out in the small bed, she felt a bony knee from the girl in bed beside her. Cicely was asleep where she had crawled in at the back of the bed. Charlotte smiled as the first soft snores filled the air and she watched the girl gradually release her grip on the edge of the bed.

Charlotte knew by morning the girl would be snuggled close, just as her youngest sister Dorothea always ended up back home. For a minute she felt a great wave of homesickness, but she refused to tolerate the feeling. This is what she had wanted. To go into the wilderness to help others.

Relaxing, accepting the comfort of having someone sharing her space, she surrendered to fatigue. Tomorrow might be as frightening as today, but in a week school would start and she needed to be ready to welcome her first students. She had a journal and tomorrow she would plan her first week's lessons. There was so much to do.

Even as she tried to urge her mind to work a little longer, she smiled, imagining the tall, bearded young man smiling down at her.

CHAPTER THIRTEEN

Charlotte woke early, picked out her plainest dress to wear today. She was determined to get her cabin and the school in perfect shape. School would start in a week.

Hair pulled back, her pair of braids looped and secured at the back of her head, she scurried down the path to the school outhouses, which Mizz Dovie had explained were amazing. Each side was a two seater. There had been endless debate about it, but positioned where it was at the edge of town, it had been argued that Saturday visitors and Sunday church goers would all be grateful to have such a large public facility.

Charlotte had shaken the sleepy girl, but Cicely had still been in bed when she left. She smiled at the memory of the dark face buried in the too white pillow. She was still smiling when a dark form made her freeze and draw back. A man, a big black man, stood between her and her cabin.

"Who, who goes there?" she said, grateful that the deep breath had given her voice enough power to not emerge as a squeak.

The man scowled at her, made up his mind, and bowed his head, pulling a soft gray cap from his fuzzy mound of hair. "I'm Big John, from Sneedville. I've come to fetch my sister by law Bessie's gal, Cicely."

Charlotte stood still, not bowing, but raising a hand to her heart. There was something terrifying about the man. She wasn't afraid for herself, but even as she thought of her, the slim girl emerged from the cabin. She was dressed in the same clothes she had worn during their whole trip. Charlotte remembered what she had planned to do before the child left.

"Wait, please, both of you."

Without explanation she stepped into the cabin, climbed up using a shelf as a ladder to reach the smaller hat box. She was relieved to find the stiff, round bonnet, just where she'd packed it. Her mother had insisted she take it, one never knew when a plain straw topper would be needed. Charlotte had protested that she had worn it as a child and it made her look ten years old, not like a teacher.

Satisfied, she stepped out to where the two dark faces were scowling at each other. If they had been talking, she hadn't heard a word.

"Here, I found it." She said as she set the hat on the small dark head. "I told mother it was too small for me, but I see it fits you perfectly."

When Cicely started to reach up to take the hat off, Charlotte caught her hand. "Something to remember me by. A small payment for all your help on my journey."

Cicely bowed and Charlotte pulled her up and gave her a swift hug. "Safe journey. When you find time, send me word of how you are doing. I will miss you."

The big black man puffed up like a snake, ready to strike, but Cicely raised her head and tied the ribbons into a nice bow beneath her chin. In the soft morning light, her bright smile changed her appearance.

"Beautiful," Charlotte said, but the big man was already tugging the girl away. In moments, they were gone.

◇◇◇

Charlotte wiped her face, surprised at all the dust that had accumulated in the new building. For a moment, she wished that she could shed her long-sleeved, over-blouse and breathe a little easier in the hot room. Instead, she moved to the long windows on one side and tried to ease the stiff frame open. When it didn't budge, she walked to the double door at the end and propped it open with a heavy rock from the overgrown school yard.

She stood in the open door, eyes closed as a warm breeze swept over her. She could feel the perspiration dampening at her bunched sleeves and the tight collar of the plain blouse.

"Morning," a familiar voice interrupted her delight in the breeze. As she opened her eyes, her sense of peace escaped.

"Morning, Mr. Monroe," she said, unable to keep the scowl from her face.

He smiled, hesitating before speaking again. "Surprised to see you and Cicely up and hard at work so early."

She wiped at her face and was surprised to see his face break into a wide grin. She looked at her hand, and knew what he was so tickled about. She turned back into the school building and walked up to the bucket of water she had carried in earlier. Dipping a cloth into the gray water, she hoped the wet would at least help as she squeezed the cloth, then wiped her face, neck, and hands.

As she turned around, she jumped to see he had followed her inside.

"Be cooler if you opened a window or two."

She snapped. "I tried, but they seem to be sealed shut."

He moved over to the first one and reached up to feel for a latch. Then giving a heave, opened the window to allow a heavenly breeze. Charlotte stood, mesmerized as his shirt billowed at his slender waist and strained tightly across his broad shoulders.

He caught her look and grinned even wider. "Do you want all four open?"

She nodded and he tried not to gloat as he worked on the last three, making sure to give her something to look at.

When he finished, he turned to see she had stopped gawking and was busy dusting the student desks in the blazing light.

She raised her head, spoke softly. "Cicely is gone. Her uncle came for her at daylight."

"You don't look pleased, I thought you couldn't wait to get rid of her. You as much as said so last night at Mizz Watkin's house."

Charlotte shook her head. "The man was frightening, and you are wrong. But, like my arriving here, I know she will be happy when her journey is over and she can settle into her new life. She was very unhappy at home."

"So, you should be celebrating her moving on."

She looked troubled as she raised the slate, then made a quick stack of the ones on the first row and carried them forward to the bucket. "You didn't see him. There was something wrong there."

"I think our chatter-box got under your skin. Did you make her sleep on the floor, like you told Mizz Dovie?"

Her eyes widened as she stared behind him. "Where else did you think she could sleep?"

She looked over to the image of the woman they were talking about. "Of course, why are you so interested? Good morning, Mizz Dovie."

Delmar turned, removing his hat to bow to her.

"Young man, what are you doing here with your ox?"

He straightened up, looked around as though expecting to see the ox in the school house. "I'm assisting a lady to open the windows. Going to be another hot day."

"That's a smart answer, but I was asking where you were going with your ox and tools," the older woman asked.

Delmar debated. He was sure the reverend's wife was as kind and generous as most in her role, but he hated answering questions from every busy-body in town. At least, if he answered her, she would probably tell the rest and save him time.

"Davis Daniel promised me a good walnut tree that stands on the edge of their yard." Before she could ask another question, he volunteered. "If I would bring the ox to help pull some stumps that are in the way of where he plans to expand his still."

"Expand it. Why the man makes too many gallons to sell as it is. He's going to make every man in the community as big a drunk as he is, just you wait and see."

Delmar nodded, backing toward the door where he swept his hat to the ladies before disappearing.

◇◇◇

"Mizz Stewart, I do remember my husband reading the school board rules to you yesterday. Association with any young man would be frowned upon, but especially a scoundrel like Mister Monroe."

Fighting the corner of her mouth, knowing not to smile at the outrageous comment, Charlotte managed a mere, "Scoundrel?"

"A man of his age, roaming the country, playing music at any excuse for a party. Encouraging dancing and drinking and foolishness. I would think an educated young woman like yourself, growing up in the home of a minister like your father, would know to be wary of his sort."

Charlotte nodded her head obediently. Every word was one she had told herself the last two days. However, there was something about his speech and manners that made her doubt if they were right in their assessment. Then there was his concern for Cicely. Certainly scoundrel was too severe a word.

Mizz Dovie was expounding upon a set of books that already rested on the shelf. "I know you said you wished to establish your own, progressive curriculum, but these little books by McGuffey are by far the most brilliant teaching aid of these modern times. Your older students will be familiar with them and already reading successfully from the stories.

Charlotte returned the first row of slates, gathered another. When she approached the table she turned over the empty coal bucket and sat down at the knee of the woman who had claimed the teacher's chair.

For an hour, Charlotte listened and nodded, but her mind was following a tall, slender man back up the trail to a big house on the ridge. She wasn't a betting woman, but if she were, she would bet he would be drinking and fiddling in the yard again tonight. It might be days before he came down the ridge again. With luck, she would be properly settled by then, and so busy she wouldn't even notice his return.

CHAPTER FOURTEEN

The woods were sweet smelling, with honeysuckle vining along the trail. A row of trees wrapped in grape vines grew half-way up the ridge. He paused to gather handfuls of the tart, ripe fruit. Without the two young women, the trip was silent and easy. In little more than an hour he emerged into the bare earth yard where the Daniels were just stirring about.

The two half-grown men were just coming across the yard from the back of the barn. They greeted him first with firm handshakes and jostling.

"Wow, you must have flown up the mountain. Didn't even hear the hounds barking you were on the way."

"That's 'cause Pa had us put 'em up last night. The way they charged at us when we came into the yard," Eb said. "Go on, let 'em out."

"You don't say. They tried to bite you?" Delmar asked.

Ned opened the barn and a pack of a half dozen hounds broke out, circling the yard and barking at the men and the cart. The big ox put his ears back and rolled his eyes before bellowing.

Davis came out onto the porch and yelled for the dogs to settle down. They did instantly, a few even tucking their tails as they slunk over to lay down below the porch.

"Twas that bar meat. That's what Ivey figured out. They didn't act that way for us. Reckoned it was the smell of blood and that bar meat, made 'em go off that way."

He stepped on down from the porch, extending a big meaty hand to shake. Pointing toward the outhouse, he took a step in the direction. "Go on in, Ivey's up, tell her what you'd like and she'll cook it up. She does real good at cooking eggs and such. Her biscuits don't match up to my Alma's, but the rest is good."

◇◇◇

The table was crowded, the three Daniel men were all elbows and reaching arms. Delmar sat quietly, listening to their loud quarrels, waiting for one or the other to ask some question of him. He was surprised to notice how quiet Ivey was. Even her hair seemed tamer. When he'd stepped into the cabin, he had seen her standing in her bedroom door, still in her nightgown. As the boys stepped up behind him, she disappeared.

Eb had been the one to elbow him. "Don't let on you got an eyeful, else Pa will flatten you."

"She do that a lot?" Delmar asked.

"Oh yeah," Ned said. "She ain't in the trade no more so you ain't goin' to get anything, but she still likes to remind you what she's got."

Now he noticed Eb fingering his beard, eyeing his father's fuller, red beard. Eb turned and glared at Ned who was talking and eating at the same time. "You're staying for dinner, ain't you Delmar. Ivey's cookin' up a huge batch of bear stew," Ned said.

"And a vanilla drop cake," Ivey spoke for the first time.

"Glad to stay. I came up to help Davis pull stumps. Hope you two can help me take down that big walnut you talked about."

"She's giving us all hair-cuts. Going to shave our beards off so we can go down to the town school," Eb said.

Davis shook his head. "You both can shave your own faces."

"Aw Pa, we might cut our necks too. Remember the story you told us about Harley Boggs, how he let a drunken Indian shave him one time, like'd to bled to death. Shot the man for trying to kill him on purpose."

"Did he kill the Indian?" Ned asked.

"No, it's that old man, hangs around the landing fishin'. He only shot off two of his toes."

"All right. I'll let her shave you if you shut up, won't you." Davis ran a big hand over his face and tugged at his own beard. "I'm going to stretch out in the parlor, you boys holler when you got everything ready to go stump pullin'." He stood over all of them. "And keep the racket down until then."

Delmar looked at Ivey, noticed she was staring at her plate. Davis' face was glaring hard at her and Delmar wondered if Davis was the kind of man to beat a woman. He certainly had his hounds cowed enough.

"Sure, we'll be glad to help, 'cept we don't know nothing about logging and such," Eb said while Ned grunted in agreement.

"Good. Maybe we can get a stump or two. You need a hand with the dishes, Ivey?"

Her big eyes widened and she shook her head, grabbing and stacking the plates quickly. Delmar watched how she glanced in the direction of the parlor. He could hear like the others, the soft snores of the man inside.

Outside, the hounds quietly rose to their feet, one by one nosing his hands for pets or treats. He made the mistake of petting one, and the young dog stayed close on his heels as he walked about. When he spotted the towering walnut tree, he walked over to check it out. At least thirty feet high, the trunk was only about two feet around, but the tree was tall and straight as an arrow. The only marks were several sharp gashes in the trunk, probably made by some big animal.

Ned found him first, and soon the boys were standing, watching him examine the tree. "That's where Nadine's weddin' hog sharpened his tusk. Alma was up the tree when he did it and she tried throwing walnuts down on him to shoo him away. Stead, made him mad and she told us how it sounded, the way he was working his teeth around first," the boy imitated the grunts and gnashing sound of the big boar.

"Your little sister climbed this tree?"

"Naw, not Nadine. Alma shimmied up it. She's eighteen, nearer nineteen," Eb said.

"Oh, the one who married a Melungeon?"

"Yeah, done run off toward California with her wild Indian, Gabriel Bridger, least that's what Pa called him."

Delmar was surprised to hear how wistful the boy sounded when talking about his sister. Alma was the biscuit cooker Ivey had been compared to. Their sister must be some woman, to be so missed by this rough family. Surprisingly, he had heard none of them talk about their mother. He had heard from the store owner that the girl

Alma had been wed the same day as the funeral for her mother.

He was tempted to ask the question that had been on his mind all morning. Did their Pa beat Ivey? He feared they would misinterpret the question as a sign of his interest in Ivey, of which he had none. He left the question unasked, hoping to get the tree cut and limbed up for the ox to pull, and enough stumps pulled out of the ground for Davis to let him take the log.

It was dark. Delmar drug a piece of bread through the thick stew and let it set on the rim of the bowl. He was too tired to lift it.

Davis raised a jug from behind his chair, slammed it onto the table. The angry man stared at Ivey, as though daring her to say anything. When she didn't, he hoisted it on the back of his crooked elbow to a comfortable pouring height, and took two deep swallows.

He passed the jug to his oldest son. Eb took a drink and passed it on around.

Finally, it reached Delmar. He remembered what Dovie Watkin had told Charlotte. He had walked out, but left the door open a crack. The words had seemed louder than if he'd been in the room. She'd called him a scoundrel. A drunken scoundrel. He pulled the cork, tried to get the angle right, but had to set it down again. Ivey leaned over and took the jug, hoisted it to show him how to do it, but he noticed she didn't take a drink.

When he tried the next time, he noticed Davis had squinted his eyes and was staring at him harder. This time Delmar lifted the jug perfectly, held it right so that the cold strong liquid poured into the side of his mouth. He set it down before swallowing, remembering from the last time the hot kick the liquor would give his throat.

Davis took the jug back, demonstrated how to chug three or four slugs, then set it down in front of him. Delmar knew it was a dare. What would he win if he bested the man in his own house at drinking? A beating? Instead he shook his head as though drunk, instead of exhausted. "Nope, another slug of that potent brew, and I'll be sleeping with your hounds on the hearth."

Davis had laughed, and Ned had slapped him on the shoulder.

"Better not get him too drunk, Davis. He won't be able to play you a tune," Ivey said.

Davis stopped laughing and stood up. In a minute, he was back shoving an instrument case into Delmar's lap.

Suddenly, the exhaustion fell away as he realized he was being commanded to play for his supper. He unlatched the sides and drew out the guitar. Hadn't the big oaf noticed the difference in size. No one said anything as he sat, carefully tuning it. When he had it right, he began to strum and sing in a mellow baritone voice, the old ballad, "Barbara Allen."

Ivey rose while he played, to make quick work of clearing the table. It was too long and slow a song to dance to, but he noticed she was swaying and swishing gracefully as she made trips from the table to the small kitchen. When she came back out, Davis managed to stand and pull her onto his lap. She seemed to have no objection when the man pawed her breasts and turned her in against him for a kiss. The boys hooted, but were smart enough not to reach for the jug or to make a call that was loud enough to drown out the song.

Davis stood, carrying Ivey in his arms toward the back room, his finger hooked in the handle of the jug. "Night boys, better get to bed."

Ned stood and raised the lantern while Eb pointed. "Your room will be our sister Alma's, just one bed in it now. It's to the top of the stairs on the right."

Ned handed him the lantern. In the dark, quiet room, Delmar raised the case and put away his guitar. He noticed it was Eb who whistled the hounds out of the house and into the yard.

When he reached the landing, he paused as he heard Ivey give a giggle and Davis a whoop. Shaking his head, he made his way to the large room on his right, happy to find clean sheets and a quilt. At least he wasn't having to stay up and sleep on the floor to bolt the door.

CHAPTER FIFTEEN

Delmar and the boys ate a late breakfast. Ivey was talkative this morning, nagging all three men, "You need to take a shower and wash your hair and beards, if you expect me to trim them up. I'm not goin' to comb out your nits or fleas, no sir."

She set out soap, towels, and a change of clothes for the two young men. For him, only a towel and soap. He noticed she had a fourth set, older and larger than their overalls. If she was going to command the big man to bathe, Delmar was glad he had enough work to keep him away while she and Davis had that conversation.

They had sawed through the big tree the afternoon before. Delmar had taken a long time, notching the log on the back side, to make sure it would fall away from the house. He had even paced the distance from the tree to the house to make sure if anything went wrong, it wouldn't hit the porch or house. He and Davis had worked the cross-cut saw first. The impatient boys had been so anxious to try it, that the men had gladly surrendered the long, two-handled saw to them.

He would need to leave the ox cart and his tools behind. The boys promised to pull it down when they came for school. Then Eb and Ned left to get their change of clothes, towels, and soap, leaving him to harness the log up. He could hear them teasing and hollering at each other as they ran to and from the house. He thought he might have heard Davis and Ivey arguing.

He'd used harnessing the big cedar as an excuse not to bathe with them. He'd cut three limbs into usable rollers. With eight of the short logs, he hoped he could control getting the big tree down the mountain. Neither Davis nor the boys had volunteered to help him, and he knew it would probably be easier without their help or their Pa's jug.

Delmar didn't connect the chain to the ox yet, knowing the animal would be easier to manage if his big gut was full of the vines and grass chomped at the edge of the yard.

When he saw the boys walking past, already dressed, he followed a worn path from the house, down past the barn and around a cliff. A nice cold waterfall made a natural shower on the back-side of the rocks.

Davis didn't come roaring up, which Delmar kept expecting. He was dressed and on his way back to the cabin when he realized why.

A scolding Ivey was trying to brush out Eb's hair and short beard. The coarse language she used would have made a sailor blush. Satisfied, that she had it curried as good as she was likely to, she raised a straight razor in the air, and ordered the boy to sit still.

She was dressed in another of her low-cut blouses that let a man have an appreciation of what a fine woman she was. Her green eyes were shining with mischief and her bright red hair seemed to glow around her. Delmar tried not to smile as he looked from the growling man to his grown sons, who were doing what men always did, trying to sneak a look.

"Sit still, or I'll cut it," Davis said.

Eb froze. Sawing with the blade, Ivey sent shorn hair flying everywhere. Delmar reminded himself he wasn't a coward. As she continued to saw at the red hair, she moved around the boy, leaning against him a time or two.

By the time she finished the haircut, Delmar was seeing pink scalp in several places. She repeated the sawing, catching big handfuls of his short beard in her hand to work around his jaw a little more carefully. She took a minute to go inside for the basin and some hot water.

Ned and Davis were laughing at Eb until he was ready to come out of the spindle-legged chair he sat backward in.

Ivey was back, shoving the cake of soap into the big cup of hot water. She poured more hot water into the basin she'd set on Eb's lap. "Hold it steady, so you don't slop it all over them clean overalls."

Eb stiffened his back, clasped the bowl tightly so there was no chance of an accident. While he was distracted, Ivey made quick work of lathering up his butchered cheeks and chin. Then ignoring his shudders, she scraped both cheeks clean, taking more time on his chin and his upper lip. When she finished, she slapped his face with some of her own cologne, smoothing it over his scraped cheeks. Sitting spradled against the back of the chair, with his long legs sticking out front, Eb had no way to escape or look at her again.

She took the bowl from Eb, slopped the water out onto the ground. "Ned you're next."

Ned was backing up, shaking his head when Davis grabbed him in a big bear hug from behind and Eb took his legs. Only when his brother was pinned in the same position he'd been, did he move in front to taunt him. "Tain't so funny, is it, when you're the sacrificial lamb."

Davis swung a big hand at him, yelling, "Baby. You're the one wanting to go back to school. Even that dumb Yankee woman has enough sense to not let you enter the schoolroom. Boys ain't got beards," Pa said.

Ivey was ignoring them both, knowing how set to fight Davis was. She'd been tiptoeing around him all week. All because she'd complained that she was getting tired of his sons sniffing around her like a couple of tom cats. He boxed and roared at the boys, then turned to yelling at her. Renting the cabin to the fiddler seemed to be the last straw. That and the fact that she wasn't turning the money over to him. He'd blustered and threatened, and she reminded him he was the one wanting no strings between them. But now, with his sons eager to pursue another woman, he was looking forward to having Ivey to himself all day.

"You're next, music man," Ivey called with a laugh. "Then the three of you can hold down this bear while I trim him up a little. That's, if'n he's taken that bath he promised."

"Told you, you heat the water and fill the tub and I'll take a wash, even though it ain't healthy. Reckon it's still hot enough this time of year, I won't take the lung fever and die from it. Though plenty of people has, and that's a fact."

"That natural shower you folks have was wonderful."

Davis shuddered and shook his head in disgust. Delmar smiled and looked at the chair, all four legs sitting in pools of water with scattered tuffs of red hair. He looked at the boys, how young they looked with their hair cut short and their big ears showing. Their faces were baby smooth but still red and smelling of the cheap cologne the woman had dowsed them in.

"Well, make up your mind. I've got work to do."

He had tied the long hair he'd pulled back. His great uncle wore his gray mane in the style of the colonials. Delmar had enjoyed copying him, if only to annoy his family back home. Now he was thinking of the snooty teacher and he knew it made him look foolish to her. "Fine, but begin with cutting the queue. Let me study how it looks and we'll go on from there."

The boys stood, their overalls hitched over bare chests and arms, their ruddy faces and big grins making him sure they'd be copying his manners and words for the rest of the week. He leaned forward, exposing his neck.

Ivey grabbed the clump of hair, pulled off and passed him the black ribbon that'd held it. "Sorry, I don't have shears. Davis' girl Alma took off with all the sewing stuff, including the only pair of scissors. He's been promising to buy me a pair, but ain't happened yet."

"That razor seems to work," Davis said, staring critically at the newly shorn boys.

She was already sawing at the light brown hair in her hands. In seconds, she was passing him the cut hair rather than dumping it onto the ground like she'd done for the boys.

Davis was glaring at him, all squinty eyed. Delmar studied himself in the mirror, watched as she fluffed out his hair to give him a better idea. He sat stiffly at attention staring over at the log with its deep gashes from an angry boar and wondered how long the moonshiner's teeth were.

"Well?" Ivey asked.

"Do you think you can take another inch or so off at the bottom, leaving it fairly even?"

She stood with her hands on her hips a moment, before saying, "I'm willing to give it a try, if you put down that mirror and stop gawkin' while I'm a workin'."

Twenty minutes later the perspiring woman stopped, puffing at her own hair. All three of the Daniel men had taken a low crouch before him, the three of them grinning in a way that had dared him to squirm. Taking in a breath or two, Delmar finally managed to raise the mirror and look. Other than looking ten years younger, the cut was as even as a Washington barber could have done.

He started to rise and she asked imperiously. "You wanting me to scrape off that silly feather-duster chin decoration too?"

Delmar stared at his carefully groomed and cherished goatee. He'd copied it after the style of a French ambassador and it always got a rise out of his father. He could hear the strident voice even now. 'Don't you know you are the son of a future senator and have the blood of a president in your veins? You need to look like a Monroe at all times.'

Smiling back at the grinning Daniel men he said with a shrug. "Go ahead, take it all."

It was dark when he and the weary animal arrived home. Leaving the cart and tools hadn't sat well with him. He already needed them, going over in his mind the dulcimer pattern he'd copied from the preacher's wife. Still, as sore and tired as his back and shoulders felt, he could use the rest. He had the more flexible tiger eye maple, and he could use the hand tools to work the fronts and backs for the fiddles he already had planned. The necks he'd make chestnut, if he found the kind of tree he'd come after.

He released the ox, rubbing its neck and back, then checking that its legs weren't as scuffed and barked as badly as his own. What he had thought would be manageable had proven nearly impossible. He'd had a hard time holding the log and keeping the rollers under it, especially on the steeper parts of the grade.

Still, as he walked down the quiet sleepy street past the school to his rented cabin, he wished the schoolmarm were still awake. The Daniel boys had teased him about looking young enough to go to school with them on Monday. He'd like to see what she thought of his bare face. Annoyed at himself for caring, he made quick work of releasing the other dumb ox, though as he rubbed the chafed shoulders of the beast, he wondered which was dumber.

CHAPTER SIXTEEN

Charlotte rubbed the table she had spread with warm bee's wax. Like Dovie had suggested, it made the big surface glow impressively. She had to admit, the table was more practical than the traditional desk she had expected. She had even agreed that the store owner who had done most of the woodwork on the school and the cabin was more than capable.

Dovie explained, "Don't expect much from the man. He can build most anything, is a middling fair blacksmith, and can pull teeth when needed. But Jasper Sykes has never been much of a talker, even before he went off to war. If you can imagine it, he seemed to resent his great uncle's dying and leaving him a thriving business. Why, the man does nothing but shout down at most people, if he speaks at all."

Charlotte wondered why the woman was telling her about the man, since she had no intention of spending that much time in the store. "He's also on the school board," Dovie added.

Charlotte nodded and let the woman continue to talk about him and the strange little woman he'd taken to live under his roof when her husband disappeared. "They were foreigners, French," she leaned even closer. "Catholic, with a new baby." The woman drew the words out slowly, waggled her eyebrows at her, and Charlotte shuddered. She prayed that she never had to travel anywhere, for she knew the woman would be gossiping about her all around town.

It had been a miserable week. Cicely had left with the horrible man who claimed to be her uncle, but Charlotte still was almost never alone. Mizz Dovie came every day, although Charlotte had been careful not to give her any indication that she was needed.

It was Wednesday before she had her lesson's planned out for the first week. When she showed her completed plan to Mizz Dovie, the woman burst into laughter.

"I don't know what sort of teacher's college that place was, but teaching in a one room school is different than teaching by grade in the big city. Did they not have lessons on that?"

Charlotte bristled in outrage. "My father is the president of Newton College. It is the most prestigious school of theology in Boston and more than half of our graduates become teachers, the others respected ministers. I was the first woman to graduate with a teaching certificate." Charlotte didn't add that she had attended over the board's protest and that it was her continued battle with her father that had persuaded him to request that the other professors acknowledge her superior work as a student there and to grant her a special, honorary teaching certificate.

More importantly, if she hadn't been ruffling through his papers she would never have seen the request by a Reverend Watkin for a fit young man to come to Kyles Ford and teach at their new school, built to the specifications of the missionary grant.

"I was a star pupil there," Charlotte added, not eager to answer questions on what she was not. True she wasn't a paying student, a normal graduate, or a man, but as far as she was concerned, that shouldn't matter.

Dovie raised her hands in a shushing motion. "Not disputing it. Just think there are a few things I can share from my experience that will be of help."

Charlotte swallowed her anger and listened. She was embarrassed not to know any of the things Dovie shared, but wise enough to know that they would make her job easier and her teaching more effective.

Dovie pointed to the rough log bench at the front of the room. "That's the recitation bench. First, you teach in four groups. First and fifth grade lessons, second and sixth, etc. Greet the students, you all pray, pledge allegiance, sing the anthem or a hymn. Say, students be seated please."

"Wait fifteen seconds after you tell them what to do, if they haven't done it, shake the bell and frown at them. They know what that means." She held the bell in her left hand and gave it one firm shake. Her face looked like she'd bitten into a pickle. Charlotte wasn't sure what the consequences were supposed to be, but she could tell they would be dire for any student still standing or talking.

"Then you say, 'First group, rise, pass, recite'." Charlotte was still as eager as ever to try all the new methods from college, but this made the task of teaching such a diverse group actually seem doable.

Dovie raised her voice. "You're teaching the three R's-- readin', writin', and 'rithmetic. I love literature and the classics, and always included those with a dose of music, art, and history, when there was time. But you're being paid to make sure they learn the basics."

"To your first group, you teach the little ones how to make three of the letters and give them a short list of words that use those letters. I always start with at, bat, and cat. Then send them back to their seats. The older students, you teach their lesson on reading. Then send them back to help the little ones with their seat work before going back to their own seats and completing their work. You call up the second group and go through the same steps, on a harder lesson. About eleven, you take a recess break. Girl's go to the outhouse first, boy's next. If they brought food, they may sit and eat it.

"Second half of the day, teach groups three and four. Those last two resume and finish their work the next day since they present last. As I told you, we have enough McGuffey readers. The older children are familiar with them. The board wants you to use them."

Charlotte stared at the woman, full of disbelief. They had had this argument by mail, and again each day since she had arrived. Suddenly, she felt hot and uncertain, and unwilling to argue again. Perhaps Dovie was right and these children were going to be unusually wild and unruly.

Maybe draconian measures were necessary. Dovie had shown her the circle on the chalkboard, used for the first transgression, the ruler and how to apply it for maximum effect. Now she raised a paddle in the air and was explaining the procedure for applying it. Charlotte shook her head. She had been paddled and had her knuckles rapped when she was in elementary school. For some reason her earliest teachers considered her argumentative and disrespectful of authority. She intended to teach as her father had, with a sense of importance that demanded respect.

Dovie was about to rap the paddle on the polished table and Charlotte raised a hand. "Then I will give them a try, with the understanding that I can use my other textbooks if they are not successful with them."

Dovie actually clapped her hands with glee, then sighed. "Drat, I presented one of each level to the Bridgers, Alma and Gabriel, for a wedding gift. Well, maybe you will get lucky and the right number will show up to make it work."

It was the end of the week, as ready as Charlotte had been for school to start, now all she could think about were the last minute details to finish. How such a small space could have blossomed into a world of its own she wasn't sure. The back benches had shelves behind them for the older children to work at as desks when needed. The front two rows were backless. She assumed the younger children would sit on the floor and use the bench surface for their desk.

She intended to use her remaining two hours of privacy before Mizz Dovie arrived, to go through the remaining lessons. She had been imagining teaching them, then the successful recitations the following days up until the last day of the week. Although the books were pedestrian, and full of moral platitudes, she had found a lot of value in the debated textbooks the woman was so proud of. She consoled herself with the fact that this was her first year. Using a text that was so widely admired and adapted, was probably a good place to start, not a bad one.

She made a face, as though she again heard Mizz Dovie clapping in victory. When she looked up, she almost screamed. Standing in the doorway, smiling and clapping at her was a strange man. He grinned, and she recognized the irritating musician.

"You," she said. "There is a door, you do know how to knock."

His mouth turned downward and she felt smug, but it vanished when he laughed. "Too good a show to interrupt. I especially love your teacher face. Best be careful it doesn't freeze on those pretty lips."

Charlotte stopped and took a breath. She wasn't used to men who flattered her. Most of the ones she knew were studying to be ministers or teachers, and even if they were aware she was a woman, they never commented. Suddenly, she felt how hot and stuffy the classroom was. That had to be the reason for her cheeks being flushed. She couldn't speak.

He was looking at her so closely and when he stepped inside the room she felt suddenly faint. "Don't, don't come in," she said as she sank down onto the recitation bench. "It's not allowed."

"What, what's not allowed?"

"I can't have congress with any young man. It's in my contract."

Delmar laughed again, swept into a bow with his soft hat held out before him. "Darling, I suspect you need to consult your contract and your dictionary. I'm pretty sure that it's keep company with a young man."

"That's what I said," she managed to say.

He placed his hat back on his new cropped hair. She noticed how soft and blonde it looked, now that it wasn't tied back. There was something different about his face. The mocking grin was the same but, the rest looked younger and more innocent.

"You've shaved and cut your hair."

"Ivey Boggs trimmed it up." He waited, hoping she liked it, but she volunteered nothing. At Ivey's name she stiffened and looked disappointed. He settled for the pleasure in having her focused on just looking at him. If her eyes deepened to purple, he might rush in to explain the difference in the word she had used, compared to the correct one. He heard the older teacher rushing his way.

"I got back the other night. Felt too sore and weary to get about yesterday, but I did promise …"

"Mr. Monroe," Dovie Watkin said, her voice as cold as her expression. "What did you promise?"

He stepped back out and stared at the meddling woman, tempted to not answer. He turned to stare at the woman inside, who had changed from relaxed and happy in her moments of pretense. Now she looked afraid. "I promised Miss Stewart the day she moved in, I'd try to build her a place to store her luggage. That trunk of hers takes up most of her room, keeps her from folding down her table. If I add a board or two, she can set it up in the rafters until she needs it again."

Dovie relaxed a little. "That sounds like an admirable idea. We would store it, if we had an attic."

"I'll go see to it now, while you two ladies are busy here." He touched the brim of his hat in farewell to the older woman, managing not to turn and look back at Charlotte. If she was angry at him, he didn't want to know.

CHAPTER SEVENTEEN

Delmar had borrowed a double saw and ax from Jasper Sykes, after telling the man his problems the day before. Jasper had wandered into his yard to return his straying ox. Delmar stared at the big silent man, wondering if he'd tell him what was bothering him. Finally, Jasper spoke.

"Nice log. What happened to your cart?"

Delmar had wanted confirmation that he'd done the right thing in trusting the two Daniel boys. At the end of it, he was surprised when the man roared out, "Borrow mine. Should of thought about that sort of thing when I was building the place. You need a hand, give a holler."

◇◇◇

This afternoon while he was busy inside the woman's tiny cabin, he wished he'd taken Jasper up on the help. The man could have just reached up to move the logs. It was strange, finding men as tall as himself in the mountains. Most were the sawed-off variety, but the Daniels and Sykes all had an inch or two on him, and Delmar wasn't short.

He'd measured twice, still the raw curved edge of the first board was refusing to fall into place. Standing on the simple pine chair rails, he hesitated before moving his foot over onto the rush seat. It was tightly woven enough that it gave only a little under all the weight. Delmar dropped down, trying to decide what to do next. He worried and tilted the log across the rafters so the end was near enough to the door. He stood balanced on the chair rails again as he sawed two inches off the end of the log.

He walked out, measured and shortened each of the other three boards he'd made from the outer curve of the big walnut tree. He had needed to square it up anyway before trying to split the thin boards he needed from the huge log.

Before lifting the others up, he notched them where each would cross one of the three rafters, then returned inside. He worried the log over the narrow path, so he could notch it to match and the chips and dust wouldn't fall on the fussy woman's bed. This time he climbed up on the boards framing the sink and made quick work of it.

An hour after he'd started, he had all four boards in position, and swept the last of the wood shavings out the door. He became aware of her, standing and staring up at him. He felt the usual jolt she gave him, attributed it to the fact that she seemed to be the only pretty woman for miles. Back in Richmond, she would of had too much competition. He probably wouldn't have noticed her at all. He studied her, watching as the pink blushed her cheeks again and her eyes seemed to sparkle with anger. Oh, he would have noticed her.

Delmar grinned at her, leaning cockily against the door frame. "I've finished the platform, but the trunk seems to still have things in it. Thought you'd probably want to be the one to empty it before I shove it up there."

"You opened it," she shrieked.

Delmar laughed as he stepped down into the yard beside the disputed luggage. "No, ma'am, I did not, but I could tell from the weight that it probably wasn't empty."

"It's my dresses. Mama and my sisters insisted I pack them all. They would have had to alter them too much for the others to wear them anyway, but the drawers under the bed are full, and I've nowhere else to store them."

"If you had a closet?"

She shook her head. He watched how her curling dark locks brushed her ivory pale neck, swallowed, then agreed. "I could nail some pegs on the back wall for you. They'd look kind of pretty, hanging there on display."

She blushed, "It would take a lot of pegs."

"A line then. I've got some heavy cord, only take a few minutes to tie enough. Then you could hang as many as you need."

She smiled and Delmar forgot to breathe. "Wonderful," they said together.

"I'll be back in minutes," Delmar said, unable to keep his eyes from hers, looking for the subtle shift in color from dark blue to purple, but they didn't change.

◇◇◇

Charlotte tried not to think about the added weight of the boards and the trunk overhead. Delmar had assured her it was safe, and had even hung off the edge of the platform to prove it. She'd tried not to watch the way his shirt shifted to expose his belly and a dark line of hair. The same as when he'd been sawing the log earlier in her doorway, she was unable to look away from the sight. The ripple of muscles displayed had her hypnotized.

She had turned around before he could catch her gaping and tease her. Worse than Charles Newcomb at school, the man delighted in bedeviling her.

Suddenly he was back, and horror of horrors, he shed his shoes and clambered atop her bed to hang the line. She fled the cabin in shock. Not surprisingly, Dovie Watkin was walking her way and she was relieved not to have been caught inside the cabin with the bare-footed man.

"Well, isn't he done yet? I was going to invite you to dinner, but saw you fleeing your cabin."

Charlotte leaned closer to whisper. "I thought he was, or I would never have gone inside. When he entered too, I thought it more appropriate to flee."

Dovie leaned toward her but spoke loudly. "Of course, dearest. Some men have no concept of what such an act can do to a maiden's reputation."

Delmar strained to hear the last remark. Grimacing, he tied off the last knot over the fourth rafter, then dropped down from where he'd been hanging. He sat on the hard board that framed the end of the bed, perfectly measured to form a seat for the drop down table. Sykes might act like a dolt, but the man was a capable carpenter.

As he pulled on his boots, he thought about Dovie's description of Charlotte. If he hadn't already been aroused, the word maidenly would have done it.

He turned and stared at the high mound of clothes the woman had removed from the large trunk. As big as it was, he was still amazed at all the trunk had carried. He tried to imagine the petite girl hanging the gowns on the line but couldn't. Sighing, he removed his boots again to walk across the bed to hang the heavy gowns. He left the rest of her things piled on the bed as he finished the job before leaving.

Charlotte sank onto the edge of the bed and looked around in relief. She stared in amazement at the dramatic sweep of her dresses against the plain wood of the cabin. The bare wall by the door looked different too. With the board down, it looked like she had a real desk or table. She'd position the candle holder and her books at one end, a china bowl of apples at the other. Lovely. A small but lovely room.

CHAPTER EIGHTEEN

Jeanne LeSouris rushed to empty the dust before the store owner came rushing back for breakfast. She stopped short, almost tossing them on the handsome young man sitting on the porch chair. Some of the fine dust drifted over the black of her newly dyed clothes. She moved to the edge of the porch to empty the dustpan and shake her skirt clean.

The man hadn't spoken, he was concentrating so hard on tuning the fiddle that rested on his knee, but he kept raising his head to stare down the road.

As Jeanne raised a hand to shield her eyes, the seated man beside her seemed to have his instrument tuned where he wanted it. Jeanne waved to the children, counting them, then stopped as she spotted Sykes. The tall man carried a large deer draped over his shoulders and anchored in place with his long rifle. He strode along with two tall boys flanking him, talking loudly. She frowned at the look of annoyance on his face, as the fiddler beside her ran the rosined bow over the taunt strings to play a bright tune.

She looked at him and smiled. "Delmar Monroe, I remember."

He bowed, "Morning Widow Mouse. Let's give the boys and girls a welcome."

"Froggy Went a Courtin'," carried on the fresh morning air and after the first stanza some of the children sang "un, huh, un, huh," along with him.

The Daniel boys ran ahead of Jasper, waving at the little widow.

Delmar dropped off the edge of the porch, still playing and singing, with even the youngest children joining in on the chorus this time. In the distance, Delmar smiled at the pretty young woman ringing a bell.

He'd been troubled the night before, worrying about the woman across the hill. If he walked to the edge of his yard, he could see into her small cabin when she lit the lamp. He had been pleased Saturday when she'd sat there smiling at the wall of dresses. The next day, he'd watched her leave the cabin early, not surprised when she returned with a fist full of flowers. He'd imagined her pumping water to fill a glass to hold them. He couldn't see them, and wondered if she would stand them on the drop-down table, maybe arrange the books.

Sunday morning on the way to church, he'd managed to look through the kitchen window and observed all the little fluffing and arranging she'd done.

Last night he'd done a foolish thing, and started wondering what she would be thinking or doing. He'd heard Mizz Dovie warning her about how wild some of the mountain children were. Finally, he'd hit upon a serenade. Music to soothe the savage beast so to speak. He figured if he had them in an agreeable mood, she'd have an easier time controlling them.

At the store, Jeanne noticed that the teacher looked annoyed at the fiddler, and wasn't surprised. Jasper stepped up beside her, scowling as though he were annoyed about something. Before he could scold her loudly on the street,

Jeanne said, "I bet she's angry. The last thing our teacher liked was when we were all excited." She looked up into his intent gaze.

"Course she's mad, won't want them moving around and talking. They're keen enough, those Daniel boys liked to talk my ears off already."

"Look, at all the people. Come out to see how pretty the children look."

He was staring at the fiddler still sawing away. He could tell the moment he realized his mistake. No, he wouldn't want to be Delmar when the teacher pulled his ear. He grunted at the little widow beside him, not having listened to her this time. He turned to the back of the cabin as she waved a stained hand at Mizz Meany.

Jasper stopped at the end of the store, ignored those commenting on the deer, trying not to hear them. He watched the little widow smile and switch her dress at the mean old gossip, then extended her darkened hand to the old woman for help. Shaking his head in wonder, he finally noticed the little man touching the deer and talking to him about its big rack. Sighing, he let the others follow him around to talk at him as he dressed the deer.

Charlotte stood, rod still, her eyes wide in disbelief. Did that fool have any idea what he was doing? The first day of school, and the children would be too excited to listen anyway. Mizz Dovie had lectured her enough on having the proper stern demeanor and to never smile the first week. Charlotte had thought she was joking the first time she gave her the advice, but after hearing it again all week, she had wondered if the woman weren't right.

Charlotte gazed at the man, dancing down the path like a pied piper, but he had a fiddle beneath his chin and a smile on his face as he used those long legs to jump about. He sang another chorus, the words clear and warm on the morning air. Now he had all the children skipping along and singing that idiotic song. It was one of those tunes that stayed in your head all day, the song drifting out anytime you relaxed. Heaven help her if it ever spilled out of her mouth.

Suddenly they were almost running into her. Charlotte rang the bell loudly, then stood with her hands on her hips.

"Quiet, line up. Boys wait, girls stand still." The children continued to move for a minute and she heard another line on the fiddle. "You, sir, I said that's enough."

Delmar stopped, the bow held up in one hand the fiddle by the neck in the other like she'd drawn a gun on him.

She lowered her gaze to the waiting children, some of their mouths had dropped open when she yelled at Delmar. "Remember, when you hear this bell, you are to be silent. In class you will be silent unless called upon by me to speak. Do you understand?"

She tried to make eye contact with every child and nodded as she did, waiting for their answering nod. "Ladies line up on the right. Gentleman on the left. Every time we go in, it will be ladies first, then gentlemen. Now young ladies, follow me."

With her skirt bunched in her hand on each side, she stepped up the two stone steps into the schoolroom and turned to hold the door open for the five frightened girls. The youngest looked to be six, the oldest maybe twelve. "Girls find your seats on the right, you youngest two on the front row, and you dear, on the third row." She pointed as the little girls found their seats, then waved her hand at the oldest girl.

She looked outside at the restless boys, noticing the tallest two, the Daniel boys, were already pushing and teasing some of the younger ones. "Gentlemen, now it is your turn."

As the boys entered, she divided and seated them by age on the left. The overgrown Eb and Ned came in and she scowled at them as she pointed to the long bench at the very back of the room. "You gentlemen, have a seat and no more of this talking."

Charlotte walked to the front of the room, aware that she was yelling at her students, when she wanted to berate that irritating musician. She drew in a breath, slowly released it, making each breath longer as she strolled to the front. All along the way she noticed the tense children, fidgeting, looking around at everything.

When she reached the front, she turned, eyes sweeping from one clean washed face to the next. Each seemed to have their hair oiled and parted precisely, even the girls. She was most surprised by her oldest students at the back of the room. Their clean shaven faces were pink, and their combed hair shone like copper pennies. Only Mizz Watkin's endless sermons about what was proper kept her from smiling at them.

Instead, she raised her eyes toward the ceiling and said in her softest voice. "Please rise for our morning benediction and remain standing while we swear our oath of fidelity to our country. If you do not know it yet, please pay close attention. You will be expected to recite it with us the rest of the year."

Charlotte opened her Bible, read the verse for the day, bowed her head, watching until all heads were bowed and then said, "Heavenly Father guide us in your light to be strong, honest, and good Christians. Amen."

She watched the little heads come up and slowly turn to look at the picture of President Polk with the national flag and its thirty stars behind him. "Who can tell me the name of the man holding the flag?"

One of the boys on the third row raised a hand and Charlotte nodded at him, aware that she still hadn't taken names and ages to form her register. That darn blonde demon outside had made her so angry, and this was to be the result. Instead of revealing her ignorance, Charlotte smiled at the boy and held her hand raised, then lowered it to grant permission.

"He's the greatest President ever, James K. Polk, because he's from Knoxville, Tennessee." Several of the children whispered to each other excitedly, and Charlotte tried not to smile in surprise. Her father would disagree with that appraisal, as he didn't like the little Democrat at all.

"Yes, he was our eleventh President of our thirty state union. Can anyone tell me who was elected in his place?" The room was silent, except for shuffling feet as the boys and girls looked from one to another.

Charlotte looked at the clever boy who had answered, but he shook his head.

Charlotte answered, glad politics had been a favorite topic in their home. "Zachary Taylor, a Virginian was elected, but died of cholera after only a few months after being sworn into office as President. His Vice-President is now the leader of our country." As the children were now looking at the floor and the top of the bench's made from half-logs, she knew she needed to wrap this up and get onto the business of collecting names and organizing the students. "Millard Fillmore is our new President, and I will grant a favor tomorrow, to whichever student can tell me the state he is from."

A loud voice at the back of the room said, "Millard Fillmore. That sounds like a girl's name." The children were suddenly giggling and Charlotte was demanding attention to no avail. It was several minutes before she had her class in order again.

She knew it was all Delmar Monroe's fault. There was a silly name if she'd ever heard one.

CHAPTER NINETEEN

The little widow was standing at the open door of the store, when the children were released from school. They were no longer singing and skipping down the road. Jeanne smiled and folded her arms across her waist, watching as the new school teacher followed the children. Jeanne gave her a bright smile as the woman climbed the porch steps.

Remembering something Mama said, "Looks like something took the starch out of the lot of them."

Charlotte ignored the strange greeting, feeling even more wilted than her children. "Oh, bless you, this store is so cool. Do you have any refreshments for sale?"

Jeanne slipped under the counter, "I can offer you a glass of cold buttermilk, or some clear spring water."

Charlotte brushed back her curls and wrinkled her nose at the idea of buttermilk. "If the water is cold, that sounds fine." While Jeanne produced a glass and poured, Charlotte looked around.

"I've been meaning to come in here since last weekend. However, there have been so many things to attend to in getting ready for school, and Mrs. Watkin has been so attentive."

The teacher smiled and extended one hand to shake, took the glass with her other. "You must be the Widow Mouse. It's a pleasure to meet you. Some of the boys were telling me how pretty you are. I'm Charlotte Stewart, the new school teacher. You're not from around here either, are you?"

Jeanne blushed. "I'm Mrs. LeSouris. Henri could never get Mr. Sykes to understand what he was saying, so he translated it for him. He always called Henri, Mr. Mouse. No matter how many times I've corrected them, looks like I'll always be Widow Mouse to everyone."

The baby cried and Charlotte swallowed the refreshing cold water while the young mother rushed over to pick him up. She lifted the counter board and motioned toward the room behind her.

Charlotte hesitated, but she needed to talk to someone after this horrible day, and Jeanne seemed sympathetic. She followed, curious to see where the girl lived.

The bell rang on the door and Jeanne buttoned her blouse, smiling down at her baby.

Charlotte rose to follow her, "I'm so glad to meet another educated woman like myself. Someone with whom I have more in common."

Jeanne raised a finger to hush Charlotte.

"Yoo-hoo, anyone here?" a voice called from the front of the store.

Jeanne grabbed the boy and carried him out to return to his cradle, while Charlotte looked around the room before pushing the door closed.

"Yoo-hoo, there you are," called Dovie Watkin. "I was looking for Mizz Charlotte, you know, the new school teacher."

Jeanne took her time settling down the baby into his cradle. "Good afternoon, Mizz Watkin. Mizz Stewart and I were just getting acquainted," Jeanne answered coolly. Mizz Watkin had been kind to her on the day she found Henri gone, but then she had offered no help or shelter.

"You were," she stared over Jeanne's head and called. "Oh there you are, you darling girl. I couldn't wait to hear all about your first day of school. I made a fresh pitcher of tea and some lovely shortenin' bread. I expected you to come right over."

Charlotte smoothed her dress and stepped forward as Jeanne again lifted the counter for her to walk through. Jeanne grinned at the solemn face of the girl as she slipped through. Charlotte rolled her eyes back at her while her back was to the minister's wife. She leaned forward and impulsively hugged the tiny woman in her neat black dress and scarf. Then whispered, "Until tomorrow, mon Cherie."

"Adieu," Jeanne whispered back.

Dovie Watkin stood staring between the two young women. Her face drawn down so that Jeanne thought she could actually see a dark cloud over her head.

As they walked out, she knew she would probably not see the young woman again. Dovie was whispering loudly, "What is wrong with you, associating with that woman."

Charlotte protested and Jeanne held her head high as she watched the two walking down the street arm-in-arm.

"What are you talking about? Jeanne is a young, educated woman like me. She has four sisters, I have three, why, we each have a sister named Rebecca who's sixteen."

"Shh, people are watching and listening," Dovie scolded.

Charlotte felt like one of her young students. She hadn't rapped any hands today, but she had waved her ruler. That was what Dovie was doing now. Rebuked, she bent her head and bit her tongue as they hurried along.

She didn't want to go into the kitchen, resented the woman, but took a deep breath and let it out slowly as she did. She had been hired for this job because of the grace of this woman and the good Reverend Watkin. She would be respectful and pleasant at all times, even if it killed her.

"I'm sorry to displease you. I had no way to know speaking to the store clerk would be inappropriate," Charlotte protested.

"Clerk?" Mizz Dovie clucked as she set out small plates on the table and took the pitcher of tea from the cold box under the floor.

Charlotte swallowed hard as she watched the woman pour the cloudy dark liquid into the glass. She carefully pulled out a chair for the older woman and then settled in one herself. At least, she would have something sweet to wash the bitter moment down with.

She accepted the flaky crisp bread, delighted in the buttery flavor, then sipped the cool, sweet tea.

Slowly, carefully she went over her day. She described the fiddler and his parade, although Mizz Dovie rolled her eyes and whispered, "I saw that. Shameful wasn't it. Bet it made your day difficult."

Charlotte almost choked on the powdery sweet, and her hostess rose and ran to get a jar from the top shelf. "I almost forgot how dry these can be. Here, she stood a spoon in the jar, then reached into the tray for a pair of forks. Add a little wild strawberry jam, then you won't have to worry."

Charlotte was grateful for the reprieve in her interrogation. After a bite of the overly sweet concoction, she had taken a sip of the tea and felt overwhelmed with all the sugar. She forced a smile on her face and resumed her description of her new students. "I only have five girls, Philomena, Constance, Faith, Glory, and Sue. You probably know the older girls, since only Glory is a first year student."

Dovie nodded, took a large bite of her red glistening square and Charlotte gave her time to swallow before continuing. "They are all sweethearts, except Philomena. You'll need to watch that girl. She's near the turning point, and these mountain girls can go a little wild when they first blossom."

Charlotte used her fork to take a small nibble of her own desert, grateful to have a way not to respond to such a comment. "The boys, there are eight. I can already see two are going to be a special challenge."

"Eb and Ned Daniel?" She cut another square, held it out and Charlotte shook her head.

Charlotte watched as the woman sat and loaded it with jam before continuing.

"They were my students, years ago, didn't even last the year. It was their big sister, Almira Maeline who wanted to learn. Alma was such a darling child, thin as a rail, big eyes and the prettiest hair." She looked at her plate. "I've nothing bad to say about the girl or the boy she married, Gabriel Bridger. He was a remarkable lad." She put her fork down, looked ready to cry for a minute. "But he was a Melungeon, poor dear."

An hour later, Charlotte left, wearier than ever. It was amazing, knowing that Cicely was persecuted for her skin, but so were people of mixed race. From what Dovie had said, Gabriel was only part Indian, and yet he was badly bullied by the other boys. At least she wouldn't have that issue with this year's class of thirteen. All could have come from the same family, they were so much alike. Fair skinned, light eyed, and none with hair as dark as her own. They were surprisingly poor, the girls dressed in simple cotton dresses, the boys mainly in bib overalls and brogan boots.

Charlotte stopped at the school outhouse on the way home. She would have preferred to stay home and make a simple meal, but in two hours, it would be dinnertime with the Watkins. Why they had given her the darling little stove and sink was a mystery, since she was expected to share her meals with the couple every night.

As she opened the door to leave, she gave a squeal of surprise. A familiar face was staring at her.

CHAPTER TWENTY

"Goodness, you!" She pushed out past Delmar. What had he been doing, lurking about, waiting on her? Why?

He disappeared from sight and she looked over her shoulder, expecting to see Dovie Watkin, hovering as always. She walked on around the facility, stopped to snap at him. "Are you determined to annoy me more today? Haven't you done enough, or do you plan to destroy the serenity of my day at every opportunity."

He held raised hands, his arms wide to prevent her escape again, "I'm sorry."

"You're sorry. Do you have any idea how hard it is to settle children down for a day of learning when they've been whipped into a singing, dancing frenzy on the way to school?" Her eyes squinted in outrage.

Delmar studied her face, noted her pale skin, dark hair
and how her eyes looked almost purple in the light.
"Honestly, I was remembering how nervous and unhappy I
was my first day of school. I thought if they were in a better
mood, you'd have an easier day." He held a hand up to stop
her, "I'm sorry, though you looked like you scared the devil
out of them quick enough."

His language made her even angrier. "I had not intended
to begin with such a fierce tone, but you gave me no other
recourse. I had to establish order, seating arrangements,
record names and ages, and begin with the first lessons
today. One must establish a routine quickly as to the manner
class will be conducted every day."

"Sounds like Mizz Dovie. Is she your role model?"

"One can learn a lot from experienced teachers, and no,
I was quoting my father. He is a master educator and I've
witnessed him taking that tone with students many times."

"Then why did you tell them such a joke? Jasper Sykes
was helping me with my log when we both heard them
carrying on, and you calling for order over and over."

Charlotte knew her ears were burning as well as her
face as she struck out at his hand and marched past. "I did

not tell a joke, I assure you. I merely introduced them to the current President, Millard Fillmore. One of those Daniel devils said it sounded like a girl's name. Goodness, with names like Ebenezer and Nedabiah, you'd think they'd know better."

Delmar stood there and laughed too. "No wonder they go by Eb and Ned. Admit it, Millard does sound a little silly."

Charlotte stopped at her cabin door, one foot already on the top riser. "I'm sure our President's name is a family one, no more ridiculous than Delmar Monroe, to those who know him." She had the satisfaction of watching his mouth drop open on her emphasis of his first name, just before she slammed her door.

The nerve of those two, lurking outside the schoolroom and waiting for her to make a mistake. She paced back and forth, then saw him look through the window at her. Furious, she turned, lifted out one of the ironed sheets her mother had sent with her and frantically tried to hang it over the rough edge of the window frame. Finally, when it was covered, she sank onto the edge of the bed, shouting the words, "I hate all men."

Suddenly the horror of it all registered. Jasper Sykes was one of the men on the school board. What if she couldn't do this job? What if they asked her to leave?

Dreading school the next day, she had trouble sleeping after the plain but heavy dinner. The next morning, she was pleased when she rang the bell and the children remembered and entered respectfully. There were only a couple of snickers when they saluted the flag and President Fillmore. She was in the middle of praising them when Ned whispered something to his older brother that made him cover his face to keep from guffawing.

Charlotte had to make a choice, and she chose to pretend she hadn't heard the crude joke about the President's last name. She had heard the boys at college whispering it in the same manner during the election, dropping a 'her' in the middle of it.

"Children, you displayed beautiful deportment. Remember to keep your backs straight as you sit, good posture is also important. Gentlemen," she looked pointedly at the third grade boy with big ears, "gentlemen, remember to remove your hats inside a building. Ladies," she turned to the little girls who giggled at the title. Ladies may keep their hats on, but," she stared directly at the Daniel boys, "there is to be no talking once you enter the school, unless I address you and request that you speak."

She straightened and held her back stiff as she quoted her father. "If you're not looking, you're not listening, if you're not listening, you're not learning."

"Remember these rules. Next week, if you forget, you will have to write the rule on your slate or the blackboard ten times to help you remember it. Do not get out of your seat without permission and raise your hands to request my permission."

"Now, group one, please 'rise, pass, and recite.' The rest of you work quietly on yesterday's lessons, until called upon."

The morning sessions went well. At lunch she had to reprimand the Daniel boys for playing too rough in a game of leap frog. Back inside she turned and wrote the golden rule below the quote about listening. "Group three, rise, pass, recite." As soon as the boys and girls had settled on the bench, she called for a volunteer to read the top message to the group. She was surprised when Sydney, the boy with big ears, rose first. "If you're not looking, you're not listening, if you're not listening, you're not learning," she clapped and the others finally clapped too. She pointed to the bottom rule and then at Eb Daniel, "Eb please rise and read this new rule."

Eb rose, head bowed. "'Don't put 'ur weight on smaller boys, 'cause they might fall down and cry.' But I didn't know he'd fall like that, Mizz Charlotte, honest."

Charlotte compressed her lips, shook her head at him. "I'm disappointed in you, sir." She looked about and the same little boy rose to read the golden rule.

The first grade girl rose and it was clear from her restless little dance what she needed. Charlotte kept herself from smiling. "In the future Glory, raise your hand and ask, 'May I please be excused?'"

The child continued the dance and Charlotte was afraid she would be too late, "Repeat the words, dear, 'May I...'" The child shouted them rapidly and bolted for the door. Charlotte stared as Ned started to reach over to hold it shut, then he nodded at her and pushed it open, holding it for the child.

"Thank you, Ned."

"You're welcome, Mizz Charlotte," he said as he sat down.

Charlotte stared at him, not sure if he was being mocking or respectful. She decided to drop a curtsy in response and saw the girls on their benches elbowing each other. Of course, they did not know how to curtsy and bow properly. She felt a moments satisfaction at the thought of passing on all the rules for behavior that her mother had fought so hard to instill in her.

She started each grade on their copy work on the slate. Each student then came up beside her to read aloud. When she found them illiterate, she read the first paragraph to them, then had them follow along and read it. Then she assigned it to them to read at their seats, trying to keep straight in her own mind when to say morning class and afternoon class.

When it was time to dismiss them, Charlotte rose. She looked at all of them. "Please rise. Ladies curtsey, gentlemen bow as I call your group. Group one and four, she dropped a curtsy and watched Glory and her friends struggle with the step. Out of the boys, only two managed a correct bow. She had the one who did it best approach. She made mock motions to indicate removing her invisible hat, sweeping her arm across as she bowed from the waist.

As soon as the room was empty, Charlotte relaxed her mouth enough to actually smile. She noticed all students hadn't finished their copy work. She recorded a grade in her book for the ones that had finished, then washed their slates clean for the next day. The ones who hadn't finished, she would have to get the work done quickly before she cleaned them in the morning.

CHAPTER TWENTY-ONE

By the end of the week, Charlotte had grown to love each bowed head and hopeful eye of her students. She examined their penmanship before wiping each slate, setting work done wrong at the top of the next day's assignment. It was letters for younger students, the original sentence at the beginning to be copied five times for older ones. They had to raise a hand, and if done right, erase it before starting on the day's work. On the back side of the slate, it was numbers for the youngest and Daniel boys, arithmetic problems for the older children.

She was excited to be adding reading to next week's instruction. For now, she read the Bible at the beginning of class, one of the favorite tales from Dovie Watkin's "Anthology of Fairy Stories" at the end. She knew she was expected to add singing whenever there was time, but she had never been a songbird, realized no one else in her family had been either. She would have to bend her neck to ask the musician to suggest something appropriate and teach her the words and tune.

The loud scream of the little girl Glory was as high and sharp as a knife. Charlotte rose in front of her pew of shocked students and dashed out of the room, pushing some of the older children back inside as she turned the handle on the door.

Glory, her pigtails caught over her head was jumping and crying hysterically. Charlotte immediately folded the girl into her arms and helped the child step out of her dangling pantalets before any of the boys peeked out of the room. She folded and rolled them into a damp slender package that she tucked into her skirt pocket. Still it took several minutes for the girl to describe what had happened.

She had climbed up onto the box as usual after lowering her pants, but as soon as she started to pee, something cold and alive jumped up and smacked her bottom. Scowling, holding the child in her arms, Charlotte marched up to the outhouse door and held it open so it wouldn't strike the girl and frighten her even more. Glory pointed to the offending toilet and Charlotte walked over to look down to see if she could see what had caused the commotion. One did hear of the occasional snake getting under the floor and crawling inside, but that was a lurid tale told to make children go before nightfall to spare the bed covers.

The opening was as dark and malodorous as she had expected and she looked over her shoulder to beckon the frightened child forward to see there was nothing there. As Charlotte turned to look back, a blue bandanna bounced out of the opening and a frog croaked to startle her. Charlotte jumped back with a yelp and little Glory pointed and laughed. "It's just a frog," but she reached out an arm to grasp Charlotte's legs tightly, still afraid.

Charlotte marched back inside the schoolroom and sent Ned and Eb to remove the frog. When she saw the two slapping each other on the back, it was too much for her. She walked to the board, picked up her chalk and stepped onto her chair seat to draw the circles as high as she could reach on the front of the board.

She marched back outside and called them forward. Neither would confess who had pulled the prank, but it was clear they both shared equal guilt. She instructed the troublemakers to stand on tiptoe, put their noses in the circle, and not move until recess, an hour away.

Every time one of the children looked at another and whispered, she and Glory would look around, Charlotte whispering 'shh'. Trying to be discreet, she snapped at the children to focus on their lessons and slipped the offensive bundle into her desk drawer. When one little boy giggled again and Ned turned to stick out his tongue at him, she rose, summoning the lad up to join them. She told him to stretch up on tiptoe, motioned him back a step, drew a circle, and motioned him forward, making sure the tip of his nose touched in the center of the circle. "That sir, is for being nosey."

She ordered Ned to hold out his hand. She gave a sharp rap and said, "face forward and keep your nose in that circle, or it will be three whacks next time." Eb chuckled, but swallowed the sound as Ned shook his hand and faced forward.

Charlotte stared at the boys, stretched on tiptoes in their embarrassing positions. Looking at Ned who had his hand tucked in front of him, she could not believe these boys had provoked her into striking another person. She slapped the ruler on her own hand, moved to wipe her hand on her skirt at the surprising sting from even the light tap. Eb was behind her desk and when he passed gas, she turned away and heard one of the boys on the pew complain. All she had to do was raise the ruler and all became quiet.

She wondered if she would ever feel the same about corporal punishment again.

At the end of the horrendous day, Charlotte hesitated, looking down both toilets first before being able to use the outhouse. At least the Daniel boys seemed embarrassed enough to remain calm and leave the other children alone the rest of the day.

Outside, she expected Delmar to pop out again to scare her, but there was no one at the little house. She was muttering to herself as she opened the door to her cabin. Really, the man was always around to pester her, but impossible to find when she had a question to ask.

If there was anyone in this small community who would know about music, it would be the strange young man who had already made trips to different ends of the community to look for his great trees.

She was so preoccupied by her thoughts, she almost didn't see the blood on the floor inside the cabin. Too frightened to scream, she backed up and sat on the edge of the bed, tilting backward toward the sagging middle before gripping the edge enough to pull herself upright. She drew in a ragged breath, ready to scream as loudly as possible, when a dark head popped out from the curtain at the front of the sink. Cicely waved a skinny hand in the air, pleading, "No, don't, don't scream."

Charlotte leaned forward, clamped one hand over her mouth to smother the sound. All she could see were the whites of the girl's big frightened eyes. Cicely was shaking her head, her mouth a perfect circle as she pleaded. "No, no, no…"

Charlotte sank forward on her knees and pushed the curtain all the way back. The nearly naked girl was wedged on the skinny shelf under the sink, her arms and legs scraped and bloody. Charlotte managed to free her own skirt enough to rise onto her feet. In a minute, she had made certain the little curtain she'd sewn from her sheet was pulled together in the center and no one could see in the cabin window.

Stepping back to give her room, she extended a hand to take Cicely's and tugged her firmly out of the narrow space. She resisted the impulse to hug her, instead whispered in a firm voice, "Are you running away? Is someone following you?"

Cicely nodded, big tears streaking down her muddy face.

Charlotte turned to bar the door, then leaned in to pull twigs and leaves from the girl's nappy head. Wrapping a blanket around the shaking girl she sat her on the edge of the bed as she stirred the coals in the stove and added wood before pumping water. She filled her kettle and a pot, then kept pumping water. When the big sink was half-full she said, keeping her voice at a whisper. "Take off your clothes and climb in. We need to wash you first."

Charlotte removed her own dress, hung it on the coat peg by the door. Standing in her petticoat, looking back at the girl, she said. "I have to wear it to the Watkin's later. I'll try to pretend to not be hungry and bring a dish home for you later."

She was grateful to her mother for letting her help bathe her younger sister, Dorothea. The frightened girl didn't complain about the cold water and Charlotte was careful to test the water before pouring some of the heated water in later to warm it. Carefully, tenderly Charlotte bathed her, taking notice of each time she winced or shrugged to escape.

She again wrapped her in the small blanket, helping to brace her until she stepped down. "I'm sorry, Mizz Charlotte, I didn't have nowhere else to go," Cicely said, her voice hoarse.

Charlotte wondered if it was from screaming or crying. She tried to remember how long it had been since the girl left with her uncle. Almost three weeks. What had happened to change the high spirited, sassy girl into this?

She got a glass of water for her, then remembered she had the small can of tea and took a minute to make them both a cup. She noticed Cicely had turned to stretch out on the top of the covers, careful not to put her wet hair against the pillow.

"Are you going to tell me what happened?" she asked, as she set up a tray with two cups for the hot brew, carefully breaking off a bit of the tip of the sugar cone into each one. She looked at the drop down table and carried both cups there to sit down. As Cicely's gaze followed her, she wondered if she would talk.

She found and opened the tin of cookies the cook had insisted she bring along, and noticed how Cicely's interest was aroused.

Charlotte moved closer, rooting around in her drawer, finding bloomers and chemise for the girl. As she had knelt and helped five-year old Glory earlier today after lunch, she held them for Cicely to step into, but let her pull them up herself. She held the chemise above her head, threaded the bruised arms through the holes, but let the girl pull it down.

From the right drawer, she found one of the outgrown dresses that her mother insisted she bring, taking the time to dress and fasten the girl in the back before encouraging her to the end of the board, where she was blocked from the door.

As Cicely sipped the warm liquid and stared up at Charlotte, Charlotte knew she wasn't going to enjoy hearing this. Smiling softly at her, she patted the wiry curls of hair now clear of mud. Cicely started to cry and this time, Charlotte folded her against her, hugging the wounded girl tightly.

CHAPTER TWENTY-TWO

Cicely ate one cookie, and washed it down with tea. Charlotte refilled the dainty cup. Each garment in the portmanteau had held a piece of the tiny set designed for two to share a cup of tea and a bite of cake. She could still hear her mother insisting, while cook packed cookies, tea, and a small cone of sugar, "You will be in the wilderness, but you mustn't forget to behave like a civilized lady."

She crumbled a generous amount of sugar in the cup and Cicely smiled crookedly at her. Charlotte could see the red gash inside her mouth when she did. She would need to borrow salt from Mizz Watkin to make a solution. She could remember whenever Mama had pulled a baby-tooth, she made her gargle several times a day so her mouth wouldn't get sore.

Charlotte sat, studying the dark bruises around the girl's face, the lump on her head. Her uncle had beaten her severely.

"What happened? Tell me everything." Charlotte whispered, running a feathery hand across the top of the girl's hand beside her. Cicely winced, drew it back as Charlotte caught it and turned it over to see the bruised knuckles, and the torn fingernails. She knew what she was about to hear was terrible.

Cicely drew in a deep ragged breath and then whispered. "He raped me."

Charlotte looked at the curtained window, then over her shoulder at the locked door. "Is he out there?"

"Not any more. I think … I think I killed him."

On the way to dinner at the Watkin's, Charlotte replayed the horror of Cicely's confession. The first week at her aunt's had seemed wonderful. Mammy Buford, as her aunt was called, loved having Cicely and fussed over her. Kept telling her how pretty, smart, and strong she was. Her aunt was six years older than Cicely's mother and had the rheumatism. That was one reason she was so happy to have Cicely come live with them and help.

It was the next week that her uncle started nosing around her, accidentally bumping into her, telling her what a pretty woman she was becoming. Charlotte felt rage again. How could an uncle, a man who was married to her aunt, commit such an act? The brutality of it made Charlotte so angry, if the brute weren't dead, she would want to kill him herself. The tale of how, when his wife was sick, he had encouraged Cicely to walk to town to get the doctor. As soon as she was out of sight of the house he had appeared from nowhere.

He beat her, tied a rag over her mouth, then did what he wanted. Cicely had fought and struggled, but been hit or pinched until she stopped and just lay there. Later, worse, was the fate he told her he was taking her to.

When a twig snapped in the dark, Charlotte's blood ran cold. A man like that, one who would sell his niece to a brothel, was capable of anything. What if he weren't dead?

Charlotte ran down to the parsonage and rapped on the door frantically. Dovie Watkin opened the door, and asked her what was the matter. Charlotte tried to laugh her terror away. "I heard a noise outside and got frightened. May I come in?"

Dovie stood in the door, staring outside. Charlotte fought the urge to grab the woman and force the door shut. Instead, she stood there, looking over her shoulder. The night was dark, but the warm breeze of summer blew against her face and a katydid called nearby. She relaxed and took a deep breath.

She really didn't have to pretend to have no appetite. The reverend had already risen and excused himself, since she was taking so long. After pushing the food around her plate she looked up at her host. "I'm sorry, may I take this home? I will bring your plate back in the morning."

Dovie looked at her, saw nothing to complain about. "Of course, but if you want desert, you need to finish it."

Charlotte shook her head, and stared at her in surprise, wondering if the woman was sincere. When Dovie came back with the plate covered with a cloth, there was a smaller dish on top with the stewed and sweetened tomatoes.

Charlotte was rising when there was a knock on the door. She felt her knees bouncing against the skirt of her dress.

A tall man stood outside the door unlit by the dim light in the room. Charlotte was ready to scream a warning, when a familiar voice spoke.

"Come in Mister Monroe," Dovie said as she turned to holler at her husband. "Reverend, there's company."

"Still? I thought the girl was leaving?"

"It's Mister Monroe, come to bring you a present."

They all heard the man muttering under his breath, as he fumbled back into his pants and shoes. When he finally came into the room, Charlotte noticed he had his black frock coat on, but there was no shirt collar showing.

"Evenin', Delmar."

"Good evening, Reverend. I'm sorry to wake you up, figured you folks would still be eating supper when I saw the light through the window. Here," he extended a bottle.

The preacher woke enough to accept it, turning the green bottle over and over in his hands.

"I was up on the eastern ridge, at the Bridger's place. Joseph Bridger asked me to bring you this bottle of wine, for use in the sacraments. Seth's baby is getting over a bad cold and they weren't sure they would be down the mountain for services."

The embarrassed man cleared his throat, pointed to the table still loaded with serving bowls. "Come in, come in, we've still got food on the table. You must be hungry."

Dovie sucked in her breath and Delmar hesitated, then said. "I am at that. Don't worry ma'am if there's not much left. I'll be happy for anything that's not hardtack and jerky."

Charlotte smiled and sank back into her empty chair. "There's plenty, isn't there, Mizz Dovie."

"Of course, of course there is." She turned, grabbed a plate, and carried it and silverware over for him, then turned back to get the small bowl of sweetened fruit.

While the men talked, Charlotte tried to be patient. At least the man didn't have a fiddle with him. She closed her eyes and bowed her head in prayer. With the heat of the room and the emotional evening, she had trouble keeping her eyes from staying closed.

It seemed natural for Delmar to volunteer to walk Charlotte home, especially since it was only a few hundred feet from the parsonage and both of them would remain in sight the whole time. The clouds were still overhead, hiding the moon. Charlotte was grateful to accept the man's elbow as he kept an eye on the trail.

When Charlotte saw someone moving down the main street, she grabbed Delmar's hand and pulled him to the overgrown side of the road. "There's someone there," she whispered.

Delmar looked, then laughed. "That's Jasper Sykes. Do you want me to ask him what's he's doing outside at night?"

She swatted at him in answer, flinging his hand and arm away.

"Charlotte, are you going to tell me what's wrong? I haven't seen you so nervous since that bear climbed into the cart with you."

Charlotte laughed, finally able to stop trembling. "Cicely's come back."

Delmar took his time before answering, wondering why that had her so bothered. "I know that's probably not what you wanted, but you seemed to like the girl well enough. If she wants to go home to Boston, maybe we can help."

"No, it's not that. Of course she's welcome, why do you think I don't care for the girl?"

When he shrugged instead of answering, she continued in a hushed voice as they walked toward the cabin, telling him all she knew of the girl's ordeal.

When Cicely finally opened the door, Delmar remained on the doorstep while Charlotte made sure the girl was hidden at the end of the bed. She set the warm plate down in front of her and told Cicely that she had told Delmar the situation and he was going to help.

"Can't nobody save me after what I's done. But I'd do it again, I swear I would. That devil man was worse than Mistress' sons back home. They never forced themselves on me."

"Are they the reason you wanted to leave Boston?" Charlotte asked.

"They's why I can't go back there. But there ain't no way to hide this dark face among all you lily white folks. They's going to come beat me and send me to that whore house, or worse, hang me."

Charlotte looked at Delmar's golden face, darker now with only the lantern to see. Still behind her, she knew Cicely's smooth black skin would be as impossible to hide as she claimed.

Delmar spoke. "I have an idea, but it may or may not work. How did you stay hidden so long? It's been nearly three weeks."

"I slept all day, wherever I could find cover. Stole food from folks' gardens at night and kept walking this trail up hill. I knows folks claimses to eat bugs and such, but I ain't seeing no need when there's sweet corn, 'maters and such all around. I didn't stay put long enough for folks to notice what was gone. Reckon they figured twas deer or rabbits been eatin' their garden truck, if'n they noticed."

"I'll be here before sunrise, if you trust me, Cicely, be ready to go. Goodnight, ladies," and he was gone.

CHAPTER TWENTY-THREE

Delmar arrived before dawn to take Cicely back up the mountain to the Bridgers. He knew if the body of her uncle was found, men would quickly find and follow the girl's trails. Even if no one had seen her, it would only take minutes for hounds to pick up her scent. He had high hopes Shep's wife Bailley would know how to hide the poor girl.

He was rewarded with his early arrival by seeing Charlotte with her hair in braids, her eyes half shut. Even with her wrapper pulled on and belted, she still looked adorable to him. He wondered how she would react if he swept her warm, sleepy body into his arms. Behind her he glimpsed Cicely rushing from the warm bed, scurrying to put her thin shoes on again. "Not those. Charlotte loan her a different pair."

Charlotte looked surprised at the demand, but found her oldest pair and held them out. "I doubt they will fit her."

"They's a little snug," Cicely said. "Youse feet must be missing some toes."

"Shh,"He tugged the girl out the door and rushed back toward his cabin, before angling behind it. He had already imagined working around the few cabins in town to avoid any chance of the girl being spotted.

"Go with God," Charlotte called after the pair. As soon as they disappeared from sight she headed to the outhouse and dropped the abandoned slippers down a hole.

He guided her downhill of the Daniel place, grateful for the light fog that clung around the foot of the hills to give them cover. The fewer people to spot the girl, the less likely someone would talk or give her away.

They walked up the cold, narrow stream between the ridges, working their way toward the path he had followed the day before wrestling the last log home. It had been almost impossible coming off the sharp ridge at Bridger's place.

Today, going the long way with the gentler grade was far easier, but by the time they reached the path up the ridge, Cicely was worn out. He knew she had eaten all the food Charlotte brought back, and had noticed them tumbling out of the same bed so knew she had slept for several hours. Still, he figured it was best if she took a break. He helped her up the hill and into a shelter beneath an overhanging rock that formed a little cave above the creek.

Leaving the girl beneath the overhang to rest, he went back down to fill his canteen and carry up cold water for her.

Straddling the stream, he smiled at the memory of how shocked Charlotte looked to see the girl wolfing all the food down last night. She probably had planned to share only half. Since he had his travel pouch, he had slipped her a piece of jerky and hard-tack, and was pleased when she accepted them gratefully, unlike the first time he had fed her.

He sat resting, thinking of Charlotte, while the runaway slept. After two hours, he woke Cicely and encouraged her up the rest of the mountain. If there were any place where she might be safe, Bridger's Ridge would be it. He hoped the Melungeon family here let her stay.

Entering the bald, the cleared area around the cabin, they walked through an acre of trellised grape vines. The smell of the young fruit was faint but made both of their stomachs' rumble. Bees were buzzing lazily to and from the conical hives placed at the front of the vineyard. In the clearing, dining on the tall grass was a small herd of brown and white spotted goats, their long white hair glowing in the morning sun. Warily, Delmar escorted Cicely toward the cabin, avoiding the billy goat who bleated a challenge at their approach.

It was the older man who hailed him first, following them out of the vines. The two men exchanged greetings, both surprised that they had passed each other unnoticed. Cicely shrank behind Delmar, at the billy goat's new challenge. Papa Bridger picked up a rock and flicked it at the animal as he waved his arms shooing him away.

"Figured you wouldn't be back for awhile, Delmar. You have trouble with that big log after all?" Cicely kept her eyes on the goats, their conversation as comforting as the buzzing bees.

"When I realized the ox couldn't help, might end up falling on the way down I did sit and comtemplate the situation awhile. Finally, I lined that chestnut log up on the top of the ridge and shoved it with the broad heavy bottom trunk leading the vertical drop. I prayed all the time I heard it crashing down that it would make it without cracking or getting hung up."

The older man was curious about the girl walking in the fiddler's shadow, but continued talking as though he hadn't seen her.

"Figured easing that ox down the ridge would be worse than working that animal up the mountain side in the first place."

"Let's just say, it took a lot of cussing and praying. Then when we were both down safely, it took an hour to locate the log hung up on the ridge and maneuver it to where the animal could drag it down the valley and the long way back to Kyles Ford. Just got home last night."

Bailley Bridger and her mother-in-law emerged from the pretty white house on the hill, with little Joseph Gabriel riding on his grandmother's hip. At sight of the black woman, he gave a little cry and was switched from the white woman to his dark mother. Shep was the last to leave his work in the garden and approach them, clearly happy to see the musician again so quickly.

"Back again. Thought that big chestnut tree was going to be enough to keep you busy the rest of the year."

He extended an arm and clasped Delmar's hand warmly, denying the teasing words.

The house was warm, so they all settled on the long porch in the rockers and in the kitchen chairs carried out for the company. Cicely sat on the steps, knees drawn up. No one asked, but it was clear they were all checking out the bruises on her face and her bulging lower lip and swollen jaw. Mama Bridger rose and called Cicely into the house behind her. Those left on the porch could hear the older woman preparing something, then demanding that the girl gargle and spit out the salt water into the sink.

With the noise for cover, Delmar whispered, "She's a free girl that came down from Boston with the new schoolmarm. Was supposed to go live with her aunt and uncle in Sneedville." He rolled his eyes toward the screen, then whispered. "The bastard jumped her last week, did everything a man can do to hurt a girl."

All the faces staring at him darkened and he watched Bailley start to rise. He motioned her down as he heard voices rise inside as the woman told the girl to sit so she could feel her head, check to see if her skull was cracked.

"He told her he was going to sell her to a bawdy house, to keep her from telling her aunt what happened. First time he turned his back, she struck his head with a rock. Thinks she killed him."

They heard the women inside approaching, and were not surprised to see the girl holding a tall glass of water tinted purple with wine. Mama Bridger carried a tray with glasses and poured the same drink for the quiet people on the porch.

"What are your plans?" Shep asked.

"Delmar told you?" Cicely watched and could tell from their faces that he had. "I been hiding, living on what I snitched from yards. Shouldn't of done it, but I went back to Mizz Charlotte for help. I'm afraid I might of brung trouble on her, if they follows me back to Kyles Ford."

Delmar turned back, clutched her hand, turning it over to look at the pink palm, then back over so the black skin with its torn knuckles showed. "You did the right thing. Charlotte wanted to help you. But you're right about hiding in town."

"I ain't got papers or nothin'. Heard Reverend Watkin and his missus ask Charlotte about her owning me. She told them I'se free, but they didn't seem to believe her. She planned to write my mammy and ask her to get proof I'se free. Don't matter now. I can't ask them folks back home for nothin'. Not when I'se wanted for murder."

Bailley, the black woman, spoke first, "Why you so sure you kilt him?"

Cicely lowered her head, stared up at them with her eyes half-moons in her face. "Cause I wanted to, kept thinkin' how I was goin' to escape. Then uncle started braggin' 'bout he was sellin' me to a place he knew above

Cumberland Gap. Goin' to tell my aunt I done got lost or runned off, complainin' about all the work. I never complained, I liked Mammy Buford. Sides, I had nowhere to run to. There weren't no black folks in Kyles Ford atall."

"Anyhow, I was mumbling and praying under my breath when my toe hit this big rock." She pulled the tight right shoe from her foot, showed them the black and bloodied toe. "I knew God was listenin' and this was his answer. So I picked that big rock up in both hands and I ran at him as fast as I could and whacked his head, wantin' to break it open. Let all his meanness run out."

"You're not that big a girl, your hittin' him might have only put him to sleep," Shep said.

She sat still, her bare foot swingin' off the porch. "He kinda' groaned and moaned and fell down like he was dead. I waited, holdin' that heavy rock over his head. I was prepared to hit him again and again if I needed to. But he just lay there, his eyes open, his mouth closed. And I know'd he was dead, and I kilt him. Nobody was there to know what he said, what he'd done to me. I would be a little negress, with no papers, no people to argue for me, or nothin'.

"Finally, I set down that rock. All I could think was gettin' away fore somebody passed by me, or found him dead. I rolled him over to the side of the road, and covered him with weeds alongside the ditch.

"I didn't know which way to turn, where to run to escape. Then I minded myself we'd been walkin' downhill all that time. If'n I just kept walkin' t'other way, I knew I'd reach Mizz Charlotte. I counted on findin' her. But it done taken' too long and I'm all tuckered out. Even if his body is rolled off the side of the trail, and covered with brush, he's probably smellin' bad enough for somebody to notice and find him by now."

Mama Bridger filled her glass again, passed it to Cicely. Delmar noticed this time the wine wasn't watered. In the hot breeze blowin' across the field, they all watched the girl wind down her talking and fall asleep.

"Poor child," Mama said. "One of you men tote her on in to the bed in the back room there."

All three started to rise, but it was Delmar who scooped Cicely up and carried her inside.

CHAPTER TWENTY-FOUR

"Best bet is to get her past Newman Ridge, up to Vardy. There's plenty of Melungeons she can blend in with," Joseph Bridger suggested.

"Don't know about that, them people ain't too social, you know. I don't know anyone there to ask," Shep said. "Might get shot at for sneaking up there."

Delmar stared at the young man, and saw his papa shake his head as well.

Bailley had been inside whispering up a storm and helping Mama get some food on the table. She appeared at the door to ask them in, staring between the three men, smiling as she saw the way Shep held the sleepy baby. The boy's soft big body was loosely cradled a straddle his knee, his round head hanging forward over his papa's arm. "I reckon we're a little kin to Big Haley. If we got the girl up there, and Mahala would let her stay, ain't nobody goin' be able to get her out of there."

"Big Haley," Delmar asked as he extended a hand to help Shep rise with his sleepy son.

"She's a moonshiner. Pretty fierce woman," Shep said.

"She's a big ole gal – why don't you tell him that," Papa said.

Shep looked at his father and grinned, "Well, she's about the biggest woman in these parts. Over 300 lbs and growin'. She don't make the quality that Davis Daniel does, but she sure makes the quantity of hooch. Reckon since Harley Boggs died, she's the one to see if you ain't particular what you're drinkin'."

During a big meal of fresh green beans, chopped and wilted salad, served with cold roasted goat, there was a lively debate about how to best shield Cicely. It was clear Kyles Ford wasn't safe, and although the Bridgers could shelter her for a while, once her uncle's body was found, everybody knew she would be easily found here. Although Shep and his parent's looked white, Bailley looked almost as black as Cicely. Delmar had already learned Melungeon didn't tell you that much about a person, other than they weren't pure white.

Hopefully, they would able to protect and defend her, since she had been assaulted and the man was only a black man. No one said it, but all stared at each other before settling on baby Joseph. It would put everyone here at risk for harboring a runaway and a murderer.

It was agreed it would be safer to move her to the Vardy community. There were mainly dark Melungeons like Bailley living there. The people had taken in escaped slaves before, and since Cicely was free born, it should be a lot easier to convince them to make room for the frightened girl. Bailley felt sure she could get her parents to take care of the girl, if no one else would.

Later, Shep, Bailley and little Joseph headed out for Newman Ridge with Cicely in tow. She had the same woebegone look that she had when they started from Charlotte's cabin. Surely, Bailley's optimism would sway her. Sixteen was too young to believe life was over.

Delmar headed for home, dragging the reluctant billy goat along, as the senior Bridger advised. He could see the sense of it, hiding the trail the girl had traveled. He had already tried to do that when he had Charlotte give the girl a pair of her shoes. He smiled, as he remembered the way she had looked kneeling to put her shoes on the hurt girl's feet. Cicely wore clothes, old ones true, but clothes the woman had carried with her from Boston.

He was relieved when he could release the ornery, creature that had fought and tugged at the end of the rope all the way. Amazed, he watched the animal jumping from rock to rock on the way back up the steep cliff part of the ridge. Thanks to his help, even if they brought hounds to trail after Cicely, the only scent they would track would be the rank smell the billy had sprayed as they walked down beside the creek. At least the animal had been able to decorate most of the trees and bushes once he reached unknown territory.

Satisfied that he'd done all he could, Delmar headed back toward Kyles Ford. He was half-way there when he encountered the first stranger. The man held his rifle at a downward angle to seem unthreatening, but there was enough in the way he stood, the ready set of his shoulders and hands and the way his eyes surveyed every inch of the music man that betrayed him. This was a lawman on the hunt.

Delmar heard an excited animal barking up ahead, and lowered his head to force the fear back down his throat.

"Mister, who are you, and where you coming from up that holler?"

Delmar said a small prayer and tried to summon his father's bearing. He raised his head, his eyes cool, blue, and full of warning. Carefully he held out an open hand until the man was forced to take it. "Delmar Monroe, pleasure to meet you...?" He continued to hold the hand until the man mumbled his own name.

Delmar released the hand, grateful that it had worked. "Nice afternoon for a walk, don't you think, Sheriff?"

"Nice enough. Bill come back here with them hounds."

Delmar waited, features frozen, until the big, raging hounds stopped their snarling and leaned in closer to him. They ran their cold wet noises over him until they'd smelled enough, then shook their heads making their long ears flap and curl. Delmar relaxed, held up both hands and asked. "Scary dogs. Will they bite if I pet them?"

The Sheriff smiled, "Don't know, never had no one ask to do that before."

Delmar was running his hands over the big squared heads, straightening their folded ears as the sheriff answered. After a minute, one, then the other of the big dogs laid down on the bare earth of the trail, rolling to encourage more petting.

The other man had moved up closer behind him. "Yeah, reckoned I'd heard tell of you. Eb Daniel was bragging about how they had a top fiddler in Kyles Ford these days. That be you?"

Delmar smiled and nodded, "Been known to saw a tune, pick a few on the guitar and banjo too. I've come down here for some special wood. Want to make my own instruments."

The man leaned back a little as he looked up to him, his mouth relaxing into a grin for the first time. "That's what Eb was telling us, just couldn't believe him, never heard of nobody doing anything like that this side of Gatlinburg."

"You know someone who makes instruments around here. I sure would love to meet him, learn what he can show me."

The sheriff shushed the other man away. "That can all keep. We're here, looking for a murdering, runaway slave."

Delmar stared at him, giving nothing away. One of the hounds raised a knobby head for him to fondle and pet.

The sheriff continued. "No need to answer, Eb done told us you brought her to town with the new schoolmarm. Reckon she might be hiding the girl somewhere, this Mizz Charlotte Stewart?"

"Guess you better come on into town. Take me a while to go there to ask and come back here to give you an answer."

The man didn't look to be amused. He snapped and the hounds were back on their feet, but the snarling was gone as they whipped against Delmar's legs to give him better access to pet them.

The street and town looked deserted as the three men walked up to the General Store. Delmar introduced the two men to Jasper Sykes and then sat down on the porch with a hound near each knee. Maybe that old billy's rubbing and butting against him had done Delmar a favor. The hounds seemed attracted to the foul scent. One planted its big head on his knee and stared up at him with soulful brown eyes. He gave in to petting it, looked toward the school and wished there were some way to warn Charlotte before she was confronted by these two men.

Widow Mouse appeared at the door, carrying a pail and dipper of cold spring water. When it was Delmar's turn, she looked at the big dogs, then over to the clean shaven musician. "What happened? This is the first time I've seen you without a violin or guitar."

He stared at the small woman, her face almost hidden by the brim of an ugly black bonnet. As he recalled, her eyes were even darker than the hounds. He recalled someone remarking that she had Chincapin eyes, her and the baby. That's what made her so pretty.

He hadn't learned what a Chincapin was until he'd been given one of the small chestnuts, found in a prickly pod on a short bush of a tree. As a breeze caught the brim of her bonnet, he got to see them. They were as dark, round, and shiny as a wild chestnut. "I'll go get it Mizz Mouse. Make sure to play you a special tune."

When he looked up he saw Jasper Sykes glaring at him. With a finger raised to the two lawmen, he left the big store owner behind.

CHAPTER TWENTY-FIVE

Charlotte had been tired and too restless to go back to sleep after Cicely and Delmar left. She had finally lit her lamp and opened the little reader that Dovie Watkin insisted was the best way to get students to read.

By the time she finished, she had decided to introduce reading today after reviewing yesterday's work with each group. She knew from Dovie that there were several returning students who were already reading.

Dressed and bed made, she lay down for only a second to rest.

The loud male voice carried through the glass pane, "You think she's dead?"

One that was almost identical answered, "Nah, might be sick or drunk though."

Charlotte jumped to her feet. Checking her hair to make sure it was still pinned, she grabbed her notes and opened the door to burst into the area in front of the cabin to the sound of the children laughing.

Cheeks flaming, she wanted to race to the schoolhouse but instead checked the impulse, and carefully pulled the latch rope as she closed the door.

"Sorry children, I got ready so early this morning then fell asleep reading. Have you been waiting long?"

The day flew by. If the Daniel boys were upset at their treatment the day before they didn't show it. Instead, catching her oversleeping seemed to make them and the other children like her better. She wondered if she would be having less problems with the children if she had followed her own instincts instead of listening to Dovie Watkin. At the thought, the door opened and there was the preacher's wife, looking very sternly at all of them.

Charlotte knew the old cat must have learned that she was late this morning. Whether one of the children had said something when they were on their first break, or someone else in town had seen the children milling around outside the school this morning, Dovie knew. Without meaning too, Charlotte rolled her eyes skyward and Philomena started to giggle and quickly raised a hand to cover her mouth. Charlotte struggled, but managed to hide her own smile by reaching out to clutch the older girl's hand. The girl was so startled, she started to hiccup.

Mizz Dovie reached the front pew, standing so her round hips were propped against the desk she said, "Pinch your nose child and close your mouth tight as long as you can. That should stop them." She gave Charlotte a stern look. "You're giving a reading lesson, already?"

Charlotte straightened her back before turning to look up at the woman. "Yes, I wanted to assess student levels today. I've already established a chart for each showing their beginning levels in writing and arithmetic. It seemed to be a good activity for this warm Friday."

Perhaps it was her confident answer, or the mention of charting student progress that had stopped the woman in her tracks. Charlotte didn't feel the need to constantly be supervised by anyone, especially this woman.

Dovie rose immediately, as though she had some urgent errand to run. Charlotte especially disliked how the woman presumed to enter the room at any time without knocking or at least making a civil greeting. She wasn't surprised the woman was leaving without a civil goodbye, either.

Dovie walked briskly back up the aisle, but turned at the door and called. "I wondered if you had a preference for supper, roast pork and potatoes, or fried pork and green beans."

"They both sound wonderful. I'm sure whichever is less trouble for you would suit equally well," Charlotte answered sweetly.

She was grateful for Philomena's loud hiccup, that hid her stomach's growl in response to the thought of food. She had slept through breakfast and packed no lunch. Maybe if she hadn't been so abrupt, Mizz Dovie would have brought something to share at noon. Now, she would have to eat the few dry crackers in her desk and pretend to be full.

◇◇◇

After lunch, she organized the children and they played blind man's bluff. She put Eb in the center of children with the blindfold on. She had expected he would be familiar with the game and save her from having to explain the rules. Neither of the boys did, so she carefully recited the rules as they began. Ned tied the blindfold and spun him the usual three times, then added a couple of more before releasing him. With Charlotte calling out the first question, "How many horses does your father have?"

"None." Came the answer as Ned spun him again and Philomena asked the next question, "How many hounds does he have?"

"Eight," and as his brother spun him, each student according to their age, asked the next question. By the time they were finished asking details about the hounds, Eb was weaving and Charlotte yelled. "Let him loose."

Pandemonium ensued as the big boy tried to catch one of the other children, reeling crazily as he grabbed for one and they giggled as they eluded him. Finally, he nabbed, and identified Sydney. Eb blindfolded the smaller boy and was set to make him sick with spins when Charlotte called out a simple question. "How many children does your mother have?"

"Three," came back before she finished. Resuming questions by the next oldest child in the circle, he quickly named his brother and sister and Eb had to release him.

Eb was almost caught again, but he pulled and shoved Ned in his way and Sydney managed to call a name. Charlotte broke up the game, sending the complaining children back inside with a single shake of the bell.

At the last break before the end of school, Charlotte stood in the warm sunshine as she cleaned the few dishes and cups that they had used. She allowed Glory and Steven, her two first graders to carry back the dishes, one at a time. When she looked up the street and saw Delmar strutting along with strangers and no Cicely, it made her shiver.

At the end, when Charlotte rang the bell, she saw the big boys in the back grinning at each other. She knew it was probably another comment between them about her oversleeping. Sternly she said to all the children who were fidgeting about, getting ready to bolt on the last ring.

"Let's not be in such a hurry. As I said this morning, we are starting things that we will now do every day. That includes a song at the end of class." At the excitement in raised voices, Charlotte waved her ruler and brought it down, stopping it at the last moment. Still the children gasped.

She turned toward the oldest girl. "Name us a song, Philomena."

"Yankee Doodle."

"Everyone knows the words?" Charlotte asked.

The children all nodded and she raised her hands for them to stand and nodded at the girl, "Lead us."

She rang the bell on the chorus and sent the children out on the last words, "Mind the music and the step, and with the girls be handy."

"See you all next Monday," she called.

Charlotte walked along behind them, wanting to stop at the store and talk to Jeanne, but seeing the strangers still standing, leaning against the porch posts stopped her. Instead, she turned back and rushed past a disapproving Mizz Watkin toward home. Delmar startled her when he appeared, halfway between the school and the privies, then ducked out of sight as he saw Dovie headed their way.

In a harsh whisper he said, "I met those lawmen on the trail, they're looking for Cicely. No one seems to know anything, so far that they've asked. Guess I'll go back, see if I can get them turned around and headed back home."

"Is Cicely safe?"

Delmar hissed at her and disappeared at the same time Charlotte heard the breathless voice call, "Wait up Mizz Stewart. We need to talk."

Charlotte froze, wanting nothing more than to duck into the nearby outhouse and lock the door to keep the woman away. An even louder voice called from behind the preacher's wife. "Wait, Mizz Stewart, we have some questions for you."

Charlotte turned to look past the nosey woman to the commanding figure with a small silver badge proudly pinned to his jacket. Cicely had been right. The law would be looking for her if her uncle's body turned up missing.

She held out a hand toward Dovie Watkin, who seemed surprised, but took it.

Charlotte moved over beside the woman, knowing how shocked Dovie would be since she had clearly had a list of things to berate her about today. It didn't matter, Charlotte knew the woman would not let this man treat her with less than respect, and she needed her support right now.

CHAPTER TWENTY-SIX

It was such a short distance to her tiny cabin, but it seemed to take forever as Charlotte led the way, arm-in-arm with Dovie Watkin.

When the Hancock County Sheriff introduced himself he told her he had some questions to ask about her slave girl, Cicely Turner. Charlotte had merely nodded and invited him to join her in her cabin for tea. When Dovie would have protested, she had tucked the woman's arm in hers and led the way.

As she pulled the loop of rope in the door opening, she reviewed her steps from the night before. After she had thrown away Cicely's worn shoes, she had returned and gathered the girls bloody, tattered clothing and carried them to a similar fate. She debated putting them in the boy's side, but figured neither side would be too closely examined. It was also unlikely the hounds, if the men brought dogs along to search, would be able to catch the girl's scent.

She had spent the early morning hours, changing her sheets, washing them and her towels in the small sink before wringing them repeatedly. She didn't dare hang them out, she had heard from Mizz Dovie already how outrageous it was that the foreigner in their mist, Jeanne LeSouris, had done laundry on a day other than Monday.

Instead, she folded the damp items with her dirty linens and dresses and added them to the laundry bag under the end boards of the bed. Surely this man wouldn't want her to bring her things out for a dog to sniff. If he did, would the harsh soap hide any lingering scent from the black girl?

Now she was glad she had scrubbed the sink and floors as well. Of course, it would have been better if she had been able to stay awake and not be caught sleeping, but as she held the door open wide for the lawman to enter first, she was relieved to see how neat and spartan the small room appeared. Even Dovie Watkin commented on how well she kept the place.

Charlotte indicated the board at the end of the bed and invited the officer to sit first. Instead, he insisted Mizz Dovie go first. While they were settling, Charlotte pumped water and started the stove, hoping it would catch quickly. The faster she waited on her unwelcome guests, hopefully the sooner they would be gone.

Aware of the sheriff looking around, she separated her curtains and then stepped up on the under sink shelf as usual to reach and open first one window, then the other. Mizz Dovie's plate rested on the shelf atop her own two, the woman's silverware lay gleaming on the counter.

"I don't have a lot to offer you, sir, I'm afraid. I take most of my meals with the Watkin. I've no milk, but do you prefer sugar or honey with your tea?" The man rolled his shoulders and Charlotte guessed he'd never taken tea before. She hoped the fragile cup would survive.

"Would your deputy like to join us?"

The man laughed, one of those insincere gestures. "He's busy with the hounds, hunting for any scent from the runaway. Now, do you mind answering some questions?"

"Maybe Mizz Watkin could tend to the tea and you could sit and tell me all you know about your girl."

Charlotte moved forward with the tray of tea things for answer. She carefully set it on the end of the board, then leaned across the man's big knees to shift the lamp to the other end, pressing the vase of flowers even closer to her books. Satisfied, she set out the dainty flowered cups and saucers in front of them. She left the teapot on the tray, waiting for her to add steaming water.

"First, she is not my girl. No one owns Cicely. She was born a free negress in Boston. As you know, slavery has been illegal in Massachusetts since the 1780's. No, my family arranged with the family her people served there in Boston for us to share passage so that Cicely could act as a proper chaperone. Of course my father, President of Newton Seminary College, secured our agenda. He arranged with many of his former students, who are ministers along the way, to provide us escort and shelter."

"So," Charlotte poured the steaming tea into his cup, then took Dovie's and poured her a cup as well. She added the amber colored sugar to each cup, grateful that this time she had been able to cut a reasonable amount from the cone without crumbling it everywhere. To her cup at the end by the door, she added honey. "Cicely can't technically be called a runaway."

While talking and waiting on the tea to steep, she cut three generous slices of bread from the small loaf Dovie had sent her home with on Monday. She spread each with the dark sweet blackberry jam that one of her student's had brought to school for her. Carefully, she cut each slice into four triangles and carried the plates proudly to hand to each guest. She drug her chair across the floor to the end of the shelf near the open door to hide her stomach's growling as she set her own plate down.

She managed one small tip before the man's next question floored her. "Her aunt, Mammy Buford, been driving us crazy the last week. Hollering her man went to fetch the doctor last Friday and neither of them came back home."

"My, it seems so long since we arrived here. Let me see. Why it was three weeks ago today, wasn't it Mizz Watkin? I mean that was when I arrived. Cicely stayed and helped with the unpacking and everything, but then the weekend before school started, a very big, mean, ugly man appeared and said he had come for Cicely. He claimed to be her uncle."

"Not quite three, I think she left the day following your arrival. Wait, that would be three weeks, you're right."

"Yes, that's so. Mizz Dovie got to meet Cicely, she was a good worker but hardly a willing one. Wouldn't you say that described her, Mizz Dovie?"

"Exactly. She made a lot of faces and gestures behind my back. But she did do a credible job of the tasks asked her."

"She stayed in here with you how long?" he asked in disbelief.

Charlotte wished she dared answer honestly. Instead she retold they had agreed upon. "She had a little bedroll that she rolled out onto the floor there, between the sink and my bed. It wasn't much space, but she wasn't more than a half-grown woman."

"Can you give me a detailed description. If we don't turn her up in the next day or so, then we'll need it for a wanted poster."

"Tiny, but about my height. She had very dark skin, hair, and eyes, and wore a simple dress and plain shoes. She ate like a sparrow," Charlotte said with her fingers crossed where she held them beneath her skirt. "Oh, and she was wearing a black straw hat with a round crown tied with ribbons under her chin when she left. Very pretty."

Dovie rose, looking from the sheriff to Charlotte. "I must get home and start supper. I'll walk you out sheriff," Dovie said.

With the door and windows open, there was a little breeze from the cool shadows under the trees that made it tolerable, sitting and sipping tea. Charlotte looked at the last triangle of bread on her plate, wondering if she dared take the remaining bread and eat the end crust with more of the sweet jam.

When she walked down for supper with the Watkins, she was surprised by the four men in the room. Delmar, the sheriff, and his deputy had been invited by the reverend to join them.

Charlotte had dreaded the confrontation with Dovie, expecting to be thoroughly drilled on her behavior today. Instead, the two women had no chance to talk. Delmar volunteered to go back with the lawmen. The most surprising moment came when the reverend interrupted their conversation to suggest that the uncle might have liked the young niece better than the aunt. Cicely was attractive, for a negress. What if the man had taken off with her?

"If he thought he could make money out of her somehow, he might of. Mammy even hinted she was worried he might try to sell the girl, claim she was a slave. Told her not to worry about that. If he tried, a big buck like him, they'd slap him in chains first," the sheriff answered.

"Really, do you think he might be dumb enough to try it. If Cicely's aunt thought he might, maybe she had reason," Charlotte said and all four men stared at her. She blushed and looked down at her plate. How could she have forgotten that most important rule of etiquette her mother had drilled into her and her sisters so often. Men do not like to hear what a woman thinks, especially in the presence of other men.

"Guess we can look into that angle a little when we get back home. Delmar, you sure you got time to walk the trail back with us," the sheriff said. Charlotte sat sipping her tea.

"No problem, I planned to go visit the Bridger's again. I cut a big Chestnut tree up there and promised to take them a circle from the trunk when I get it worked up. Mama Bridger wanted it for her daughter-in-law, Bailley."

"Don't understand those people. Now that's a crime in every state in the union," the reverend said.

"What is?" Delmar asked.

"Misanguination, the mixing of races. A crime against God, the state, and man."

"Bailley is a Melungeon," Delmar protested.

"What the hell do you think that means, but mixed race, subhuman. All the Bridger's are, though most of 'em claim they're half Indian, not Negroe. Like that's ary bit better. If I was you mister, trying to build a reputation and business, I'd advise you to avoid trash like that." The sheriff stared at Delmar hard, then shook his head.

"You sure don't look like a man that would welcome that kind of trouble. That's a little like Mizz Stewart defending that little negro gal. You folks from up north got some peculiar ideas about nature. Bible points out the children of Cain will bear his mark, they're all close to animals. You act like they was regular people."

"Maybe you're mixed race too," the Deputy said.

Delmar had to bite his tongue to keep from protesting that in his blood flowed the blood of a president. Instead he grinned, and then roared with laughter.

At the change in mood, Mizz Dovie asked him if he was going to play. Delmar opened the fiddle case he'd brought, requesting she play her Dulcimer to accompany him. He tried to tease Charlotte into singing, but she apologized, telling everyone about having to ask students to lead the end of day song since she had such a terrible voice.

Nothing would do but that she prove it. Once she did, she noticed, no one asked her to sing the next song.

CHAPTER TWENTY-SEVEN

Delmar ended up inviting the sheriff and deputy to stay the night. This time he would keep his bed, let the strangers bunk on the floor.

"I'll see Mizz Stewart home, then be right back for you fellows."

"We can go along," the sheriff said.

Delmar was stumped for an answer when Charlotte put down the knife beside the cake plate. "Drats, I was just slicing more cake. Is it that time already?"

Mizz Dovie stared at her, and Charlotte knew it would be added to the rest of the day's sins the woman intended to berate her for. "Nonsense, you two hurry on and I'll finish serving these two gentlemen."

"Sounds good to me," the deputy said.

The sheriff ran his tongue over his lips and stared at the stack cake, before nodding. "Don't dally."

Charlotte was already at the door, "No need, Mr. Monroe if you want to stay for coffee and cake with these gentlemen."

He shook his head, looked at the sheriff, then gave a rough bow of acknowledgement and followed her out. The sky was black, the familiar path invisible. They were both aware of the sheriff watching them up the hill. They were nearly at the school before the man turned away.

"The Bridgers are moving her to the community of Vardy. Have you been there?" Delmar whispered.

Charlotte shook her head, "Of course not, "how would I get to travel?"

Delmar was a little surprised, after what Jasper had told him the school board was expecting of their little teacher. He didn't want to be around when she figured it out.

"Bailley knows a woman where the girl can stay. If I delay enough, maybe the fools will give up. Can't do much tracking in the dark, at least."

"Maybe I should ask Dovie to pray for a heavy rain," she said.

"Well, if you think she has the connections?"

"My problem is, I don't know how to take your irreverence sometimes, Mister Monroe."

When she pulled the latch on the door, something flew past and she let out a squeal of fear. Delmar entered first. Whatever it was, another brushed past his head.

"Where's your lantern?"

Charlotte squeezed past him and found it in the corner. She held it toward him and he struck his flint to it and turned up the wick. Delmar took it from her hand, their fingers brushing as she backed toward the door. He set the lamp down by the sink, noticed the open curtains and windows. A little click and eek sent her flying out the door and made him sure of the visitor.

Charlotte jumped when the sheriff appeared beside her, pistol drawn. "What's the matter?"

Delmar swung the broom, connecting and sending the furry intruder toward the door. "Bats." He took the lamp, lifted it high enough to inspect the loft, then low enough to check under the hanging desk and bed.

Firmly he closed both windows, and pulled the curtains closed.

"No need for the gun, sheriff. She forgot and left the windows open, and a couple of bats got in."

Charlotte entered reluctantly, excusing the men. She noticed the deputy had finally appeared on the trail and closed the door on the three men staring in at her. If the deputy had stayed hoping Dovie Watkin would serve him a third slice of her famous cake, he had quickly been disillusioned.

As she lay on the bed, lantern still lit on the sink beside her, she studied the six dresses hanging on the wall, staring carefully at the little pockets of darkness at the edges of each, the sinister ruffled pockets of shadow at the bottom. The little flying mice could hide anywhere. She didn't want one to drop down on her in surprise. Beside the bed, stood the broom, her only weapon.

Reflecting on the long day and the interrogation by the sheriff, she wasn't sure he was satisfied by her answers. Had no doubt that was why he and the deputy had shown up at the Watkin's for supper.

Just remembering the appalled look on Dovie's face made the endless evening worthwhile. Luckily, she had cooked the large roast and there was plenty for everyone.

Later, their host had seemed to enjoy playing music with Delmar, although the tunes were old ones. "Whistle, Mary, Whistle," and Delmar had asked her to sing. Well, they couldn't say she hadn't warned them. For a moment, she wondered if he had only wanted her to sing the last refrain. The thought made her heart speed up.

Sighing first, she sang, "Whistle Mary, whistle, and you shall have a man. I can whistle, Mother I just found out I can!" Everyone had laughed, but afterward, he asked Dovie for the dulcimer to play the second song alone, a nice rendition of "Columbia, the Gem of the Ocean."

Charlotte woke late, relieved to know there was no class to teach. She wanted to speak with Jeanne LeSouris, but wondered if the nosy lawmen were gone. By the time she was dressed and ready to go down to the store, Dovie Watkin was at her door, knocking.

Determined to not get upset, Charlotte opened the door with a big smile and urged the woman inside. "I'm sorry, I meant to return your things yesterday when you and the lawmen came to tea. I felt so guilty last night when you had such a table full for supper."

Dovie managed to smile in turn. "It was a challenge, but there were only six of us. I have a service for eight."

"If you would just sit down, Charlotte, I have important school business to discuss with you. I've been waiting for an opening to tell you about the board meeting, but there always seems to be someone or something to interrupt us."

At the serious tone of voice, Charlotte sank onto the bench. She knew she wasn't going to like this. The woman unrolled a long sheet of paper and started to read. Charlotte hated being right.

Even after Dovie left, Charlotte was too restless to sit. Instead she picked up her drawstring bag with the board's memorandum folded neatly inside. This was Saturday morning. If Dovie had delivered the message as she was supposed to have, Charlotte would have already been able to complete one of the scheduled visitations.

It didn't matter. She was going to visit Glory. She had made sure of the directions the day of the outhouse incident with the Daniel boys. This was an added complication. But with the family living so close to town, she thought she might be able to meet the board's requirements and still sleep in her own bed.

Walking down the wide trail through town, she passed one family headed toward the store, and noticed another was already there.

The Goin's family had been busy, the house noisy and less than clean with two younger children and little Glory running around. Charlotte was pleased to see how surprised the little girl's mother was to see her come for a visit. After the blonde woman, who looked like a not much older version of her little girl, stopped apologizing, Charlotte spoke.

"Well, I really should have told you to expect a visit or come home with Glory on Friday. As you know, it's expected that a teacher will make time for a long visit and get to know everything about her students. What their parents are like, what their home life is like, what she does outside of her school work. It lets me help Glory learn to the best of her ability."

"No, I ain't heard of it before, but you're most welcome to come and stay as long as you like. The little ones can double up on the floor and you can share the bed with Glory."

The woman rushed over to where a thin screen of planks had been constructed that held a short little square bed. Now it held only a very fat, sleepy cat on the rumpled covers. The children's room and the parents were both open to the fireplace and main room, although the parent's bed was longer and there was a tall bureau wedged between the foot of the bed and the wall. In the main room, there was a round table with four chairs and a stool.

"Thank you," Charlotte curtsied and the woman tried to copy her motion. Glory ran around and surprised Charlotte when she copied the little bow perfectly. "I only live a little distance away from here, beside the school. I couldn't think of putting your children out of their bed." The other two, a boy about four and another little girl somewhere between two and three came up and managed to grab their mother's skirt.

"Let's just spend the day together, then I'll walk home before dark. I can come back and meet everyone on the way to church. Doesn't that sound like fun."

Glory clapped and ran over to grab Charlotte's skirt and she let her hand rest on the tousled little head.

The mother looked at them and smiled. "Well come sit, have a cup of coffee, while I string my beans."

Charlotte settled, after watching for a minute, took a bean and copied the motion of snapping the tip and pulling the long string down the side, then repeating it from the other end. She snapped the pod into four pieces and was given a nod of approval. While they worked, Glory and the young children tried to help, then gave up and ran outside to play.

"I should have come over last week, when the Daniel boys played that awful prank on Glory."

"Yep, would have been nice. Her pa was ready to go to your school and give them two pranksters a thrashing."

The woman didn't add, and 'you too,' but Charlotte read condemnation in her eyes. Charlotte had made another mistake, not coming soon enough. If these two parents had been that angry with the way she was handling school, why hadn't they come to her and complained? Her hands shook as she picked up the next bean and the string broke somewhere along the side.

The woman took the bean, snapped it before the break and used the short piece to pull the rest of the string along that side. She handed it back to her, shaking her head in wonder.

"What?" Charlotte asked.

"Well, you act like you've never snapped beans before."

Charlotte shook her head, and blushed.

The woman smiled again and said, "Well, when we complained to Mizz Dovie about them bad boys and how upset Glory was over it all, she said we had to remember it was your first year to teach. She also said anyone would have trouble with Eb and Ned."

"She said all that."

The woman nodded. Glory came running into the house, cradling a big hen. Charlotte jumped up and moved to the other side of the table, keeping the woman between her and Glory and the strange pet. The children laughed so hard, the little ones rolled on the floor. Only after the little girl begged her to pet her hen, did Charlotte reach out and touch the big red bird, delighted at how soft the chicken was. She even enjoyed hearing the hen cluck softly.

All the way home after the surprisingly good dinner and visit with Glory's family, all Charlotte could think about was the generosity of the bossy woman who had been hovering so close at hand. Dovie Watkin had stood up for her and that was important. She wasn't sure how she could repay the woman for all the resentment and resistance she had shown her, but she was determined to try.

CHAPTER TWENTY-EIGHT

Monday came, and though she didn't look for him, she was aware that Delmar had not returned. Determinedly she focused on the lesson. Reading aloud was her favorite part of each evaluation, with each child taking a turn standing at the table beside her. She listened for errors in pronunciation or misread words to correct as Sydney read a story in the second McGuffey reader.

She sat beaming as the thin blonde boy stood erect and enunciated each word clearly. When he finished the story of the boy who learned not to be afraid of the dark, since it was only a shadow, Charlotte clapped. She rose and wrote the slate work for the last two groups to copy, making sure her lettering stood firmly above and below the lines she had ruled on the board that morning.

Beautiful faces are they that wear,
The light of a pleasant spirit there;
Beautiful hands are they that do
Deeds that are noble good and true;
Beautiful feet are they that go
Swiftly to lighten another's woe.

As they finished their copy work, she sent the students out on break, watching as the girls headed straight for the outhouse and the boys darted toward the woods.

"Mizz Charlotte," a man's voice said.

Charlotte was busy working with the next group of readers when she looked up, startled to see a familiar face. She realized his chin was covered with blonde down and his blue eyes were shadowed, but the thing that drew her to her feet was the boy beside him.

Sydney's face was tear and dirt streaked and one overall strap was unfastened. Delmar motioned her toward the door.

"Continue to work children," Charlotte said as she closed the door behind them, noticing that the Daniel boys were giggling.

She pulled out her handkerchief, shook it so the lace was out of reach and wiped the boy's face, then handed him the hankie to blow. She examined his shirt and clothes, looking for any bruises or wounds. Satisfied that all was well, she buckled his strap as she squatted before him. "Can you tell me what happened?"

He folded his mouth into a tight pout and she leaned forward to smooth his hair and stare into the eyes that were already blinking back tears. She stood and asked Delmar the same question.

"I kept hearing a noise. When I walked out, I found him hanging from the limb on an oak tree, way above the ground."

"But how, when…?" Charlotte blushed with guilt. "I'd just let the children out for their break, to get a drink or visit the facilities." She squatted again to look Sydney in the eye. "Darling, I'm so sorry that I didn't notice you were missing. I would have come running."

"Wouldn't have done you much good," Delmar said over her head. "You would've had to find someone tall to help, real tall. I had to climb part way up to reach and rescue him."

"Those Daniel boys! Is that who did this Sydney?"

He shook his head, looking miserably down at the ground. "So they threatened you too if you told, is that it?"

He stared up at her in surprise. Charlotte held out her hand to grab Delmar's, and shook it fiercely. "Thank you for being our hero." She looked toward Sydney, took his hand and replaced hers with his. Delmar shook it and ruffled the boy's hair. Charlotte reached out her own hand to smooth it back in place. There was a loud noise inside and Charlotte curtsied and herded the boy back inside, closing the door when Delmar would have entered.

"I told you all to work quietly," she snapped as she walked Sydney to his pew and then marched back to finish the lesson. "Eb, Ned," she motioned to the boys.

She checked all students had copied their writing lesson, erased the board and then wrote, "I apologize for my barbaric behavior."

"Each of you write that 20 times, then stand as before in your circles of shame." She stepped up and drew the same two circles as she had used the week before.

Working with the other distracted students, she managed to check their work, then complete their new lesson. Before hearing the children read, she turned and said loudly to the Daniel boys. "I am deeply disappointed in your behavior and ashamed of you."

The two had finished their writing and were elbowing each other into position with their noses near the top of the chalk board. They actually grew still.

Charlotte could only hope they were ashamed too. Her ears pinked again as she imagined what would have happened if Delmar hadn't heard Sydney's cries for help. As upset as Glory's parents had been, she could only expect that the Tate's house would be even more upset tonight when their son told them what had happened at school. Poor Sydney, the terror he must have felt, and what if the broken limb had broken again, he could have been injured or worse.

"Mizz Charlotte, did I do good?" Leonard asked as she closed the book.

"Yes, Leonard, very good." Although, she honestly hadn't heard a word. "You children all did a good job."

One of the boys jostled another and rolled his eyes. Charlotte rose, called all the students to their feet to end class with a Bible verse and prayer.

She stopped the Daniel boys when they would have followed the others out. "Remain in your positions until I finish checking work and tidying up the room. I will let you know when you may leave."

They had been standing nearly an hour before she ran out of reasons to delay and released the brats. Again she repeated her shaming words, delighted to see them slip out of the room with their heads hanging. Even if it was only to release the crick in their necks from being pilloried so long, she was glad to see them shuffle out.

As she pulled the door to the school closed, she jumped. A man moved from the shadow, his hat in his hands.

"Sorry to startle you. Figured it might be best to linger and make sure those two didn't give you any more trouble today."

"Thank you, Mister Monroe. But I know how to handle those two scamps."

"You do?" Delmar asked.

Charlotte bristled at his tone, for clearly he didn't think she did. "Certainly." She fluffed her skirts around her as she circled him.

"Wait," he said. "I think I better show you the tree, in case the parents come tomorrow and ask to see it."

Charlotte looked around, expecting Dovie to pop out of nowhere to conduct her own inquisition over what went wrong today. The whole thing set her teeth on edge and made her stomach ache. Why had she been so bull-headed and insistent that this was her true calling? She could have been suitably married to Charles Newcomb by this time.

As they walked, Charlotte forgot convention and followed the man to the edge of the woods where the boys had disappeared today. She was curious to see the tree.

"Aren't you going to ask me about Cicely, now no one is around to overhear us?"

Charlotte stared at him, shook her head at her own obsession with what others might be thinking about her. If there was one message her father had drilled into her head it was to think about other people, before yourself.

"Yes, please." She stopped inside the tree line beside him. Please Delmar, is she all right."

"As good as can be, I suppose. The Bridger's got her settled in with a fierce woman called Big Haley, a moonshiner like Davis Daniel. Don't see how anyone can get her out of there, now the big woman's sworn to protect her."

"You saw her settled," Charlotte asked, looking at the long shadows forming in the woods around them and remembered the boy who was afraid to go into the attic. She shivered and Delmar offered his arm. Eagerly she grabbed hold and he pointed with his left hand.

"It's that tall tree at the end of this clear spot." Charlotte stood frozen, clinging to him as she looked up to the limb at least twelve or fifteen feet in the air.

"Those devils," she whispered angrily.

Delmar laughed, pulled his arm and hers closer to his side. "It's your own fault for being so pretty. They just want to make sure you're noticing them. Guess they were a little jealous of Sydney. He's your smartest student?"

"Why yes, he reads perfectly." She looked into his pale eyes. "I guess I did praise him a little too lavishly today."

Something in the way he smiled at her made her tremble. Foolishly she asked the question. "What do you mean I'm too pretty?"

He raised one of his hands, ignoring the resin still on his fingertips from the balsam boards he had been planing. "It's your skin, white and smooth like fresh milk."

Again Charlotte trembled, and tried to swallow.

"Your hair, all dark and shiny with those bouncy curls. Boys told me all about how much they liked those. Made them think of hard coal."

His voice had deepened and Charlotte felt transfixed, as hypnotized as though he were a big snake.

He bent down to the ground around them, came up with a handful of some small flowers, dirt and all. "And your eyes, your eyes when you're excited or angry, they turn as purple as these violets."

Charlotte felt dizzy, breathless, hoping he was going to kiss her.

"Charlotte! Charlotte Stewart!" They separated at the raucous voice, Delmar pressed the ball of flowers into her hands, and melted into the woods.

"Here, I'm in here Mizz Dovie." She turned and ran out into the open path toward her cabin, gulping the sweet mountain air.

Clear of the trees, she looked down at the crushed violets in her hand and relaxed her grip to prevent ruining them all. "I was collecting a few flowers, have you seen these before."

"Wild violets, of course?" Dovie said.

"I thought they only bloomed in the spring."

"Usually do, but this little pocket is protected. The mountains do that sometimes, lie about the seasons. I saw the Daniel boys leaving late and wondered what had happened. Are you all right?"

Charlotte reminded herself of her resolution after the weekend visiting Glory. Dovie Watkin was her ally and mentor. She needed to remember that and trust her. As they walked together toward her cabin, she shared the details of her day. All except her conversation with Delmar.

Inside, she looked around for a vase or container, settled on a small pottery bowl from the few dishes the school board had provided. Gently she potted the bruised flowers while talking to the preacher's wife.

When she finished, she pumped water to wash her hands and face, and to splash the little plant. For the first time, she noticed the light blue band of color around the simple bowl, how it matched the color of the flowers in the fading light. She pushed the curtains open to let in more light. Maybe the circle was lavender instead of blue.

She wished Dovie would hush and leave. She needed to find her hand mirror while there was still enough light. She wanted to see if he were right, if her eyes did match the little blooms.

Dovie had been talking in an agitated manner and Charlotte tried to stop smiling long enough to hear anything the woman said. Finally, her voice came through.

"Well, I can see there's no sense talking to you. Go on and rest dear, you're clearly too exhausted to listen to me now."

Charlotte nodded, dried her hands, and took Dovie's arm to usher her out again. Confusing them both, she leaned over to kiss the woman's soft, round cheek. "I'll be over for dinner, you can tell me then. Good day."

She closed the door before the surprised woman could get her second wind.

CHAPTER TWENTY-NINE

On her next weekend, she planned to go home with Sydney. At dinner, Dovie suggested she write a letter to his parents before her visit. "Always write, especially after you have to discipline a student or if something happens to a child under your care. Keep a record of such matters in your journal too. You do journal, don't you?"

"I have a nice one and write in it every day. Actually, I use it to record my lesson plans." Charlotte guiltily remembered the diary her mother had enclosed, along with the nice stationary folder to encourage her to write home often. Charlotte had only written one letter, since it was difficult to send in a community without a post office.

When the meal ended, she rose quickly, eager to get home and to her writing. The knock on the door surprised her less than Dovie.

Delmar doffed his hat and bowed to the reverend and his wife. The reverend acknowledged his elaborate courtesy with a gruff nod. "Sorry to arrive so late, Reverend Watkin. When I was returning Master Sydney to the classroom, I quite forgot I had a letter for Mizz Charlotte from Boston."

"A letter, oh do sit down darling, and share it if you can. We get so little mail here in this out of the way little burg."

The reverend harrumphed again. "How'd you get the letter?"

Delmar had entered at Mizz Dovie's invitation, accepting the offer of coffee and a dish of rice pudding. He unbuttoned his coat as he sat down. "It and a flyer for the store owner were at the post office in Sneedville. You remember me going with the County Sheriff and his deputy, to look for that runaway girl?"

"Certainly, I'm not addled, but thought you were going to walk the trail with them, although for the life of me, I don't know why they thought an outsider like you could be of help."

"Not sure why myself. But since they were walking that way, and the deputy mentioned the girl's aunt played a diamond shaped banjo, I decided to tag along when they reported they couldn't find the girl."

"Diamond shaped?" Dovie said.

Delmar swallowed the spoonful of rice and raisins cooked in heavy cream before answering. "She made it herself and showed me how to play it. Which was surprising, seeing as how disappointed she was to learn the girl and her husband seemed gone for good."

Charlotte had opened the letter, pleased to see there were three pages enclosed, written on front and back. Each family member had written her a note. She held it near the lamp and read, trying to concentrate over the babble of voices and Delmar's occasional "yum's" as Dovie refilled his bowl. When she read about Charles, she let the letter drop to her lap to keep from showing her reaction to the fluttering pages.

"Well, Mizz Dovie asked. Is there any news to share?"

"Mama writes that all are well, and the girls are growing. They had a coming out party for Rebecca on her eighteenth birthday, and for Elizabeth too, since she will be seventeen in a month. Dorothea is the baby at fifteen and is furious that she wasn't included."

"You look sad, dear, was there bad news?" she pried.

Charlotte felt her throat tighten and shook her head so her curls bounced. She stood up, so the lamp wouldn't reveal the tears she was holding back.

"Just Papa complaining how much he missed me rifling through his desk and sitting in the back of his classes," her voice choked and she cleared her throat and curtsied to her hosts.

"I must get home. Tomorrow will be another long day."

Delmar rose, gracefully retrieved the scattered pages of the letter to hand to her. "Thank you for that, Mizz Dovie. I do believe you are the best cook in this county."

Dovie raised her head, looking smug. "While you're not the first to make that comment, I do thank you."

"Do you need to take the lantern," the reverend called.

"No, I'll see she gets safely home," Delmar said, but Charlotte walked on ahead before he could put his hat and coat back on.

She had tucked the letter into her purse, her cheeks stinging with rage. All this time she had always counted on

Charles. If her teaching career should falter, if she needed to go back home, counted that he would be waiting there to marry her.

To read that Rebecca was now engaged to Charles Newcomb was too much to bear. Rebecca was such a conniving…

"Wait up, Mizz Stewart," Delmar called but she didn't slow down.

Charlotte had passed the school before he caught up and reached out to touch her shoulder and turn her around. Charlotte shrugged his hand off and kept walking.

"Whoa, why are you mad at me? I didn't write the damn letter."

Charlotte stopped and turned in horror. "Do not swear, Mister Monroe. Although I was not angry at you, if you continue to behave in this vulgar, coarse way, I will be."

Delmar stopped, as peeved by her snooty tone as her storming off and leaving him. He took a deep breath before letting out a string of profanity that would really shock this prudish little schoolmarm.

"I thought you might wonder why I really went to Sneedville," he managed to whisper, aware as always that the Watkin's back door was open and the light still revealed their shadowed figures.

"I thought you said..."

He raised a hand, shook his head in the direction of the open door to call her attention to the woman watching and listening.

Whispering he said, "I did that to keep the law from going up to the Bridgers, although when the dogs picked up the goat's scent, they lost the girl's trail entirely. No, I wanted to let her aunt know why her husband wouldn't be coming home and to let her know Cicely was safe."

"You told her that while the sheriff was listening?"

He pointed toward her cabin, "Keep walking, she looks like she's going to come out to hear us."

They started walking again and he continued to whisper rapidly. "No, the banjo was my excuse to go back and tell her the truth. She honestly didn't seem shocked to hear any of it, obviously knew the man was worthless. She seemed relieved and glad Cicely was safe, but also that she wouldn't be coming back. She told me there were only a few negroes in the county, and it was a dangerous place. She was thinking of packing up and moving north while she still could."

"What do you mean, while she still could?"

"There's talk about putting up even more rules to prevent negroes from traveling across the country alone. A lot of people are afraid of the free ones, believing most with dark skin are really run-a-ways and dangerous," he said.

Charlotte raised one hand and hissed. "I do not need a lecture on the Abolitionist's movement. I share my Father's position in all regards and am already in that camp."

Charlotte had listened to the debate, mostly caused by the writings and speeches of Frederick Douglas, a free negro who wanted freedom for them all. When students at the seminary asked her father for his stance, he had prepared a massive article.

Everyone seemed to gloss over the fact that one-half to two-thirds of the whites who settled the colonies came as indentured servants. They were beaten, abused, mistreated and starved, with their terms of indenture extended whenever they protested their treatment. The women were dishonored, mistreated, and their papers sold to other men if they protested. Of course, some men honored the indentured contracts, releasing those who had worked to repay their transportation costs with the acres of land, seeds, and farm animals they were promised.

These wretched poor from England and Germany came with dreams of freedom and bright futures. Nearly half died while indentured or after being freed. They tried to live on the edge of settled land where there were clashes with Indians and wild animals, with to little land to support their families.

Not until the eighteenth century did African natives replace the majority of European poor as labor. Slavery had been abolished in the north soon after the colonies united and defeated the British, but it still persisted in the south.

Charlotte stood at the house, opening the latch, certain she would not need rescued again since she had kept the cabin sealed since the bat episode. She certainly didn't want to debate the issue of slavery with Delmar all night.

"I think we are agreed on the horrors of that institution and you need not seek to persuade me. Goodnight, Mister Monroe."

Delmar stood as though shocked by how anxious she was to be rid of him. All day he had thought of nothing but the kiss they had almost shared. Like an idiot, he had waited in the dark with that blasted letter as an excuse to see her and walk her home. Furious with the conceited woman, he doffed his hat and gave a stiff bow as she swept inside. Behind him, he heard Dovie Watkin close and bar her door just as loudly.

CHAPTER THIRTY

Charlotte sat at the long shelf that was her table and desk to write a letter to Sydney's parents. She stopped halfway through to wipe her eyes. She almost wrote what she was really feeling. Despite all her efforts, her hours of study, her preparation to teach these children, it might not be enough. She was learning she might not be qualified, since she couldn't even protect them from two known bullies. Instead, she blew her nose, then carefully blotted the paper, and folded it. She sat and folded another sheet into an envelope.

Instead of blubbering, she tucked the first letter into her Bible and started the second. Carefully she addressed each family member, trying not to leak tears onto the paper. When had her aggravating sisters become so dear, her scolding mother so wise? Inside the sheet she folded to make an envelope, she carefully wrote a short note to her father.

Pray for me, Papa dearest, for I feel lost in the Valley of Darkness. No longer am I confident that I know what I am doing, and am overcome with doubt. I will think of your calm and wonderful voice, chiding me for my fears and foolishness. Tonight I will read the Bible and pray.

I love you Papa, Charlotte

After reading Job to put her own problems in perspective, and Psalms for comfort, she fell to her knees and prayed for strength and guidance.

Only later, when she had shed her dress and petticoat for a flannel gown and climbed into bed, did she relax in the darkness. Whatever tomorrow brought she would face it, no longer feeling all alone.

She called up Delmar's smile and breathed a sigh of relief for Cicely and all his efforts to rescue the girl. She prayed for both, then added Rebecca and Charles to the long evening's list. She herself had told Rebecca, that she did not love Charles enough to reside in his shadow for her happiness. As her sister, Rebecca would never have formed an attachment to the handsome young man without her tacit consent. Charlotte squinted her eyes and bit her tongue to hold back those feelings of resentment that had overwhelmed her earlier.

As she relaxed and stared at the rough loft above her, thinking of all she had to be grateful for, her mind went to the music man once more. She wondered if he would ever forgive her enough to kiss her.

The next morning, she opened the classroom early. As she started the fire and put the fresh bucket of water in the corner, she tried to feel as calm as she'd become last night. When there was a knock on the school door, she jumped, sloshing a little of the water. She took a deep breath and prayed her knocking knees would not betray her.

"Come in," she called.

As the door opened, Sydney and his father entered. Charlotte placed her hand on her Bible and said a last prayer.

Like the day they had hung the bullfrog under the girl's box and been punished, the Daniel boys behaved like perfect gentleman. Charlotte was glad, for after the lecture she had received from the small but angry man this morning, she felt on the verge of tears all day.

When the classroom grew too warm, she took the children out of doors to collect ten different leaves and identify the tree or bush they were from. She had thought she would have to consult the little chart at the back of the dictionary to help identify them, but even the youngest child seemed to know each plant.

The Daniel boys offered to knock down some mistletoe, although they told her 'it weren't potent, 'cause it didn't have berries.' She pretended to not know what powers they were talking about, but she had been kissed under the mistletoe before.

The only mischief was when the Daniels collected fan-shaped tree scale by pulling off some tree bark on a rotted log. They screamed and yelled snake as they did it. They had the younger children running and squealing, but told the curious older ones who wanted to see, that it ran away.

The day turned rainy and they couldn't go out for the afternoon break. All the children were disappointed, so she let them play button-button. Sydney held the yellow button as he walked in the center of the children who were seated on the floor, the benches moved aside. He held his closed hands over theirs for a few seconds before moving to the next child. At the end, after visiting everyone, he stood in the middle and called on a boy to tell him who had the button. It went three guesses, before Philomena guessed who had the button and took her turn walking around.

It was a perfect fall day, the rain was over by the end of school. Freddy, a ten-year-old boy, led them in singing, "Home, Sweet Home."

◇◇◇

The only incident the next day, was when one of the boys released a small ring snake while the second group were up for recitation. Charlotte wasn't the only one to react, but she managed to stifle her scream when the only second grade boy, walked over and picked it up.

Mesmerized, she watched as the thin black snake wrapped around and through the boy's fingers. When he offered to let her see it, she nodded, holding out her hand, ready to squeal if it were wet or slimy. Instead, the small animal with a bright gold band around its neck, felt like a leather belt. It curled up in the palm of her hand, ready to sleep. She slipped it into the pocket of her skirt and the children all laughed. Charlotte grinned, and the rest of the day was hers to command.

She now had a student in each of the first groups who could read a paragraph without error. Even the Daniel boys could read the word list of at, bat, cat, hat she gave them, correctly.

It was not until the end of the day when she was walking around, checking work at their seats, that she saw the Daniel boys drawing instead of writing their sentences.

When she asked what it was, Ned answered. "Poles and holes."

Charlotte shrugged and said, "Erase it and focus on your school work, not your farm work."

Several of the younger boys started to giggle and two of the older ones laughed out loud.

Eb said to Ned, "See, she don't even know what it means."

Unsure, but tired of their nonsense, she ordered them to the board to write an apology to her and the other students for disrupting class.

"Tain't fair, you're always yelling at us. Don't see you pickin' on nobody else," Eb said.

Charlotte crossed the last "t" and dusted her hands. "I apologize for being disrespectful to my teacher and fellow students." She read it out loud and said, "ten times."

When Ned started to argue too, Charlotte lost her temper.

"The others were quietly doing their school work, not being crude. Twenty copies, and hurry, so you don't have to stay after to finish today."

"Pa liked to whipped us the last time you held us over, said he would the next time," Ned said.

Charlotte knew her cheeks were red, her mouth pursed, and she probably looked like Mama in a temper, but she shouted. "Twenty-five copies, and stop arguing."

She sat down with her back to them as she worked with the four children on the recitation bench. There were only boys in the group, and when the last finished reading, Eb threw down his chalk. In horror Charlotte watched the piece shatter, wondering if he knew he had just destroyed five percent of her school supplies for the year.

Eb had only written four sentences, Ned three. Charlotte rose, checked the small watch pinned to her blouse and lifted the bell to ring three times. "Class you are dismissed, all but the Daniel boys."

CHAPTER THIRTY-ONE

As soon as the last student left, she turned on them. "Explain yourself."

"I'm tired, and I ain't going to write it anymore," Eb said.

"Besides, you didn't even know what we were drawing," Ned said.

Charlotte had her ruler and demanded he hold his hand out. When he refused, she grabbed the wider paddle and began smacking at his arms and his legs. When Eb tried to intervene, she did the same to him. All the time she was backing them toward the door. Only when they were hollering for her to stop did she pause.

"Go home, you are expelled from class. I do not want you to come back, unless you are ready to apologize and behave."

She slammed the door after them. Realizing that she was all alone and they might return, she lifted the board to bar it, then drug their bench over in front of the door.

Minutes later, Dovie Watkin was at the school door, calling her name, and knocking. Charlotte sat there, heart pounding, trying to hold her breath until the woman left.

It was over, she had done it now. Even if the school board didn't fire her, which she expected they would, she would have to give up her dream of teaching. In her wildest nightmare, she had never imagined striking another person. She could imagine her parent's horror if she told them. Today, she had wanted nothing more than to make those boys suffer as much as she had from their nonsense, and she had loved hitting them.

Catching her breath, she shook her head. Not yet, surely things weren't as bad as she thought. If only there were someone who could look at things objectively.

As soon as she could, she headed for the store, praying she could talk to the little Widow Mouse.

Later, she had not only been able to see Jeanne, but to persuade her to return to the cabin with her.

"Jeanne, thank you for coming. I don't have anyone else I dare tell this to." Together they sat, each pushing, not eating, the tasteless greens the girl had cooked, while Charlotte went through everything.

"All I've ever wanted was a chance to learn and to teach. If you only knew how hard it was to convince Mama and Papa of that. Then it was the same, fighting to persuade the university that I deserved a teaching certificate, and that I was qualified for this job."

"The children who come in the store with their parents seem happy with you. I know little Kitty Meany can't wait to be big enough to start school so she can have fun and learn to read and everything," Jeanne said.

"Thank you, all I've heard from parents so far have been complaints." She tried to keep from crying, hating how sorry for herself she felt.

"Mama wanted me to stay in Boston, to teach at one of the finishing schools. But not me, I felt I needed to go where education was really needed," her voice broke. "I can't write them, say they were right, I was wrong. They're not rich, how can I ask them to pay for my return passage?"

Jeanne patted her shoulder. "It can't be as bad as all that. Tell me everything."

Charlotte did. She detailed each incident with the big boys and how she'd dealt with them. How she had confided in Mizz Dovie, only to have the woman popping into the school nearly every day to observe how things were going. Dovie had handed her the list of rules and families she had to visit.

Then, embarrassed, she told her how Glory's parents and Sydney's father had been upset because of the boy's pranks.

"It sounds normal to me. I know our teacher had problems with students from time to time."

Charlotte raised her hand, "Not like today." She told her about the way her day had ended.

Finally, she paused and Jeanne asked, "They went?"

"Oh yes, they went. Then I hid from Mizz Dovie. When I heard her run off, I ran over to see you. It's cowardly of me, but I didn't want to come home alone and have them show up here."

Jeanne laughed, and Charlotte stopped crying in surprise. "I would love to have seen that, those good for nothing rascals getting chased out of school."

Charlotte hugged her, then sent the girl home with the rest of the turnips in her pot. Maybe there was still hope.

At dinner, she expected Dovie Watkin to pry more than usual. Blessedly, the woman said hardly anything until afterward.

"I saw that French woman going home with you. I'd wondered where you were, when I went by after school to talk and you weren't there. You let school out a little early, didn't you?"

"The trails are muddy after the rain, and I didn't want the children to get caught outside if it rained again."

Charlotte stood, helping to clear the dishes. "Jeanne's husband was French, but she is from New York."

"Remember what I told you, the woman's a Catholic. You're already an outsider, it's not wise to build your friends from non-locals."

"I thought you were from the east, not a mountain girl?"

Dovie sputtered, but finally managed, "It's different for a preacher's wife."

Charlotte tried not to gloat, remembering her resolve to treat this woman who was backing her with more warmth. "Jeanne offered to show me how to cook turnips. One of their customers harvested a lot from their garden."

The conversation quickly changed to gardening, cooking, and recipes, and Charlotte used the rain for an excuse to leave early.

Walking home from the Watkin's, she was surprised when Delmar called out "Good evening, Miss Stewart."

She sighed, then nodded and walked on. She knew Dovie was watching them, wished she could ask this man home. It had been wonderful to have Jeanne offer her sympathy, but a man would have a better idea of how serious her predicament was. He might even know what was so funny about the Daniels' drawing.

The next day was tense, but she was better able to handle her students. After she called their names, one of the boys asked about Eb and Ned. Standing straight, she announced. "They were told to stay home, until their manners improve."

She was surprised when the children were no happier at the news than her.

At lunch, they got in a quick game of drop the handkerchief, another circle game. The circle seemed smaller, but the play was quicker without worrying about Ned or Eb sticking out a big foot or trying to grab and lift one of the children running by.

Charlotte realized she felt like a failure. The big oafs were impossible to teach, their writing indecipherable even after six weeks of practice. She had never met anyone dumber than those two. She scolded herself. Weren't they the type of student she had expected to find, that she had hoped to teach and make such a difference in their lives?

When a couple of the other boys wanted to step into their shoes as trouble-makers, she took Jeanne's advice and paddled each, this time on the hand but with the promise of worse if it happened again.

Today, they finished their lessons earlier than usual. She warned them that there would be a class spelling bee on Friday. It was easier to divide them into three groups for the competition. She urged all to be recalling and practicing their spelling on the way home and on the way back to school tomorrow. She would set it up then, but they wouldn't compete until Friday. She hoped to ask Dovie to make a treat she could give the winners, and was looking forward to dinner for the first time since school began.

When Charlotte stopped at the outhouse on the way home, she was startled when Delmar started talking to her through the thin walls. So embarrassed, she couldn't even pee for several minutes.

"Charlotte, are you all right?" he repeated.

Mortified, she drew in a deep breath and passed water, aware of the sound of every drop falling into the abyss below.

"Charlotte, I haven't spoken to you all week. If you don't answer, I'm going to think you're hurt and I'm going to come over and open that door."

"Don't you dare, I'm fine."

"You had me scared there for a minute."

Charlotte hissed, when she finally caught her breath. "You really have no idea of manners and civility. I cannot believe you want me to talk to you, when we're, when…"

Delmar chuckled. "The children don't seem to have a problem with it. I just haven't been able to find a way to speak to you with that chicken hawk always watching."

Charlotte rose, straightening herself as best she could, before bursting out of the confined space into the clean air. As she walked past the side of the outhouse, a hand reached out and grabbed her so they were hidden from view of the Watkin's house behind it.

Delmar continued, "I wanted to warn you. I heard talk that there will be a special school board meeting tomorrow night. I didn't want Dovie Watkin to spring it on you at supper."

Her color was already high, but she blushed even deeper. "You were misinformed. They met last Thursday. I have Dovie's hand-written notes from the meeting."

He nodded, "It's about the Daniel boys."

Charlotte stood there, shaking, staring up at him in desperation. "I had to throw them out yesterday. It was them or me."

He smiled, "I know what they're like. I'm sure the board members do too, probably all a formality."

Nervously, Charlotte pushed at her hair, turned and looked desperately at the cabin. "I have to go, what if she's watching."

"Wait," a strong hand pulled her around and into his arms. She stared up, breathless with anticipation. He reached behind her with both hands, one holding the bulk of her skirt, the other moving to free the hem caught in her pantaloon's waistband. Charlotte felt dizzy.

She was waiting for him to kiss her. Instead, he caressed her bottom before lightly giving her a quick spank and shaking her skirt down over her hips. She gasped in shock.

When he released her, she could only stand and stare at him in amazement.

"It's okay now, go on," he whispered.

Charlotte walked in mincing steps toward the cabin, her gaze unfocused and her blood threatening to boil over. When she stood on the step to look back, the devil was gone.

CHAPTER THIRTY-TWO

All day, she worried about the school board meeting to come. Delmar had been right about there being a called meeting. Last night, Dovie had served a scoop of stew into her bowl as they passed plates. She was chattering about the turnips she had used instead of potatoes in her stew and the tops she had used in her wilted salad.

Charlotte sat, enjoying the cornbread, the wilted greens, even the stew. Then Dovie mentioned the special board meeting, about dismissing those two boys. "We'll be there to support you, but you should bring your lesson plan book, and anything you have to document and justify your actions."

"I'll be there?" Charlotte asked, her voice squeaking.

"Yes, dear, we all are eager to hear your side of the events."

On Thursday morning, Charlotte rushed to open the school, determined to make this the best day of teaching she had ever had. If after tonight, the board told her she was being replaced, then she wanted to have one perfect memory.

Philomena had summed up her own feelings yesterday when she'd said, 'It's a lot quieter without Eb and Ned, but not near as much fun."

Today, Charlotte started with a greeting and benediction, followed by the normal routine of rise, pass, and recite. The morning group now only held first graders and one fifth grade student. Although she knew she would never forgive herself for failing to control the Daniel boys, she quickly realized the change in the other students. They were more relaxed and better behaved without being scolded.

At the end of the day, she was as tired as the children, but managed to stand at the door and smile at each one as they left.

When she looked behind her, she saw all the work she needed to do before leaving today and began by sweeping the room out carefully. After cleaning the board and the children's slates, she carried a fresh bucket of water from her cabin. She had never mopped, but the board had provided one and the floors had enough dirt packed in the cracks already to look dusty as soon as she finished sweeping. She planned to do it before leaving.

Charlotte sat with the school doors propped open while she took a break. Sipping a cup of cool water, she read her lesson plan book, looking for anything she could use to make a case for dismissing the Daniel boys. She knew she had recorded each disciplinary incident in her diary, realized she probably should have also written it again in the front pages. She certainly didn't want anyone to read her private thoughts while looking for the information.

A load of wood dropped outside the door. Charlotte sat up with a start, lowering her feet from the bench in front of her so quickly both benches moved.

"Know it's a mite warm now, but could be a lot cooler tonight. Thought you might need some more stove wood. Happy to carry it in for you."

She managed to nod and stepped out of the room while Delmar carried a huge armload to the front beside the stove.

"Thank you, Mister Monroe. I appreciate your going to so much trouble for the school board."

He placed the wood in the nearly full wood box and turned to grin at her. "You're welcome, Miss Stewart." He doffed his hat and swept her a bow. For a moment, Charlotte thought he might lean over and kiss her, but he was gone, bounding out the door past her. She heard his laugh as he rushed back to his work.

The children had pointed him out to her earlier as they stopped in their games for a minute. For that instant, she thought she saw a halo of gold surrounding him in the bright sunshine. Charlotte had heard Philomena whisper to the next oldest girl. "Now that's what I'd like to have when it's settling down time. A man surrounded by a cloud of dust, because he's working so hard."

Charlotte was nervous, looking around twisting her hands for something else to do as the board members started to arrive. Dovie and the reverend sat on the front bench on the right side. Charlotte wondered if anyone would complain. She had started the fire to fight the night chill, and now she was sweating, it seemed so warm. Four of the board members were already there. Charlotte smiled as the Widow Mouse settled onto her bench and Jasper Sykes yelled and asked, "Did anyone invite Davis?"

"Oh yes, heard he's coming," the other board member answered loudly enough Jasper would hear.

Charlotte had decided to sit on the front bench on the boy's side of the room, since she didn't want to hear what Mizz Dovie and the reverend were whispering about. Her stomach was roiling and she had used her complaint earlier, to keep from having to walk down and sit in that small kitchen at suppertime. Charlotte wasn't any good at pretending, and she didn't want them to see how nervous she was.

Jeanne rose, shed the man's coat she wore and carried the baby to stand in front of the stove. Jeanne reached out to take Charlotte's hand. "How are you this evening?" Jeanne asked, smiling warmly at her.

Charlotte rolled her eyes in answer, placing a hand over her heart before whispering. "Terrified, the board just met last week and gave me all those rules."

Both turned when there was a knock on the door. Charlotte turned back to look the other way as she recognized the man entering. He'd shaved his wild fuzz of a beard, and again had only a neat little chin decoration. Out of the corner of her eye she saw the golden beard bob as he entered. Her eyes widened in surprise that Delmar had come to the meeting.

Both heard him talking loudly to Jasper. "Saw the lights and was curious. Is it okay for me to be here?" he asked.

Jeanne smiled at the thick drawl of his cultured voice. "Doesn't Mr. Monroe have a wonderful accent, such a handsome young man?"

"Really, I hadn't noticed."

Charlotte kept stealing glances at Delmar, as Jeanne bubbled on about how pretty she had made the room. Jeanne pointed to the colorful collections on the shelf by the window.

Charlotte seemed to relax a little. "We collected them on our walk Monday. We went out to study the names of the trees. They knew far more than me, even the little ones. The Daniels shook down the nuts and peeled off the bark on a log, teasing everyone about seeing a snake underneath."

Jeanne nodded, looking at the day's lesson that was still on the chalkboard, with its neat drawing of states with their carefully labeled capitals.

Suddenly, the room grew silent as they heard loud voices outside. The Daniels had finally arrived.

CHAPTER THIRTY-THREE

The door opened and the cool mountain air rushed in with the noisy family, clearing the close warm stuffiness of the place. As the door closed, new scents of the late arrivals filled the air. Charlotte sniffed the dank smell of men who had worked and sweated, and the strong scent of something familiar, but hard for her to place.

There was a sudden stiffening and several whispers among those who had been waiting. Jasper stood and extended a hand to welcome Davis.

"Good that you could come, all you Daniels," he said.

"Didn't like to, we had to rush taking off a batch of whiskey today. Figured I might as well bring it to town, since we was coming. Heck, thought we just met and worked everything out about the new schoolmarm last week."

The others exchanged whispers, and Charlotte felt her cheeks stain red. She could feel everyone looking at her, judging her.

Jeanne whispered, "do you smell that, I think it's whiskey."

The baby in the girl's arms started to fuss. Ivey Boggs walked forward to sit beside the two young women, The fiery haired woman started complaining about all the Daniel men. Charlotte stared at Jeanne, but neither answered the other woman.

Jasper stood and walked forward to hand the little widow his coat so she could cover up if she had to feed the crying baby to get him quiet. The coat held the warm smell of the tall man and helped to cover the flowery perfume of Ivey as she sat fluffing, spreading her scent across the room.

Charlotte sneezed, and fumbled for her clean handkerchief before sneezing again. Jeanne turned, holding her precious son away from her sneezes. Ivey said, "God Bless," but it sounded more like a curse word than a blessing.

Reverend Watkin rose next, walked to the front of the room, and pounded on the polished table to get their attention. He began talking, and Charlotte covered her nose just in time. "Davis, we figured you might have already come storming into town, since it was your boys the teacher expelled. We only learned of the matter yesterday. But it is the power of the school board to decide on such drastic measures of discipline, not the schoolmaster or schoolmarm."

He turned and stared at her with scorn and Charlotte felt her stomach sink. It was going to be worse than she thought.

"Hell, is that what you run us down the mountain for. Been expecting her to kick them out since the first day of school. Neither one has a head for learnin'," Davis Daniel said. He continued to talk, but Charlotte bent her head to hide her own shock. Had everyone thought her a fool for not throwing the boys out the first day. Here she had put up with all their nonsense, and there was no need. She could have sent them back home and not had to explain a thing.

The reverend raised one of Charlotte's brass bookends, used it for a gavel. Charlotte winced at the solid sound of the object hitting the desk. The pair had been a whimsical gift from her youngest sister, Dorothea, before she left home, a casting of "Hickory, Dickory Dock."

The reverend raised a hand, "We'll have no swearing, not in front of women and children."

Davis looked around, looked like he was about to say something crude about the widow and her suckling child, but at the reverend's sour look he subsided and sat down.

"We'll hear from Mizz Stewart first."

Charlotte rose, pushing the taffeta of her full skirt down around her, blushing as she remembered Delmar's actions last night. She stepped forward, both women beside her giving her encouraging nods.

Charlotte walked to her desk, picked up the small, leather-bound book where she had written her lesson plans and notes. With her left hand, she fingered the bruised edge of the brass object, returning it to push the small collection of books together. She wondered if she walked out the door and kept walking north, how long it would take for her to reach home. She heard Eb and Ned say something and giggle.

Suddenly, she raised her head and began to speak in clear, precise tones, explaining why she had chosen to come to Kyles Ford to teach. She explained that for her, teaching was a calling, as strong as the call to the ministry must have been for the Reverend Watkin.

At his blustering reaction, she changed tact. She decided to merely state the facts, starting with the first day of school. It was Delmar's turn to blush as she reminded the board of the fiddler and the little parade of excited children he had led to school that day.

She talked about poor little Glory, the horror of the bullfrog hidden in the outhouse. Related how upset her parents had been on her visit with them this weekend past.

Next, she told the tale of Sydney, and how he was rescued by Mr. Monroe. He might have fallen to his death, since she never heard his calls from inside the school. This time there was less laughter from the Daniel's side of the room. Charlotte looked ready to scold Davis and Ivey, but Delmar shook his head at her, and she let it go.

"I will admit, I came to Tennessee, in part as a missionary. I wanted to teach children who might not have an opportunity for a classical education, growing up here. I looked upon the Daniels as in special need of instruction and deserving of my help. So I thought to remedy their bad behavior with discipline.

"I wrote a note home to Sydney's parents, but they did not get it before the father came into town to scold me

"I think I placated him when I explained, 'I had few rules, but I expected them to be obeyed'."

"The first time I paddled the Daniel boys' hands with my ruler. She raised the narrow wooden tool and slapped it against the desk top. All the men winced, and she wondered if they had all been paddled the same way. Even the two young women made faces and folded their hands.

"The second offense, I drew two circles on the board, as Mizz Dovie had suggested. I had to climb on my chair to reach high enough, but I'm certain the boys were uncomfortable for that hour's duration.

"Because they struggle with writing, and are not diligent in their work, I made them write their apologies ten times each on the board.

"Their conduct Tuesday, was the first time they had been rude and insubordinate to me. Eb refused to write the apology. That is when…"

Charlotte blushed, ashamed to admit her incredible loss of control that day. "I had exhausted all my patience." She lifted the heavy, wooden paddle.

"The final day, when they acted inappropriately, I took the board to them and paddled them, telling them never to come back again."

The reverend stood as Charlotte flounced back to her seat on the bench, her head held high.

He turned to look at Eb and Ned, motioning them forward. Charlotte wished she had remained standing there. She never thought of herself as short, but compared to the Daniels she was tiny. When she looked at the reverend, standing next to them, she raised her handkerchief to cover her mouth, as she had to smile.

She might have lost her temper with the young men, but she was sure Reverend Watkin or Dovie would have found keeping them seated and quietly working a challenge, too.

The boys talk was slow, with an occasional joke thrown in at her expense. When they talked about how they first saw her, leaping out of Mister Monroe's cart because the bear was jumping in there, the whole room laughed. Charlotte remembered Delmar wrapping her up, keeping a leg over hers to prevent her skirt from flying up.

She let out her held breath as the boys didn't mention that part of their meeting.

They talked about how they fell in love with Mizz Stewart, when they got a chance to dance with the "purtiest" woman they had ever seen. Eb talked about her purple eyes, perfect white skin, dark curly hair. Ned pointed out she was the shape his dream woman should be.

Delmar stood up to protest, but Charlotte was already rising. The reverend and Jasper Sykes were both yelling at them that that was enough.

After the angry men settled down, they admitted they had done all the things, the teacher had accused them of, and agreed that they had deserved the whipping.

They told the board members they were bored with school, and could tell Mizz Stewart was never going to return their interest.

When they didn't describe what their last punishment was for, and no one asked, Charlotte finally relaxed.

"I'm glad to hear that Mizz Stewart has been doing an effective job, following all the rules the school board set forth, and that she handled this matter with the Daniel boys, Eb and Ned, as well as anyone could have done. What say the rest of you board members?"

Charlotte felt like standing and cheering when the chorus of male voices saying "Yay," ended and there were none saying "Nay."

She accepted hugs from Jeanne and Dovie, ignored Dovie's scowl to reach out and shake the hands of Ivey and Davis. The boys bowed to her and apologized. She accepted the apologies with a rough shake of their arms, wished them well without saying how glad she was that they wouldn't be back.

As the others left, Delmar turned to damp the fire and close the flue for her. Ned picked up the bell that was on their old bench and rang it, passing it to Eb to do the same while Mizz Dovie demanded they put it down.

Charlotte heard everyone talking as from a great distance. She hadn't been fired. Tomorrow she would walk down and open the school as usual. Head back, eyes closed, she said a silent prayer.

As softly as a breath, Delmar leaned down and kissed her.

CHAPTER THIRTY-FOUR

It sounded like a flock of birds, the loud strident voices of the men, with the women's higher, more rapid chorus. Charlotte finally was able to make out some of the conversation. The Daniel's were talking with the store owner about building a raft to take goods down river to Knoxville. She heard Ivey Boggs interrupt them, and the crude laughter of the boys, then Davis' loud voice rebuking her.

Charlotte stood as though in shock as she heard the musician volunteer to help build the raft, and correct Davis. "I was offering the bed to you and Ivey. The boys and I can bunk before the hearth in the other room."

She tried hearing more, but the elation she had felt moments before deflated into an empty pain in her chest.

The devil had finally kissed her, without a word. Now he was acting as though it had never happened. If she had her ruler or board with her, she'd love to strike him and demand an explanation. However he was standing on the other side of the porch with the others. She realized, Dovie was asking her if she was ready to go.

Charlotte mumbled something, accepted the reverend's other arm. The sweet drawling voice behind her said goodnight to the others. The Widow Mouse called to her and Charlotte said, "Goodnight, Jeanne. Goodnight, Mr. Sykes."

Dovie clucked beside her and Charlotte realized she probably shouldn't have spoken to the woman. The man's southern drawl behind her seemed a caress to her ears, although none of his words were for her.

"Of course, you'll have to be careful. I've stacks of wood air curing about the front room, and I've taken over the dining table to use for my piece work," Delmar said.

What Ivey had to say was again lost in the whoops of Ed and Neb, so she figured it was shameful.

◇◇◇

The Watkins walked her home, waiting until Charlotte had the door open and lamp lit. Charlotte was embarrassed to let them inside to see the discarded clothes she had tried on and rejected. Dovie managed to look, but acted as though she saw nothing out of place.

"Sleep tightly, dear." This time when Dovie leaned over, the kiss was expected. Charlotte returned the older woman's embrace, and tried to find some way to thank her. Although she realized part of what she felt was disappointment that she had not felt their support during the meeting, now it seemed meaningless.

Alone, Charlotte tried to regain her buoyant mood. She put the tea kettle to warming, lifted and rehung the scattered clothes. She tried to shake off the feeling that she was a terrible failure as a teacher. At no time tonight, had anyone attacked her for doing a poor job. As she went back over all the conversations, she recalled only praise and compliments, mostly from Jeanne LeSouris.

With the room cleared, she settled on the end of her bed in her nightgown, sipping her small cup of tea. She opened and read her Bible, as she did every night. Calmly, she recorded her thoughts and her list of things to be grateful for this day. The list was longer than usual. She described the board meeting and its outcome. Charlotte listed friends who had stood by her, Jeanne, and Jasper Sykes, Ivey Boggs and even all three boisterous Daniels. Of course Dovie and the reverend, but only half-heartedly. She drew a wavery line under their names. She wrote Delmar Monroe, and realized how much that had meant to her, seeing his handsome face there staring at her. He had scowled when Reverend Watkin scolded her, but nodded encouragingly whenever she spoke up in her own defense.

When she wrote the last line, Delmar finally kissed me, she let her inked quill drag across the page. Too shivery to stand it, she laid the quill down and corked the ink bottle. Beside the bed, she threw back the comforter, knelt and prayed before blowing out the lamp.

She had been vindicated, she could be a spinster schoolmarm forever. As she lay there in the quiet, warm room, she shivered again. Looked up at the loft above her, over at the shadow of the dresses on the wall. For the hundredth time she remembered the feeling she had watching the tall, blonde man building that loft for her. Charlotte sighed in confusion and tried to fall asleep.

Delmar led his company home, keeping an eye on Charlotte and her escorts. He wondered why she wasn't laughing and smiling. He had seen how worried and afraid she was earlier, and had felt compelled to attend the meeting to be there to support her if there was a need. She had seemed so brave, so convincing, especially when she talked about how much teaching meant to her. He had felt proud of her.

The sad look on her face, the way she turned her head to accept Dovie's peck on her cheek before they called goodnight, convinced him the victory had not been enough.

Had it been that reckless moment, when the world seemed hidden by the nearly closed door and she had looked so beautiful. The moment he had finally dared to kiss her.

He knew the pressure she was under, the rules of her contract. Jasper Sykes had explained them all to him the other day when the big man had come up to help him build a curing shed at the edge of Ivey's property.

Delmar knew it was a warning, that the community had noticed how closely he watched the girl. Sykes had promised to take the shed down and reuse the posts on his place if Ivey objected. Delmar was comfortable using the space in one room for storing the planed boards and the pieces he was already working on. He'd worried that if the woman came by, she might kick him out for creating such a mess.

He heard her and Davis arguing up ahead, heard Eb and Ned talking as they watched the shadows of the store owner and the little woman beside him. He wondered what the two were plotting now.

He moved ahead of the couple, apologizing and explaining what she might find to Ivey before he opened the door. "After all," he said, "I am a bachelor, and my only company."

The woman seemed neither pleased or unpleased, too eager to continue her argument with Davis. The boy called to him, too. "Pa, we're going to run the whiskey down to the store, while Sykes is still awake and up."

"Good, don't be long," Davis called.

Delmar pointed out where he planned for them to sleep and the boys agreed, unwilling to stop, listen, or look.

In the cabin, Delmar stood at the door, listening to the boy's crazy yells and Jasper Sykes loud rant in response. He told himself he was waiting for their return before settling down. Instead, he was staring down the hill as he did every night, waiting for the lamp to go out in the little cabin.

Before she had placed the new curtains up, he had been able to see her shadow, sitting up in bed, reading a book, or writing in a notebook. When it was shining from the front of the cabin, he knew she was working at the drop-down desk. He told himself he liked to look because he was lonely.

At college, there had been someone awake at almost any time, usually trying to get someone else up to talk to or study with. At home there had been his parents, brother, sisters, and three servants. Someone was always awake and moving about somewhere when he was trying to go to sleep.

Here, in these peaceful Tennessee mountains, the only sounds were crickets, tree frogs, and an occasional animal or bird call. Tonight, the ruckus at the store made several dogs bark and one or two other people yell, "What's going on?"

Now there was only silence. All he could think about was Charlotte's sad face and soft, sweet mouth beneath his own. He wondered if she was disappointed that he had stolen the kiss, or angry because it had been so fleeting. The thought of her as hungry for more, like him, sent fire and hot blood to torture him.

Suddenly the light went out. Sighing, Delmar moved inside the big room of the cabin and looked at his own lamp, still lit on the table.

The couple in his bedroom had stopped quarrelling and Delmar strode to the table to pick up his sander. He slowly worked on the wood as he did every night, silencing his hunger.

He heard the boys, swearing and complaining as they climbed the hill from the store pushing the empty cart. Shook his head when they didn't stop until the cart bumped against the cabin wall. He rose, holding the lamp as they entered and they stopped in surprise. He shown it around the room, pointing to where he had placed a blanket for each one on opposite sides of the stove in the middle of the front of the room.

He waited, scowling at them, until both slipped inside their folded blanket and made a pillow of their arms, then he set the lamp down and blew out the light.

CHAPTER THIRTY-FIVE

Early in the morning, Ivey Boggs burst out of the bedroom, all smiles and energy. She bounced around enough, to awaken the interest of all three young men, then chased the brothers out of the way. Delmar had pointed out he didn't have enough grub anyway, and there was no space on the table for them to eat. She shooed him out with the boys.

Somehow, when they came back from answering nature and loading the tools they would need into the cart, she had made fried bread by combining all his meal and flour together with water. The stack of hoecakes smelled better than they tasted, but Delmar was grateful to have something to eat that he hadn't cooked. All were happy to have the weak black coffee and enough molasses to sweeten the dry bread. Wisely, she wrapped the rest and refilled the coffee pot with well water before telling the men she could and would out work them.

Davis seemed a lot less inclined to argue with her this morning, and Delmar was glad. Ivey might not be available these days, but she was a lot of woman and a pleasure to look at. At the last minute, he picked up and added his fiddle case to the cart. The ox stared at them with suspicion, but Delmar left him to graze. Eb and Ned made good enough mules.

Jasper Sykes called to them as they passed, telling them he would be down to join them this morning, after he got the Widow Mouse set-up to run the store.

Delmar was glad to have work on the raft to keep him occupied and away from the school. He would have been able to keep the little schoolmarm off his mind entirely, if Eb and Ned hadn't been there to remind him every few minutes.

When they weren't teasing him about keeping the woman under his eye all the time, they were teasing their pa about being wrapped around Ivey's finger. When Jasper joined them, they were happy to tease him even more about having something as sweet and pretty as the Widow Mouse living under his roof.

Other men came down to watch, rather than help build the raft. None brought any food. Most of the men seemed to light up when they saw Ivey there, her red blouse loosely tied, dropped off a shoulder or two to show her cleavage. She gave each man a familiar smile, but the men were smart enough not to smile back with Davis glowering at them.

Few were any real help, until Jasper Sykes came down. Davis encouraged the onlookers to leave, that they could handle the load. The few who had ventured out, quickly left to tend their own home and lands.

In no time, they had enough logs and then some, cut from the river bank. When Davis asked, didn't he think it was enough, Sykes had just said, he thought they might as well clear this part of the bank. Make a nice park area for picnics and what not.

When the boys started to complain they were hungry, Ivey told them there was nothing for her to cook unless they wanted to catch their supper.

The boys tried their hand at fishing, but the sound of the axes and all the talk had driven the fish downstream. Delmar wisely sent them down to the first little rapids, insisting that was where the really good ones could be found.

When the boys caught enough fish, they were surprised when Ivey refused to cook it. She pointed out she had no pan or stove, no meal or grease. While the boys built a fire out of some green wood, Delmar took the fish, cleaned them, then ran a branch through the mouth and out the end to skewer the fish.

Ivey sat down to watch it cook while the men continued to work. There was a lot of discussion on how to build the raft. None of them had done it, and they especially argued about the best ways to secure it and how many logs wide the thing should be. They ended with six timbers for the bottom frame, a dozen sizeable logs forming the length of it. Jasper was the only one who had that much experience with building, and Delmar noticed all the volunteers were curious to see how he would set the steering paddle and oars.

At noon, they stopped to eat, but Jasper took off back to the store to check on how things were going. There was a lot of speculation about Jasper and the little widow woman while he was gone. Most people in town, especially the Daniels, didn't believe that there wasn't more than a working relationship between them. Ivey contributed that the couple were too dumb to pretend, she thought it was a business arrangement.

Delmar blushed at the rough language, but Ivey didn't bat an eye. When she said if they were doing it, one couldn't blame any woman for being willing with a man like Jasper Sykes, Davis exploded. Ned and Eb roared with laughter at their Pa's expense. He was so busy chasing them to smack down that Ivey escaped anything but his verbal abuse. Delmar watched, studying Ivey. If the woman felt any shame for her past as a prostitute, she didn't show it.

When Davis hollered for his help, Delmar sprang to his feet. Only when Jasper returned did the three men corner the boys and take special delight in tossing and shoving them into the river.

Delmar realized it must be a constant challenge for a man in such a tight-knit community, to have taken home the local whore. Ivey might not be Davis' wife, but there was no arguing that they were a couple with more than a business relationship between them.

After they ate, Delmar played a couple of tunes and all the men enjoyed watching Ivey dance. While the older men stripped the branches off the trees, Delmar, Eb, and Ned shed their shoes and shirts and worked at testing the platform base. As expected it floated, and the young men took turns diving off into the cool water, splashing around enthusiastically.

As he walked back with Jasper, ahead of the Daniels who were pulling the cart and tools with Ivey riding home, he saw Charlotte head toward the store to visit with Jeanne LeSouris. He held his breath, hoping that she would stop and at least smile at him.

Delmar realized he must look disheveled, He raised a hand to smooth back his wet hair, felt his unbuttoned shirt flap against his wet chest. Suddenly Charlotte stopped. He was aware of how her glance swept across his exposed chest, the color deepening in her eyes and her cheeks blooming pink. He wished he had the power to hold his response, but he felt a slow hungry grin pull at his face.

Shaking her head at him as though shocked, she flounced into the store and Delmar laughed. He had to wonder what might have happened if he had cornered her in her little school or cabin looking like this. He hummed "Yankee Doodle Dandy" as he walked the rest of the way home.

Charlotte felt embarrassed for staring at the man, but could not fight the rise of blood pressure. The store was crowded, Jeanne too busy to stop and talk. Charlotte bought a small bag of flour, two eggs, sugar and some precious milk. Jeanne insisted she take some sweet potatoes, assuring her all one needed to do was put them in a pan in the oven when she lit a fire for her tea. They would bake and be delicious. Charlotte thanked her, admired her baby, and noticed he seemed pinker and fussier than before.

As she waited for the girl to tell her the amount due, Charlotte whispered. "Any word about Cicely?"

"None, since you told me Delmar took her away. With everyone bringing goods in for the boat trip to Knoxville, expect Shep or Bailley to come by to visit. I'll tell her you want to see her."

Charlotte nodded, accepted her parcels and rushed home. Dovie had already written out the recipe for her cookies, and she was determined to try to cook something on her own.

Behind her she heard the whoop of the Daniels and moved off the road to let them pass. "Sure 'nough lookin' purty, Mizz Charlotte," Ned called. Eb just gave a loud yell and Charlotte gritted her teeth as the boys pulled the ox cart with Ivey standing up inside, waving at her like she was a queen.

Charlotte laughed and waved back at her as Davis cut across through the store's back yard, complaining when the new flock of chickens set up a ruckus. She wondered how much longer the motley crew would stay in town. Surely they would leave when the raft was finished. She then realized the men planned to leave either tomorrow or Sunday

Charlotte took a moment to pull the latch string, staring wistfully up at the cabin on the hill above her own. Delmar would be gone all week. It seemed like if she ever had a reason to talk to him, the man disappeared. It didn't matter, tomorrow she was going home with Sydney. When he told her his pa was coming back tomorrow, Charlotte had been delighted to only have to spend one day with the family. The school board's demand of staying over two days was impossible.

Still, she stood there and wondered if she would see Delmar tomorrow, or if she would have to wait a week before finding out why he had presumed to kiss her and when he was going to do it again.

CHAPTER THIRTY-SIX

Charlotte appeared at the store to wait for Sydney's family to arrive. She was surprised to see a dark woman shopping there, with a young white man beside her. When she walked up to the counter to visit with Jeanne, she saw the young woman busy arranging two babies in the crib. Her little Henri at one end, and a larger, black baby at the other.

As Jeanne rocked the cradle the older baby laughed, the sound loud and beautiful. Both mothers laughed as little Henri stared at his visitor and smiled. Charlotte clapped her hands and both boy's eyebrows bounced, making Charlotte laugh as well. The older baby laughed again and this time Henri blew a little bubble in response.

"Jeanne, I've never seen two handsomer babies."

Jeanne smiled at her, gently rocking the cradle again. "They are wonderful, aren't they? Would you like to meet Bailley, Joseph's mother?"

Charlotte turned and her eyes widened. "I certainly would. So you are Bailley Bridger? I've longed for a chance to meet and thank ..." both women hissed to warn her and Charlotte stood stiffly and tried to resume breathing.

If Dovie Watkin or one of her sewing circle were present, she might have to endure another session with the school board and it might not go as well. Slowly she turned around, a rather insincere smile upon her face.

"I'm here, waiting for one of my students to arrive. I'll be staying over with Sydney's parents and their two sons tonight, coming back to church with them on Sunday." When no one reacted with shock, she relaxed a little. The school board must know how green she was about speaking in public and staying in the home of strangers. If they had faith in her, she should have as much or more in Delmar's friends.

While Jeanne waited on customers, Charlotte followed Bailley behind the counter with the excuse of looking at the baby boys. Bending over them, Charlotte whispered urgently to the woman. "I don't know how to begin to thank you for all you did for Cicely. The girl has had such a rough start in life, and now all this."

Bailley's voice was deep, as rich and full as her lips. Charlotte was hypnotized as the woman explained how they had wanted to help the girl as well and how they knew she would be happier now, among her own kind. Charlotte wanted to argue but knew this woman with the light brown skin, was right.

"I thought she was staying with the Melungeons?" Charlotte whispered.

"She is, oh you mean about mixed blood. Reckon she's got that, we all do. Good book said God molded Adam out of mud. Now you take dirt and add water to it, no matter how much water you add, youse still going to have brown mud. That's what happens when you mix white and dark, that baby's still going to be brown."

Charlotte shushed the big woman, as she realized how quiet the store had become as Bailley's voice became louder.

Shep over beside the door, said. "They all left before the good part. But you better hurry, I see that boy and his pa headed this way."

Charlotte clasped the woman's hand, leaned over to hug Jeanne too, before slipping under the counter again. At the door, she was surprised when the man tipped his hat. She had heard the Bridger's looked like gypsies or Indians. If she hadn't been told that, she would have thought Shepherd Bridger was European, probably Italian.

The trip up the mountains toward the Smokies passed quickly. The day was warm and clear, the leaves already changed along the trail. Instead of Sydney, his brother Zeke had come with his father to fetch her. Sydney had been kept by his ma to help get things ready for their company. The man and boy were carrying totes full of the goods they picked up at the store and took turns telling her about their part of the community. Zeke was telling her how they found the dead Frenchman, Henri LeSouris, killed and partially eaten by a bear.

"The same bear Mr. Monroe shot?" Charlotte asked.

"Reckon it was the very same," Mr. Tate said. "Oh yeah, Delmar told us the story of fetching you and that bear down to Kyles Ford when he was up our way. Nice young man, plays a right bodacious fiddle."

"Did that bear really jump into the cart with you, Mizz Stewart?" Zeke asked.

Charlotte smiled at the question, delighted when Sydney charged down the path toward her. She pulled the bright, happy boy into a hug and laughed. "Yes, that bear jumped in and I jumped out."

All four were laughing as they met Sydney's mother on the porch. Nothing would do, but that Charlotte tell the story again. Looking around the nice clean house, Charlotte was delighted. Unlike Glory's little home, it looked like she might not have to share a bed with her student.

As they were leaving the house the next morning, church bells began to ring. "Oh my, wait a minute," Ma Tate said before disappearing back inside.

"It's amazing how clear and loud the church bells sound all the way up here," Charlotte said.

"T'ain't that far, as the crow flies," said Pa. "Did you have something, Ma?" he asked as the flustered woman reappeared, a big covered basket on her arm.

She lifted the cover to let him look inside and the man actually ran his tongue around his mouth and said yum. Charlotte waited, but no one made an explanation. Instead the brothers kept up their competition to name the most dangerous animal that might jump out at them in the mountains.

After all the stories of mountain lions, bears, badgers, boars, and charging deer, Charlotte was delighted for the trail to flatten out and the little, brown church steeple to appear ahead.

Charlotte entered with the Tates but moved forward to sit beside Jeanne. The little woman was rocking her fussy baby and looking very anxious. There was a buzz of excitement through the whole congregation and Charlotte looked about, but could find no reason for it. She asked Jeanne, but the girl shook her head, her dark eyes revealing nothing.

As late comers settled, the preacher told them there would be a special ceremony for one of their members at the end of the service.

Minutes later, Delmar arrived late, carrying his fiddle case. This made Charlotte sure something special was about to happen, but Jasper Sykes glowered like someone had just poked him in the eye. Charlotte decided if they wanted to tell her, someone would, and focused on opening the thin hymnal in the back of the pew, reading the song titles. Although the singing was different than what she was used to, some of the hymns were the same.

As the sermon began with Reverend Watkin's sing-song voice, Charlotte struggled to keep from nodding. Although she hadn't shared a bed with Sydney, she had been offered the chair in front of the fire with a woven rush stool for her feet. Covered with a quilt, she had pretended to be appreciative and comfortable, but she had woken feeling stiff and tired this morning.

After the members stood for a hymn and prayer, Charlotte was shocked by the reverend's announcement. She felt all the fatigue and grumpiness leave as she smiled at the bright and excited face of Jeanne. "You're getting married?"

Shyly Jeanne nodded, grabbing her hand. "Stand up with me."

Delmar rose with Jasper and the two walked onto the dais with the reverend. Delmar set down the fiddle case despite Jasper's frown. Charlotte followed Jeanne onto the small stage, grateful that the baby still seemed asleep. They were almost through the service when Jasper took the child from his mother's arms and passed him to Charlotte.

Charlotte was so shocked, she barely caught him before he fell and the baby began to cry loudly. Delmar moved around the couple being married and took the boy from her as though he handled crying infants every day. Charlotte noticed he was quick to hand the baby to Bailley, who was rushing forward to take him. Obviously, she wasn't the only one terrified of babies, but what did a school teacher need to know about tending to infants?

Charlotte's earlier annoyance returned as she heard the reverend asking Jasper a different set of questions than those for Jeanne. Why, he only had to honor and protect, and his wife had to promise to obey his commands. For a minute, she wondered if all wedding vows were this lop-sided, or if it were only hillbilly ones. Suddenly the big store-owner was pushing back the brim of Jeanne's bonnet, and the look of love and longing that passed between the couple left Charlotte's throat dry.

Would she ever have anyone look at her that way? Feel for her such an awestruck love? She shook her head, but tears formed in her eyes anyway. Love was so beautiful, and she had chosen to teach children instead of settling for marriage. She was fumbling for her handkerchief to wipe her nose when a horrible screeching noise sounded. Like everyone else, she stared at Delmar with his fiddle raised and Dovie who was seated with her dulcimer on her lap.

As soon as the reverend pronounced the couple man and wife, Delmar sprang down from the little platform and stood over Dovie, watching her hands strum across the lovely instrument. This time when he raised his fiddle, they were not only playing the same song, but the music ran together beautifully.

CHAPTER THIRTY-SEVEN

It had been such a cobbled together ceremony, so hastily arranged and carried out, Charlotte was amazed at how everyone was rushing as one toward the church door to see the couple off. For goodness sakes, they lived only a few hundred feet from the church steps. By the time she made it through the crush at the door, her students and the fiddler were already outside.

Charlotte bit her cheek as the taunting song, "Froggy Went a Courtin'," was sung again with glee. More surprising was the laughing couple stopping to face their chorus of well-wishers. As Jasper knelt and swept his little bride onto his knee, the children went wild with laughter. Charlotte laughed too.

When everyone else rushed about, already knowing what to do to have a wedding supper, she stood, feeling abandoned by everyone. Sulking, Charlotte walked the distance from the church to her little cabin, a distance she could never remember being so long. She made it into her cabin before she started crying for real.

Later, she heard someone ringing her school bell to signal the meal was ready. Rising, she took time to rinse her face, holding the cool water over her eyes for a few minutes. Smiling at her reflection in the mirror, she quickly neatened her hair, then straightened and brushed the dust from her clothes. The dress looked sad after being worn two days and slept in overnight, but it would have to do. Biting her lips and tweaking her cheeks, she could only imagine what Mama would say about her appearance.

The Daniels came running down the path from Delmar's cabin, Ivey calling to her as they sailed past. "We're going to wake the newlyweds." Ivey turned toward the store, with Davis trying to catch her, while the boys headed for the feast set out around the front of the church.

The Tates and Dovie waved at her at the same time. Charlotte hesitated and heard the warm drawl beside her ear.

"Looks like you've got plenty of choices. Both ladies are fine cooks, but figure the Tate's conversation might be more palatable."

Charlotte stared up at him, her eyes widening in surprise. The first line made her wonder if he'd heard about Charles defection in favor of her sister Rebecca. She took a deep breath, trying not to get lost in his teasing eyes and mischievous smile.

"This weekend I spent with the Tates, with Sydney."

"You told me, remember," he said.

Charlotte blushed, amazed at how the sound of his voice seemed to crawl over her skin.

He turned, laughing, and she looked where he pointed. The newlywed Sykes were following the Davis couple, both looking shy and hastily put together. Charlotte felt the pinch of jealousy again, wondering what it would be like to share that sort of relationship.

Delmar beamed at her, and she blushed even deeper. When Zeke hollered an invitation, this time to Delmar, Charlotte accepted his arm and allowed herself to be led to join the family. Passing by Dovie she whispered. "I guess

I'm supposed to spend as much time as possible with the parents. I'll see you tonight, sorry."

Dovie looked peeved, but waved her on ahead. Delmar noted the look, seated Charlotte beside Mizz Tate, and walked around the improvised table to sit along a temporary bench between the boys and Philomena and her family. The girl surprised everyone when she asked, "Mizz Charlotte, are you coming to our house next week?"

Charlotte smiled, "I don't have a fixed order, but if that would be all right with your mother?" Charlotte looked from mother to daughter, noting how much alike the two were. She was pleased when the woman nodded and said. "Might work. We'll see what comes up."

Charlotte almost coughed around the bite of bread in her mouth, she was so surprised at the strange answer. It wasn't as though there were that many social engagements in this small town. Instead, she managed a polite smile, "Fine, please let me know when it's convenient, if not, I can visit someone else."

She wasn't surprised when the girl started to whine at her mother. It was her standard pattern of behavior if she didn't get her way, but the woman merely looked across at

Delmar, making a disapproving face as she gnawed a rib bone of some unfortunate animal.

If Delmar noticed the look the woman gave him, he made no sign. Instead, he was joking with the Tate boys about what they'd really do if they saw a mountain lion. Apparently, Zeke was planning to become a hunter like Jeanne's first husband.

There was talk and laughter up and down the table. She noticed Delmar hadn't pulled out his fiddle. Charlotte asked him, "Aren't you going to play another song, some pretty song of love, maybe?"

He looked at her strangely, then shook his head. "Sykes already said he didn't want a party yet. We finished the raft late last night, now he thinks the people need to load up if the Daniels are going to be able to make the trip in three days."

Everyone seemed to be finished with the meal. Charlotte couldn't eat another bite. Mizz Tate's pound cake with jam had been divine. She needed to thank Delmar for his intervention but he was standing up. She realized Jasper Sykes was speaking, his loud voice booming over the table.

It was Delmar's much softer one that she listened to. "Sorry, but he's right about loading the barge. Have to make Clinton by dark. I promise we'll have a party with lots of dancing and music when everyone's back."

In minutes all the men were gone and soon they saw dozens heading for the river with their arms loaded. Charlotte looked around at the tables and dirty dishes. She stepped over to Dovie and volunteered to help her clean up. At least if she was busy, she wouldn't have to fight this new wave of disappointment.

Drying the last dish and raising on tiptoe to add it to the shelf, Charlotte folded the damp towel and turned to hug the older woman. She apologized to Dovie, explaining she was still too full from the big wedding meal to eat any more tonight. Dovie smiled and packed her a plate to take home for breakfast or a late supper if she got hungry.

The older woman walked to the door with her, and stood staring at the fading light. Both shivered in the cool air.

"I heard a lot of hammering at the store the other day, didn't get a chance to ask what the noise was about," Charlotte said.

"That man, he's always loud and noisy. Guess now he's married, he'll tone it down a little. I asked the Widow... Mrs. Sykes, what he was building. She thought it was another room, but he hadn't told her about it yet. Don't that beat all?" Dovie said, giving a wink.

Charlotte laughed and stared at the store. "They seem so different, but it seems like they belong together. I hope they have a long, happy marriage. My parents have one of those."

"Good, I pray they will as well. Guess it's not the girl's fault, the way they started out. Better go on, Charlotte, while there's still plenty of light."

Charlotte obediently stepped out, heard voices and stepped back into the shadow.

"Go on," Dovie said. "Just men coming back from getting that silly raft launched. You don't need to worry, since there wasn't any foolish drinking, dancing, or singing to get folks blood up. Go on, and I'll stand here till I see you've reached your door.

Inside, Charlotte set the plate on the table, quickly changed into her gown and wrapper. Stepping back into her shoes, she started off, then turned back to grab the lantern and went out again.

Ever since those wild Daniel boys played their prank on Glory, she had been afraid to visit the outhouse after dark without the light.

When she returned, she had barely stepped in and pulled the door closed, when a man reached out to take the lamp and she started to scream. Delmar placed a hand over her mouth, whispered 'shh."

Charlotte stood there, finally surrendered the lamp and watched fearfully as he set it down on the desk beside her plate. Slowly he released her mouth, then sank down onto the plank at the end of the bed.

Instead of kissing her as she had dreamed about the last two nights, he sat looking up at her. "Is that all yours, or is there enough to share?"

She waved her hands at him, pulled up her chair to sit down and watch him gobble her food. He started to talk, and she made a face. "Not with your mouth full, please."

A minute later, she handed him a glass of water, watching as he drained it in one swallow. She brought more and waited impatiently. He stopped, indicating the dessert. When she looked blank, he raised a fork-full and held it out to her.

The smell of apples, cinnamon and toasted oats was too much. She ate the food, realizing as her mouth closed over the fork that it had been in his mouth. She inhaled and the feeling of tasting it all, of tasting him, made it hard to swallow.

Delmar put the dish down. He stood, his gaze intently fixed on her face, on her mouth. The room felt close and hot as Charlotte raised a hand to push her hair back, trying to breathe. She saw his gaze drop to her parted robe and the heat in his gaze made her knees buckle.

CHAPTER THIRTY-EIGHT

Delmar moved quickly enough to catch her before she fell. He stood, breathing as though he had run a mile, aware of her hair falling down over his arm, the silky brush of it against the back of his hand. The robe now fell all the way open and he inhaled all the air in the room in one gigantic gulp, then exhaled on a loud oath.

Carefully, he stepped around the end of the bed, avoiding the counter and sink in the small space. Clumsily, he opened the covers, pushing the quilt back, then gently laid her down. He wished the lamp were closer, not the shadows, for they were torture. The high crests of her breasts beneath the thin linen were palely painted amid the shadows around their curves.

He knew if anyone knocked on the door, or came inside, he would have compromised her name, exactly what he had avoided all week. He wanted to be a gentleman, to show her respect and remain distant more than ever. He didn't want to jeopardize her reputation or position as the schoolmarm, realizing now how important it was to her.

He sighed, leaning against the counter behind him and crossed his arms. Coming inside like this had been a mistake. He arranged himself, and closed his eyes for a minute. She was probably too innocent to notice his arousal. According to Eb and Ned, she had no idea that they were talking about sex in their dirty pictures.

He wondered what she would think if she woke and realized he was gone. He hoped she would miss him, but then he would continue to see that sad look in her eyes and he had to know what that meant. Carefully, he leaned forward to flip the edge of her robe to cover her breasts, but then he noticed her nipples were hardening in the cooling room.

He knew he was dammed, but all he could think was how they would feel in his mouth. The moment her eyes opened, he wished he was already gone.

Charlotte stared at the man in the shadows, breathed in the earthy scent of him from his sweat and dirty clothes. Of course he had worked hard with the other men. How long had it taken to prepare the raft and launch it?

Suddenly she sat upright in the bed. "Why didn't you go? I thought you were going to be gone all week?"

There was a burst of sound, either a cough or a laugh, then his gravelly voice. "Close your robe, for pity's sake."

Charlotte blushed as she sat up, pulling her wrapper tight and retying the cloth belt. She would have stood up but he held his hand in the air to prevent it.

"I needed to see you, to try to explain."

"Explain what, has something terrible happened?" She said in a rush, moving closer beside the raised hand. "Oh Del, are you all right?"

"No, I'm in Purgatory. Tortured by you," his hand cupped her shoulder, moved up along her slender neck and buried itself in her dark silky curls.

When she raised her face to his, he did the only thing possible, he kissed her. Not the soft, fleeting exchange of the other night. This time he took her mouth, invaded it with his tongue, explored all the beauty of her velvety lips.

Shocked, Charlotte stood there, enjoying the teasing beauty of the kiss, then he lowered his hands, placed one on her breast and she pushed him away.

Delmar stood there, panting beside her. "I don't think you can trust me. I want you too much, and when we're alone, all I can do is imagine making love to you."

The last words were barely uttered when they both heard the sound of a door slamming in the distance. Charlotte rolled her eyes to the door of the cabin, but Delmar moved first, blowing out the lantern still lit on her desk. Together in the dark, they held their breath.

"Who's there?" a woman's frightened whisper sounded. Charlotte groaned, stared at him in rage and moved past him, slapping his hand away when he would have reached for her. She sat at the end of the board, put her shoes on and relit the lantern. Holding it high, she reached for the latch on the door and Delmar moved past her to take position at the end of the bed in the far corner. It wouldn't matter, if the damn woman came in, they were done for.

Charlotte opened the door and held the lantern aloft to call. "Dovie, is that you. Are you all right?"

He heard the nosey old bag sigh dramatically, knew in a minute she would be at the cabin, coming inside. Before he could stop her, Charlotte stepped out and walked down the path to the outhouse where the woman stood. "Is your stomach out of humor too? Mine has sent me here twice already."

Not giving Dovie a chance to intercept her, Charlotte ducked inside the toilet, letting the door bang behind her.

Inside, she was seething. That animal, that careless, thoughtless fiend. Why hadn't he thought what would happen to her if he were seen going in or out of her cabin at night? Destroying her, her reputation and career, had that been worth a wild passionate kiss. Charlotte froze, moaning in memory of it.

"You poor dear," the woman outside called. Relieved, Charlotte made a number of natural sounds, including moans every few seconds. She raised her hands to her face when a man's voice intruded. "Dovie, what are you doing out there? Is everything all right?" the reverend called.

Charlotte couldn't wait for Dovie to answer. "Dovie, I'm fine," she yelled. "Please go on home. I have the lantern to walk back with."

"Nonsense, I'm waiting to walk you home."

Charlotte doubled up in laughter, close to tears as she sank down onto the seat. Now what? If Sykes heard the commotion and came out too, they could hold the board meeting to dismiss her on moral grounds, outside the outhouse.

As she rose, head hanging, the lantern dangling at the end of her arm, Charlotte opened the outhouse door and emerged into the yard beside the couple. Embarrassed, she didn't raise her face to theirs, but turned, and trudged toward her own tiny cabin. Dovie reached out a hand to pat her shoulder and Charlotte snorted in horror. If the reverend did the same, she would have an unbelievable scene to write to her parents.

Finally, she raised her hand to open the door, but Dovie reached past her to open it for her. Head hanging, Charlotte stepped past her into her own room, staring around in horror, knowing there was no way to avoid what was about to happen.

Dovie sniffed and Charlotte knew the rank odor of the offensive man would tell her everything, even if they couldn't see where he had hidden. Charlotte pictured him tucked above the bed behind the trunk, trying not to be detected.

"You poor dear, go on and lay down, I can stay and bathe your head."

Charlotte set the lamp down, stared past to the man outside. The reverend clearly looked uncomfortable in his hastily pulled on pants, his shirt tail hanging out.

"Nonsense," Charlotte said turning to put both hands on the woman's shoulders and turn her around toward the door. "I'm a grown woman, I can deal with a little stomach distress. You don't want to leave your husband standing out in the cold, waiting to walk you back?"

"Oh, I see you ate your supper after all," Dovie said.

Charlotte covered the nearly empty plate with the dish towel and handed it to her. "Yes, and I'm paying for it now. I told you, I overate at the wedding supper. I'm not sure which particular thing, but something has disagreed with me."

She gave an unladylike burp to convince her. The reverend held up a hand and snapped, "Come on, Dovie, you know the girl needs to get to sleep so she can teach tomorrow."

Charlotte stood framed in the door, resting her head against it in prayer. "Thank you, reverend, and thank you, Dovie. I'll be fine, now."

CHAPTER THIRTY-NINE

Charlotte stood, stiff and grumpy, and made breakfast. She sat down in her customary place with her tea and pot of oats. It had been a horrible night. She almost wished she had had an upset stomach, instead of an upset head. She had lied to her sponsors, lied to a poor woman who had come out in the night to see about her.

As Charlotte moved the teaspoon around the delicate china cup, she wondered if that was true. The woman would have had no reason to check on her, to call out in the dark, if she hadn't heard Delmar's voice in the night. Had Dovie sat and tossed all night, questioning her own judgement as well?

Charlotte had waited until the Watkins were in their own house, the closing of their door much softer this time. She had not dared to light the lamp, but had whispered

Delmar's name to no avail. She thought he must have managed to leave while the Watkins were talking to her, but she couldn't be sure. No one would have dared to take such a chance.

She had thrown back the covers, and shot out of bed, searching every inch of her cabin for the man. He was not up in the loft, nor tucked onto the shelf under the sink where Cicely had hidden before. She had looked under the raised board and the shelf board at the end of the bed. The fact that she opened both drawers that pulled out from underneath the bed, still made her shake her head in wonder.

This morning, she pushed the soft cotton and thin silk garments back in place. There was no way the tall young man could have fit in any of those places unless he was an oriental contortionist, able to disconnect his joints to fold up in impossible ways. The image of him doing that made her laugh.

Convinced, she'd crawled back into bed, straightening the covers. Breathing deeply several times, she ordered herself to relax. Her mind filled with each detail of finding him here, of the bone melting kiss, of the words he had growled at her.

Did it mean anything? Was he really as tortured by thoughts of her as she was of him? What did he mean he couldn't trust himself with her? There was the way he had looked, the way he had felt, the way he said he wanted to make love to her. Charlotte swallowed, twisted, and squirmed until she had finally climbed out of bed.

The curtains seemed to glow with the pale half-light outside. For the hundredth time, she wished the small cabin had a window on the end so she could watch the sunrise over the foggy, blue mountains.

Slowly, she ate the food that had grown cold, consoling herself that he had promised to stay away from her. Never again would she have to experience the terror of finding him in her cabin, or the joy.

The next morning, Charlotte dressed with care, as though she might encounter the vexing man at any minute. What did it matter, he hadn't worried about his attire the night before? Hadn't stopped to wash or bathe. She had opened her windows while she tidied the small kitchen, reluctantly letting out the last smell of the bothersome man.

Before she left, she took her time to secure both windows, not wanting to encounter a bat or worse on coming home. In the distance, she could hear a melodious voice singing.

She held her breath as the words reached her. She and her sisters had sung this song in the parlor. "Sleeping, I dreamed love, dreamed love of thee."

The brashness of his song sent her racing down the hill to the school room. What if someone else heard him, and started talking? Besides, the couple's love ended badly, with a ship wreck at sea. Surely, that wasn't what he had wanted her to hear.

She entered, setting about returning the normal order of things. Their first spelling bee had been a disappointment to her and the students, all but Sydney being outed on their first word. She promised them they would soon do a better job. To cheer them up, she had confessed that she had tried to bake tea cakes for them, but had failed at that herself. She had promised to keep practicing, and encouraged them to practice more too.

Of course, Philomena had offered to come by and give her a cooking lesson. Charlotte had smiled and told her when she came for their family visit, she would bring the ingredients, and Philly could teach her then. The children had liked the shortened name, and had used it to tease the bossy girl the rest of the day.

Although she didn't hear the music man again, the children pointed him out to her, as they played at recess and after lunch. They wanted to know what she thought of their song after the wedding. She had laughed and it seemed compliment enough to them.

Delmar, the irritating man, seemed to need to plane and sand all day long, busy working where she could see him every time they emerged from class. Every glimpse was sweet torture for her. As much as she tried, there was also something exciting about knowing he was out there, hoping to see her as well.

A week later, the Daniels were back. Charlotte relaxed a little. At least she would be able to see Delmar, maybe even talk to him, at the celebration. Since the Daniels had taken so long on the return trip, and arrived on a Monday, the party wouldn't be until Saturday. More people would be in town, and the weather promised to be cold enough for hog-butchering. With the kitchen add-on to the store half-built, there were plans to butcher hogs the morning of the party, and roast one of the half-grown hogs. Every day without a word from Delmar, her excitement continued to grow.

Charlotte had worn all the dresses from home but one. After school on Friday, she asked Dovie home with her. She wanted her opinion if it would be appropriate to wear to the celebration, with a scarf of course.

The older woman was less than enthusiastic, and Charlotte had to try it on for her to judge before she would give her approval. Charlotte could remember Mama insisting she wear the same gown at her graduation party, because it was her newest and prettiest. She felt embarrassed at how she had protested, not wanting to be on display for the young men at the party.

Then, she had thought it far too revealing. Now, she wished she were brave enough to wear it without the scarf. She wanted to see Delmar's face when he saw her in it.

Dovie was talking louder, and Charlotte finally paid attention. "The men are almost done building Syke's new kitchen, a wedding gift for his bride, as that ogre, Jasper calls it. Oh, I heard some unbelievable gossip, supposedly something Ned Daniel said. Someone was buying moonshine from the Daniels and heard him giving Davis trouble about it, although with that group of drunks, a tale repeated by a drunk, who knows." Dovie said as she fastened the buttons down the back of the dress.

Charlotte fumbled with the scarf, managing to tie and tuck the scarlet knot into the plunging bodice of the gown. "See, I don't think it's too immodest do you? Although I wish my scarf were some other shade than red."

"I have a large square of lace, we'll see if you can make it work. It is a beautiful gown, but this is a cook out. We will be eating pig meat and dancing over bare ground. Are you sure you want to chance it? What if someone asks for a dance with greasy fingers? I know if it were me, I wouldn't risk it."

As Dovie touched the gown, fingering the flesh-colored pink satin with envy in her voice, Charlotte hoped the woman's fingers were clean.

When the woman returned several minutes later, Charlotte had rehung most of the dresses, and opened the window to let a cooling breeze through the room.

Charlotte smiled at her, "You didn't tell me what the gossip was."

"There will be a wake and funeral for Otis Meany, who's died of lung fever. His wife is down with it too, but it looks like their little girl is over the worst of it. With the cold snap, the Tates have taken care of the body, in hopes she will be well enough to attend. We'll hold the service either way this Sunday after church, not wanting to put a damper on the celebration Saturday."

Charlotte fussed with the scarf, folded it into a triangle as she had the red silk one, then exchanged them. She only had a small metal mirror, but from the image, she thought it looked better.

"Did you hear that our gadfly, Delmar Monroe, paid the second half of the year's rent on his cabin."

Charlotte thought the last was the first good news in all the gossip. "Why would the Daniels ..."

"No, I was there in the store when Delmar paid Ivey. He told her he had received bad news, that his great uncle was ill. Apparently, it's the one who taught him to fiddle and convinced him to come here for wood to make more instruments. He told Jasper he would play at the raft celebration, but planned to leave the next morning.

"Honestly, I think it would be better for all of us if he would leave right away and stay gone. He'll just be giving the men an excuse to get drunk, and the women to dance and misbehave, all because he wants to play that wild music."

Charlotte felt as though Dovie had slammed her with a rock. She pulled the stiff horse-hair petticoat from behind the bed and knocked the dust off. Numbly she lifted the hem of the gown, before pulling the slip up to tie. She tried to rephrase her question, but Dovie clapped her hands, turning her back and forth so that the full skirt belled out around her.

"Lovely, of course you should wear it," Dovie said. "What do you think about the Daniel's tale? I think if he had married that woman, a harlot in the full sense of the word, he would have announced it, or she would have. Neither has said a word. So I think it was all drunken nonsense."

Charlotte tried to keep her face calm, swallowing down the tears dripping down her throat.

"They seem a funny couple, and he is so jealous of her. I bet it's true." She turned her back for Dovie to unbutton the dress, while she spoke.

She didn't want to add how it made her feel, to know that all around her people were falling in love and marrying their perfect partner. The first time she had ever felt an interest in a man, and he was getting ready to disappear.

Holding her arms above her head, she let the woman lift the precious satin to peel the dress off of her. Charlotte moved the scarf to drape over the dress on its hanger as she stepped onto the bed to hang it on its peg. She stood there, untying the stiff petticoat to drop. A breeze stirred the curtain and through the little slit she could see out the window. Standing frozen, watching her, was a man with blue eyes and the same sad look on his face as in her heart.

CHAPTER FORTY

Charlotte woke at dawn to loud squealing and men yelling. Quickly she dressed in one of her oldest dresses and pinned back her hair. She didn't take time to eat breakfast, she was so curious to see what was causing the big commotion.

She rushed toward the sound, heading to the new addition on the Sykes' store. It had been transformed into an abattoir, or slaughterhouse. The clean frame of the new kitchen was being stained red as big hogs were hung from the cross beams with chains as soon as they were killed. She was glad for Jeanne that the floor had not been installed. These boards would all be hidden later.

Delmar was helping butcher the hogs. She stared in amazement at the long tables set up with their big knives and hatchets. Beneath each animal, buckets had been set to collect the rapidly draining blood. As another squealing live animal was chased forward to the chute they'd made between two standing poles, Charlotte turned aside with one last look at those already dead. In the frosty cold air, steam rose from the carcasses like miniature souls escaping.

Shuddering, she turned and ran around to the front of the store. When she knocked, Jeanne opened the door and Charlotte saw how energized the girl was. Two buckets of water had been precariously balanced on top of the stove, probably with water to scald the hide on the animals.

The baby was crying and Charlotte rushed forward to pick him up and pat the small back, amazed at how soft and sweet the child felt after the horror outside. She was muttering soothing words when Jeanne reached to take down one bucket, pushing the other more firmly on the stove, and adding the large coffee pot to its usual place.

"You have him?" Jeanne asked over her shoulder.

"Yes, go on." Charlotte walked slowly, rocking the child from side to side as she sang down at him. When the back door opened, she heard the men grunting as they lifted their most recent victim to hang with the first two. She saw the boy turn his head toward the noise, his black eyes shiny and his fine dark brows raised in question. Charlotte smiled, and when the baby turned back, he seemed to wave his arms, cooing as though discussing it with her.

"Pretty scary, isn't it Henry. But you are safe, safe in here. Mama will be back in a minute."

At the word Mama, the baby's lower lip started to tremble and his eyes filled with tears. Charlotte raised him upright against her, his little head braced against her cheek. She was still crooning softly, but now he was crying. A high, sweet warble of sound that made her look around for something to give him as Jeanne returned.

Jeanne tutted at the boy and his crying seemed to stop at the sound of her voice. At Charlotte's nod, the tiny woman lifted the second full bucket of scalding water and gracefully carried it toward the back door without spilling a drop.

When the women finished their breakfast and the baby was fed and quietly in his crib, Charlotte walked out with Jeanne. Obediently she took her position next to a large kettle raised over an open fire. She stared at the glistening white slabs of fat that coated the bottom as another bucket of the same was added.

"Have you ever rendered lard? Helped with anything like this?" Delmar asked.

Charlotte shook her head, looked at his blood and mud spattered pants and shirt. "Have you?"

He grinned at her, shook his head in answer. "If I had known, I probably wouldn't have volunteered to help."

She smiled in answer, but didn't call him a liar. Anyone could see this was a major operation and too much for one man, even one as capable as Jasper Sykes, to manage. More people were arriving every minute, probably as soon as they finished their breakfasts. "Mizz Potts," he called.

A large woman waddled forward, wiping her hands on her apron as she approached. She looked Charlotte up and down, turned to spit a brown stream of tobacco at a hound that had run up. The dog howled and darted away, receiving several kicks from others to send him on his way. "First, we'll arrange your skirt, then I'll shows you what to do, dearie."

Minutes later, Charlotte stood back to catch her breath from the blazing fire. Her skirt had been raised between her legs and tucked at the waist to keep it or the petticoat from brushing against the fire. She had a broad wooden paddle to push the meat down under the boiling fat as more and more buckets of pig fat were added. In addition to the four big hogs of Mr. Tate that the Meany's had been feeding, two other neighbors had shown up whipping their hogs along the narrow street.

The smallest hog, one Jasper called a shoat, was already resting between layers of wood and hot coals. Another pit was being dug farther down the lane in hopes that another one might come to the slaughter.

Carefully Jeanne stirred the dangerous liquid, watching as brown, foamy pieces of skin and fat began to float on the surface. Mizz Potts had explained they were cracklins, best part of the hog to her way of thinking. An empty pan with several of the golden bits stood nearby as Charlotte skimmed the latest ones to add to them.

Mizz Potts had been an encyclopedia of information on the useful and delicious parts of a pig, pointing to people dropping pink brains into one bowl, brown organs into another. According to that woman, "they was going to use every bit of it but the squeal." Charlotte watched the men moving from the killing, scalding and scraping, to the actual butchering, starting with the first one slaughtered.

Poor little Jeanne was relieved from her one-woman bucket brigade.

Charlotte had never experienced anything more exhausting or exciting. It was strange, but watching the men season and wrap the hams, shoulders, and side meat that would soon be hung in the smoke house, seemed wonderful. Everyone joked, no one argued. Charlotte was proud at being considered part of the community.

Jeanne came out with clean tins, and together they managed to ladle the hot fat without anyone getting burned or any of the valuable lard being wasted.

The women divided the remaining tasks of making sausages and lunch meat using the cleaned guts. A woman volunteered to pickle the pig feet, another to make the souse meat from the snout, ears, and tongue. Another wanted to make black sausage or blood pudding from the liquid collecting in the buckets. She actually shared the recipe and Charlotte realized it didn't sound much worse than any of the others. The blood would be boiled with onions, oats, and ground bits of meat. Yet another was planning to make liver loaf.

After the main cuts had been removed to the smoke house, Charlotte was given all the little scraps of pork to stir in her empty kettle until crispy. These were served on fresh bread with a few cracklings as a snack for the workers. The women disappeared to their homes to work on their share of the sausages while preparing for the party in the early afternoon.

Delmar gave her a tired smile and she almost made the mistake of reaching out to wipe his dirt smeared face. She realized he was studying her, and self-consciously unhooked the tail of her skirt that Mizz Potts had helped her fasten. With one or two shakes, she hoped she looked presentable. The way the man stared at her, she wondered if the tobacco spitter had forgotten to mention everything that was on the menu.

Before she left, she helped Jeanne add two or three pumpkins to each pit with its roasting pig. Then they had layered silked, but unshucked corn, over the warm earth. Those living in town quickly disappeared as newcomers were assigned the task of washing the temporary tables and moving everything down toward the clearing by the church. For such a cold start, the day had really warmed up.

It was the normal time she would have been heading home after cleaning up after school. The sun was high, the day perfect and clear, leaves dancing around over the ground.

Charlotte bathed after the hard, dirty work and got ready for a quick nap. She had cleaned her hair, set it by twirling strands around her fingers and tying them with rags to curl. She might no longer wear the elaborate curls Mama had preferred, but tonight she wanted to make a special effort.

Other than the look and a couple of words this morning, there had been no chance to speak with Delmar. She hoped that Mizz Dovie had misunderstood about his leaving, but in her heart, she knew it was true.

Well, one had one's duty. Family first, as Papa would say. Family always first.

An hour later, Charlotte woke, refreshed from the short nap. Primping, she secured the ribbon in her hair, pulled to finger comb each long curl as she untied the thin rags. She set to work trying to get into the dress without a maid. She had all but the top two buttons done up in the back, and decided with the lace scarf insert, she could get one of the women to button her before anyone noticed.

Settling the skirt over the stiff petticoat, she gave a swish and opened the door to run to see Dovie. Standing outside in her path, the tall young man was tuning his fiddle.

Charlotte caught her breath at the site of Delmar, the way the autumn light softened his hair until it looked golden. He looked up at her gasp, and she knew she would never feel more beautiful than this moment.

CHAPTER FORTY-ONE

Charlotte imagined they might have a stolen moment to talk, but the hollers of Ned and Eb racing down the hill behind her made her groan instead.

Delmar gave her a wistful smile of his own. He moved quickly from the tree, whispered, "Turn around beautiful." Deftly he buttoned the last two buttons, removed a rag strip from one last curl, and pocketed it.

She could feel the blood humming between them as he stepped away too quickly. She wanted to hear him explain about leaving. Ned slammed into Eb and both tumbled in a heap in front of her. Delmar jumped even father back.

"Dear Gawd, would you look at that," Eb said.

"An angel, a sure 'nough angel," Ned said.

Charlotte laughed, checked to make sure the lace was still carefully filling in her bodice.

Delmar extended a hand, to help the older boy to his feet. "She sure is that," he said. "And I'm going to have to go back to Virginia and miss seeing her for too long."

"Ned, Eb," Charlotte said with a curtsey. "Stop running and no swearing, or I'll make sure Dovie Watkin has a word with you."

Eb and Delmar pulled Ned to his feet as well. Both boys stood, their half grown beards making their dropped jaws more comical.

"Go on boys, think they need some help heaving those roasted hogs out of the ground. Didn't you tell me you already had experience with that sort of thing?"

"Yeah," Eb said, "But it wasn't no half-grown cut pig, it was that big boar, you know the one left them long gashes in that walnut tree about shoulder high on you?"

"Yeah, we had to lift him out of that pit for Nadine's wedding," Ned said, smacking his lips. "Man, hope these pigs taste as good as that one. Pa's the one shot him after Alma told us he was there."

Charlotte shook her head and the long spiraling curls bounced, making the boys gush and swear again. Delmar swung a foot at the nearest Daniel, urging them to hurry up, before someone else tried it and the pig ended up on the ground.

Both managed to sweep deep bows toward Charlotte before whooping again as they ran away.

Delmar lifted the fiddle in his left hand, and slowly extended his right for her to take. Someone was coming up the hill toward the outhouse, but Charlotte returned his half smile as she accepted his hand and moved closer to hook her arm in his for the walk down to the church.

"Dovie already told me you had a letter and would be leaving."

"My Great Uncle William is very ill. His butler wrote and told me he had asked for me and I'd best come planning to stay awhile."

"He's the one who taught you to play and make musical instruments?"

"Helped me find the love of music that's in my blood. You've not heard music, until you've heard him play."

Somehow they managed to talk without looking at each other, too aware of the whole community staring at them, remarking on the handsome couple. "He must have the skill of one of God's chosen angels, if he plays better than you do, Mr. Monroe."

Delmar saluted and bowed, using the rosined bow to make the gesture even grander.

When one by one, parents and neighbors came closer to comment on her dress and hair, Delmar stepped farther and farther away.

Charlotte sat in one of Dovie's kitchen chairs, one of the lady's big checked napkins spread over her lap. The Daniel boys had carried her a plate of roast pork, with a spoonful of baked pumpkin, and a shucked ear of hot corn. They had each had a plate for her and argued all the way to the table where she sat with the reverend and his wife under a shade tree. Dovie had taken the first plate from Eb, and Ned had given the second one to Charlotte.

"What about me?" the reverend asked.

"Better hurry," Eb said. "Choice parts is already getting plundered. We got to get us some for they's gone."

Charlotte and Dovie laughed at how quickly the older man sprang to his feet. Delmar started to approach their table but the Sykes arrived first. He was ready to move away when Charlotte called to him, "Come on, Mr. Monroe, there's one more chair."

Delmar sat down on the end chair across from the reverend when he returned. "It was smart of you folks to move your furniture out here."

Dovie smiled at Charlotte. "Miss Stewart showed me her dress yesterday, and I just couldn't stand the thought of her sitting on a rough board, or heavens, the ground, in it."

"That's because, madam, you didn't have to figure out how to maneuver it out here," the reverend said as he took his seat.

Jasper and Delmar spoke at the same time. Dovie grinned. "See, these two young men will move it, so stop complaining. But you'll need to leave at least two of the chairs. This is my best gown as well."

While both women complimented Dovie on her dress, Charlotte extended her hand under the table and felt a thrill when Delmar gipped it and gave it a gentle squeeze.

Dovie thanked them as she sliced the pan of cornbread and passed it around. "I only brought out the one knife and six forks, so please keep up with them," she warned. "But since I didn't have to make sausage like most of the women, I figured pickles and eggs would go nicely with this plain food."

"And, be sure to try some of Dovie's special barbecue sauce. It's a wonder what it does for the pork," the reverend handed the jar to the circle of food Dovie had started around. Charlotte was relieved to see it already had a spoon.

Dovie was right about her risking her gown for all this messy, finger food, but smiling at the man beside her, she couldn't remember another time food had tasted better. Her only regret was she had to take her hand back in order to eat it.

There was still a lot of food on her plate. Delmar reached over to take half of the pork and the rest of her corn bread when she complained at all the Daniel boys had brought her. Delmar noticed Mizz Dovie wasn't having a bit of trouble finishing hers.

The Daniels were already asking when the music was going to start and were urging some folks to move back so that they had more room to dance. All four were passing around a jug, selling drafts when anyone came over with a jar or cup.

Charlotte felt suddenly sad as she stared up at Delmar. When he looked down at her, she wondered if he were imagining a delicious kiss as much as she was. Sighing, he patted his flat stomach and apologized. "Time to go pay for my dinner."

Delmar walked up to the spot where Davis had pointed for him, stood a minute, then raised the fiddle up to his shoulder. "I hope you don't expect me to be the only one playing. The rest of you musicians hurry up and eat your grub."

There was a scattered laugh or two, the sound of happy people who were enjoying a perfect fall day. Delmar continued. "Know you want me to play so early because you don't want to have to climb home in the dark.

"This is a new song, learned it when visiting my great uncle on the way to Kyles Ford for the first time. If you don't laugh, I'll try to sing the words along with it. It's called "Sleeping, I Dreamed Love.""

Charlotte looked down at her hands and used the napkin to dab at the single spot where a bite of cornbread had dropped. She was too afraid her face would reveal her emotions if she looked up, struggling between smiling and crying as he played the song, then sang a verse between playing until he reached the end. There was a big round of applause.

Charlotte had to look up when she heard him cough as though embarrassed, her gaze locked with his across the crowded picnic area and all the faces between them.

"Oh, play something faster that folks can dance too. Play that Susannah song," one of the Daniels shouted.

"I only brought down my fiddle, you guys want to run up and get my guitar and banjo, I'll play that one," Delmar answered.

Players gradually joined him, couples rose to dance. Charlotte smiled as the reverend and Jasper carried the table back inside, while she and Dovie turned their chairs to watch those who were dancing. Jeanne handed Dovie her son as she carried the scraped plates and a chair after them. Jasper met her half way and took those, sent her back to sit down in one of the chairs.

Charlotte took the sleepy baby when the Sykes moved out into the road to dance, then the Watkins and a dozen other couples joined them.

Charlotte was grateful for the sleeping child to show, when men came over to ask her to dance. Only when Jeanne came back to claim him did she finally say yes to a request.

When that dance ended, she looked up and smiled as Delmar stepped in to claim the next dance.

"You look like you belong in a grand ball room, not on a grassy field like this. I wish I had a more presentable suit to wear for you," Delmar whispered.

"Don't, I can't talk, not knowing I won't get to see you, ...," she took a big gulp of air, bent her head.

With the slightest touch, Delmar prodded her head back in place. "I need to look at you, enjoy this time, and you do to," he smiled at her and she smiled back. "It's probably for the best, anyway. I told you how hard it's been to resist you.

Then you wear this. I'll never have a moments calm when I think of you in this pink gown."

"You should see it without the scarf," Charlotte bit her tongue, her eyes widening at what she'd said.

"Oh, I'd like that," he purred. "I'd like that a lot."

Charlotte blushed and someone tapped Delmar's shoulder. He looked like he would say no, but it was Mr. Goins, the other school board member.

Delmar leaned closer as he released her. "I'll write."

With that, he was gone. Charlotte tried to summon a smile for the man across from her. "You're Philomena's father?"

"Yes, was that man being disrespectful to you, Miss Stewart?" he demanded.

"No," she shook her head, "No, not at all." She stared at the shorter, broader man who looked a little more than angry at the situation. "I'm sorry I wasn't able to come to visit this weekend. This pig killing seemed to have come up fairly quickly."

"There's always next weekend," he said.

Charlotte nodded, "Next weekend then."

She tried not to, but she turned to look at the band. All she saw amid the jostling music makers was the tall handsome man, shining as he played, and she had to look away.

CHAPTER FORTY-TWO

Near the end of the day, the room felt freezing around the edges, while smothering hot near the center. Charlotte tried to cheer up, smiling around at her students. The room smelled of wet wool clothing and tree sap from the spindly cedar tree in the corner. The children had decorated it with popcorn, tinsel, and folded red and white heart shaped baskets. Charlotte had already bought a dozen candy canes and a sack of hard drops for the little paper baskets.

The last snow still lingered outside, but today had grown colder all day. She had decided to hold the Christmas party tomorrow, early in the morning, in case a new snow fell. The children were all excited about exchanging presents. At first, it had been a big controversy for the community, but she had assured one and all that a present didn't require money. The best gift of all was one that someone had made for you. A month ago, they had drawn names. She had students suggest things they could make for a gift, and she wrote the list on the board.

They could sew a doll from an outgrown sock, make an Indian style doll from a corn cob and dried corn shucks, carve one and tie the pieces together to make a dancing doll one of the boys shouted. The little girls looked shocked at the boy who had taken over their topic. Philly said they could knit or crochet a scarf from new thread or yarn they unraveled from something torn or ruined, the carver interrupted them again and Charlotte wrote quickly, shushing the protesters. They could whittle a bird or whistle, or cow, or something else pretty. Even the boys had laughed at the idea of whittling a cow.

She reminded them, Mizz Dovie had taught them all how to make paint. They had made glue by boiling milk and flour, added tiny amounts of Mizz Dovie's powdered pigments to little bowls of the warm glue. Some of the bright art still hung around the room. When the left-over paint looked like it was drying up, Charlotte had pounded up some of the raw chalk rock piled outside the school room and stirred it into the old wooden bowls. When it dried, she had colored chalk.

They could also write a special poem or story. They could bring some little treasure they had found, a fossil or crystal, or something else interesting.

She was amazed as the group continued to make suggestions, weaving a pot-holder, quilting a doll blanket, making candied popcorn, baking a cake or cookies, making a musical instrument like Mr. Monroe. Charlotte had stopped writing at the name, forced a smile and sat down while they whispered and talked to each other about things they might make. Charlotte loved the ones who already stared smugly at the others. She knew in their minds, Sydney and Philomena were already at home making their gifts.

The two littlest ones were shaking their heads at each other. "If you got my name, don't write me nothing. The rest will be okay."

Charlotte patted the folded letter in her pocket, the paper burning her hand, she was so impatient to get a new one. She wished she could read Delmar's letter out loud, tell her students how much something you wrote could bring you closer.

Today, she smiled as she had to send one of the younger children back to their seat. The gifts many of the children had made now rested under the tree. Each morning as the children snuck the gifts to her she took them home, carefully making and wrapping them in the precious newspapers Delmar had sent.

Now, all but two were here, they seemed to torture the ones whose names had been written on the simple wrappers.

Charlotte wrote her own list inside her diary. She needed to bring the candy early tomorrow to divide. Tonight she needed to bake the plain cookies again, or try to bake a pound cake like Jeanne had advised. Since Jeanne was dying to try her new oven, she had volunteered to bake one for Charlotte if she paid for the ingredients. She decided to tell her yes, when the children were eating lunch.

Charlotte turned her book to the back, looked at the tally of her limited resources. Since writing letters back and forth for two months, postage had depleted her funds and she was even stingier on what she spent. Dovie had promised she would receive the first half of her pay at

Christmas and Charlotte could hardly wait to spend some of it on a store-bought present for Delmar. Of course, she had followed her advice to the children and used her red silk scarf and a woolen sash to sew and quilt together an ornate guitar strap. She had never seen him use one, and wasn't sure if he would like the gift.

She hushed the children, then had them all rise. Sweetly, they sang "Silent Night" as she looked out the window at the darkening sky. Her evening prayer was that all should reach home quickly, before they felt the cold, and that tomorrow would be warmer and clearer for their Christmas party.

Before releasing them she reminded them that parents were welcome, if they wanted to come. She reminded the children they would hold a spelling bee and singing if any did. She already had approval from Dovie, so reminded them tomorrow would be the last day of school for the next two weeks.

◇◇◇

As soon as the last child disappeared, Charlotte ran her errands. She picked up the finished cake, carefully cut two generous slices for the baker's dessert. It seemed cruel to leave the kitchen smelling so good, but without dessert. She took the time to admire everything again, offered to help with any chores. Jeanne shooed her away, told her she would have everything ready on Christmas Day, but if Charlotte wanted to come early, she would be welcome.

Now Charlotte worked to clean the slates, then carefully wrote Merry Christmas in the center of the wreath in the middle of all the drawings on the board. She patiently colored the green leaves, added red berries and bow. The new letter had been read not once, but twice. The irritating man had not promised to be back for the party.

Even though his Great Uncle William was dead, there were many details of the estate to tend to and much needed work about the place that he wanted to finish before starting out. Charlotte stared at the clean, glowing classroom. She tucked candy into each little paper basket, having to pick it up and rehang two of them, grateful that she had cleaned the floor first.

Even more carefully, she hung the peppermint sticks. She had thought at first to let the children take one of each, but decided it might seem more special with their names on it. She took care to hang the younger children's lower on the tree.

She had already carried in clean water and fresh firewood, carefully knocking snow off each log before carrying it inside.

On the short distance to her cabin, she stopped at the outhouse, shivering as she sat on the cold seat. In her own place, she started a fire, put on a kettle for tea before sitting down on the bed to wait, her feet carefully held over the edge of the blanket as she stretched out to read the letter yet again in the lamplight.

Beloved Charlotte,

My sweetest darling, I'm writing by firelight, thinking of you. You are right to complain to me, I was a coward not to steal a last kiss before leaving. It has made me miss you more than if we'd had a proper goodbye. As always, concern for your reputation is all that stayed me.

I would be riding there tonight if you would but say yes to my proposal. I know you have signed a contract, but I cannot imagine being back in my lonely cabin and you in yours. I must have you for my wife.

Since there will be no long sweet kisses or passionate embraces, I must linger until the latest date possible before leaving the plantation. Great uncle is dead, but there are many details to settle in his estate. The house has fallen into decay and I have been working day and night to make much needed repairs. Some of great uncle's old freed slaves have returned to help me with this work and if the weather holds off, I should have the house in order come spring.

I plan to start for Kyles Ford the week before Christmas, riding Brick. My horse has grown snappish and surly from his long idle days. There is a small mare, ten years old but sound, that I plan to use to haul my tools and instruments back. I will try to be there for the little party for your children, but weather may delay. Look for me by Christmas Day, even if I must let Brick ride on my shoulders and drag the mare behind.

Devotedly yours,

Delmar

Charlotte crumpled and tossed the letter, then scrambled out of bed to smooth it and place it with all the others. The proposal was there again, but what was she going to do.

CHAPTER FORTY-THREE

Delmar stopped first in Richmond. He was able to easily persuade the store manager of the largest music store to take eight instruments on consignment. As he played to demonstrate the quality of each, those in the store had gathered as well as many people from the street. Delmar pointed out that a unique instrument could be that perfect gift for Christmas, and the dealer had no argument with the price he listed for them. Everyone agreed they were beautiful.

Next he stopped by the office to visit his father and brother James. He tried to protest, but of course, had to go home for dinner and a visit with his sisters as well. It was not until he saw Eleanor welcome James with a warm kiss, that he had a moment of doubt. The girl was prettier than he remembered, and clearly richer. Beautifully gowned, for a minute he pictured Charlotte dressed the same, standing beside him. His father pointed to the couple. "You may kiss the bride, but don't say you didn't have your chance."

Delmar embraced his brother, congratulated him and kissed Eleanor on the cheek. "At least my sisters haven't wed without sending me notice."

Mother laughed, "Actually, Debra has a gentleman in pursuit, and Ellen will debut next spring. If you stay gone any longer, you may return to find the house full of nephews and nieces."

Eleanor blushed, gave him a sharp look, as she was seated across from James and him. The happy chatter and faces were reassuring, but Delmar had to admit it made him long for the quiet life he had left, not this one of manners and polite conversation. When his mother interrupted him with a question about his own intentions, it was Delmar's turn to blush.

"There is a girl that I'm interested in, although I'm uncertain if she can be persuaded." He went ahead to describe Charlotte, discuss her ambitions as a teacher and her upbringing. "I hope to ask for her hand when I return to

Kyles Ford. She is not from wealth, but her family is more than respectable. He discussed how the Reverend Benjamin Stewart was the President of Newton Seminary College in Boston. His mother was the only one who seemed impressed. "I've read his argument on abolition, brilliantly composed," she said.

Later, as he made his farewell's, insisting on the urgency of his journey, his father pulled him into his office to ask. "I received a copy of William Monroe's will from his solicitor. Did you know you are his sole heir?"

"Of course, Father, as the executor of the estate, I have been living and working there the last two months."

"I thought you were living in hillbilly country, pursuing your music and this theologian's, missionary daughter?"

"When Great Uncle William had a stroke, the butler sent for me. Apparently, uncle drew up his will when we all visited fifteen years ago. I was as shocked as you to inherit everything. You father, are his closest relative, and rightfully, James and I should only receive anything after your turn running the land."

James Monroe stared at him, shook his head. "No matter, Uncle William had no more head for farming than he did for the law. Was he much in debt?"

Delmar shook his head. "No, not at all. He was able to pay for the servants and provide food with the sales of his instruments and home-made wine."

"Good, I don't have a lot of ready cash at any rate. I am the Democratic candidate for State Senator. Do you know what that means?"

"It sounds like you are abandoning principal for electionability. The party of Stephen Douglas is pro-slavery. The Monroes have all fought against that cruel system. It was grandfather who proposed the law to prohibit the import and sell of more slaves."

"No, that was Jefferson, his mentor. Grandfather was for state's right, the Monroe Doctrine, and the Missouri Compromise."

"If you want to be a senator, why not do it as a Republican and oppose slavery. You know the Democrats even want to put all free negroes back in chains or ship them to Liberia."

"The capitol of which is Monrovia, for your Grandfather's work to establish it." His father sighed. "William, I guess we will have to agree to disagree. But the other Virginia state legislators are taking the pro-slavery side. To oppose all of them would be political suicide. A little like your current choices are leading to the suicide of your career."

Delmar shook his head. "Father, I must go."

"William, do you need money, anything?"

"I use my middle name now, everyone calls me Delmar." Delmar stood there, taking a couple of deep, calming breaths. Money would be a wonderful thing to have right now. He had secured a loan for restoring Sparrow Walk, the aging plantation that was now his own. But asking Charlotte to join him there when he was three-thousand dollars in debt was a problem. Straightening up, he thought of the one thing he needed that wouldn't make him feel a bigger debtor.

"I would like to take the rest of my clothes, if you don't mind."

"I'll have Asa ship the contents of your room. I can send him to join you as well, if you'll accept the gesture as a gift."

Delmar bowed his head. "I would like that a great deal, father, a great deal. It will make the perfect wedding gift."

His father stared at him, held wide his arms and Delmar stepped in for a last embrace. "I'll send him and your belongings on to Sparrow Walk."

"Delmar, son don't accept no from your girl. If she's what you want, pursue her with logic – there are children to teach all through this great nation, but you are land rich now and will be living in Virginia."

The rest of the trip was as hard as the visit home. The logging season was over, and the short line railroad was no longer in operation. Brick was still traveling well, but the mare had shown no willingness this morning to drag the small wagon with his tools and materials. He had exchanged the two, tying the little mare behind the wagon and driving forward as quickly as possible.

He hoped to persuade Charlotte to marry him and to return to Sparrow Walk with him right away, but he had thought it best to be prepared to work at Kyles Ford until spring if necessary.

It was outside Blackwater, when heavy snow on the road sent him toward the sawmill for shelter. He was able to remove two hinges to open the large, padlocked door, driving the animals and wagon inside for the night. He found plenty of wood scraps to feed the big stove and was able to have hot coffee and food for the first time since leaving the plantation. The only concern was the howl of a wolf.

He would have argued with anyone that the animals had been killed out by trappers years ago. Like anyone, he would have been amazed that a man could be killed by a bear in Tennessee, but he'd seen the bear, met the man's widow. As he prepared for bed, he prayed for the snow to stop, so he could reach the woman he loved.

Only thinking the words brought a smile to his face. How long had he felt that way? Would he have the courage tomorrow to say those words to her, to ask her to marry him? It was almost dawn when Brick whinnied loudly and the little mare kicked at the door.

Delmar woke instantly. He had left the rifle in the back of the wagon, wasn't even sure he had loaded it. In minutes he was in there, moving things, finding the gun, checking the load and waiting. He noticed how the two animals moved closer, the big gelding putting his neck over the little mare's back. A pity, but the animal had been bought in that condition. Father argued a man couldn't risk his family's safety on a stallion, and Delmar knew most men felt the same.

He wondered if he would have those feelings if he had to buy a horse for a wife or a child to ride. He smiled again at the outrageous thought.

The door rattled and he raised the rifle and yelled as loudly as he could. Someone dropped to the ground. Minutes passed before a voice called out. "Whoever you are in there, you better stand down, I'm coming in."

Delmar lowered the weapon and called, "Come on in."

Minutes later, he was sharing the bitter dregs of the coffee from the night before, waking up quickly.

"How'd you get in?" the man asked curiously.

Delmar held out the pins from the hinges. "Something frightened the horses last night, howled like wolves."

The man nodded, "Might have been." He threw out the coffee Delmar had poured him, opened a bottle, and poured some instead before offering the bottle to Delmar. "Wasn't you here last year, wanting pretty wood?"

"Yeah," Delmar said. He rose, opened the small instrument case and drew out his Christmas present for Charlotte.

The man whistled as Delmar tilted it so the light reflected off the pretty top of the dulcimer, then he sat on the wagon tail gate with the instrument in his lap to play a little tune.

The air was warmer, the sky clear and blue. The ground was blanketed with snow, but there was no biting wind or spitting snow today. Delmar had to hold the rested horses back when he too wanted to gallop them home.

It was still early when he reached Ivey's cabin. He watered, then fed the horses as he moved the contents of the wagon inside. Afterward, he hobbled the animals and released them to graze. He wondered if Charlotte would notice he was back, then decided he'd rather she didn't. He took the time to wash, shave, and change into his good suit. In his right pocket he had the ring, in his left hand, the case with her new present.

Walking down the hill he saw the white smoke from the little school house, could see the doors were standing open with grown-ups craning to look inside. He didn't bother with the porch. Instead he walked around and stared in the window. He saw the children seated, staring straight ahead. He cupped his hand over his eyes as he leaned in, pressing his nose against the glass. He still couldn't see her, and wanted to swear in exasperation.

Suddenly, he was lifted into the air, his leg caught high so that he was swaying and swearing to keep his balance. "Hey," he shouted.

Jasper Sykes put the younger man down, clapping him on the shoulder. "That's what you get for peeping in windows."

Someone was rapping angrily on the glass and Delmar turned to see Charlotte staring at the two laughing men. He watched her face change from scolding to transfixed with shock. People were coming off the porch toward him but all

he could see was the color bloom in her cheeks as her eyes
deepened to violet.

CHAPTER FORTY-FOUR

It was the reverend who suggested, "Let's move everything over to the church. That way parents can come in out of the cold to enjoy the festivities." Charlotte looked around at all her decorations, and wanted to argue. Finally, she said, "Thank you, is the church already warm?"

The reverend looked a little perplexed, then said, "I'll be back in a few minutes." Charlotte raised a finger, blew against it to shush the anxious parents outside. A tall, red-headed man leaned around the doorframe to extend a cluster of green. Delmar pushed onto the porch and ducked under Davis' arm. He leaned in as he brought Charlotte's hand down. The kiss was a loud, pucker kiss that made all the children giggle and point at them.

Charlotte looked outraged, and the crowd whispered instead of laughing with the children. As Delmar stepped closer, she leaned her forehead against his, then turned to all the whispering children. Delmar reached up to snatch the bunch of mistletoe from Davis and stepped inside.

Charlotte directed him to sit on the back bench. She was all business. She had been over what she would do, and how, all night. Now she said, "If we move the tree, some of the candy baskets might spill. So, as I call your name, come up to get your present, your Swedish basket, and candy cane. Then sit down without opening anything."

She extended an arm, "Ladies on the right, gentlemen on the left."

Starting with Glory, one by one she called their names by age and each walked forward, claimed their paper basket, shiny candy, and wrapped present. Only when the last student had been called, and seated, did she look back at Delmar and blush again.

"Reverend, just hollered, Mizz Stewart," Mizz Goins said.

"You may go on ahead. If a couple of you men would move the tree, and one of you ladies would help me move the refreshments, we'll finish everything over at the church. Please leave the first two pews empty for the children."

As orders were followed, and the last child filed out, carefully holding their treasures, Delmar stepped into the room. Charlotte was scooping up her grade book, looking around for anything she was forgetting. Then her eyes landed on him.

He extended his arm, led her out, and pulled the door closed behind them. Walking over the crunchy ground she whispered, "I see you made good time."

"Had to. Told my parents I had met the girl I wanted to marry, if she'd have me."

Charlotte stumbled, stared up at him breathlessly. "Now, now is not the right time for this. The children are waiting. There is the contract I've signed. I've given my word."

He pulled her back behind the church door and stared down at her. "Then I will wait until it is the right time, but not patiently." He pulled her into his arms and kissed her as he had wished he had weeks ago. When he released her, Charlotte swayed, taking several seconds to get herself steady. She nodded, aware that her face was red enough to be on fire, but she had children who had waited long enough. Delmar clung to the door, uncertain what to do.

He turned and walked back toward the rented cabin. At the sound of Davis Daniel's loud voice and everyone's laughing, he turned back toward the church. He opened the door, then stood there in wonder as he watched her.

Everyone shouted, but it was Davis that said, "See, he done hit her with that mistletoe again."

Charlotte straightened her back, stared at the fidgeting children, and took a deep breath as she assumed Papa's poise in his stiff black robes. The room became silent. She called a name. "Glory, come forward and open your present."

The little girl did, carefully undoing the newspaper wrapper with its chalk drawing of a blue bird. She held the paper out for her mother to take, then raised the small, sock doll high for everyone to see. "It's a pretty dolly," she looked at Charlotte.

"Who does she have to thank?" Finally, a small boy on the other side raised a hand. Glory ran over to kiss his cheek and give him a curtsy. Everyone clapped. Delmar raised his hands and clapped too.

Charlotte looked at the children, half turning to give him a smile and then called the next name. Most of the other children, merely said thank you and bowed.

Later, almost all the children had one of the hard candies in their mouth, although most had surrendered their presents and candy canes to their parents. Delmar had eased into a back pew next to the Tates, as Charlotte arranged her charges on the small platform, tallest in back, and blew her little silver pipe. Those who could manage had switched their candy to their jaw, a few held it tightly in sticky fingers.

The five carols were so beautiful, no one clapped, or moved until the last.

Afterward, she conducted a spelling bee, girls on the right, and boys on the left. It was Sydney and Philomena who were still standing after eight words. Finally, Sydney won. Everyone clapped and stomped. Charlotte pinned a little blue ribbon on the boy's coat.

At his proud and shiny face, Delmar was glad the Daniel boys were no longer going to school. It would be a cold day to be hung from a tree.

Jeanne handed Jasper their baby boy and stepped forward to help Charlotte serve cake and cookies, lifting the bucket of cold water onto the table so anyone who needed a dipper full could serve themselves.

Charlotte was apologized to Dovie Watkins for any mess they had made. The woman praised her for a wonderful Christmas program and for the job she was doing with the children. No one had any idea their manners were so polished, but come to think of it, people had commented on how much better behaved they seemed these days.

At the look on her face, Delmar wished he had a ribbon to pin on Charlotte's blouse. Sitting on the back pew, he noticed how everyone took their time folding their piece of reused newspapers as though they were special awards. She had drawn a image on each one. Zeke passed him the little red and white basket that had looked like a heart on the tree, and he studied the neatly woven paper before passing it back.

The reverend had already insisted that she leave the tree, it was way too pretty to throw out. Delmar knew it would be awhile, as parents waited in line to thank her for the program. Some shook her hands, others acted like they were old friends. Maybe there was something to sleeping at their homes with them, for it seemed to him, everyone was proud of their little schoolmarm.

Quietly he slipped out through the main doors of the church. This time he kept walking.

Charlotte looked around at the empty church, her heart in her throat. He was gone.

She tried not to look around expectantly, knew everyone would be talking if she did. People were still standing around and visiting. Head down, she walked home.

All day, she stood at the smallest sound, moved to the door, and waited breathlessly. He didn't come.

In the morning, she dressed hurriedly and rushed outside to the outhouse. Inside, there was no one in the other stall wanting to have a conversation, outside there was no one waiting to grab her hand. She forced herself to stay calm. Trying not to cry, she walked back into her cabin and made a breakfast she could barely swallow.

When no one came by, she wondered what had made her say that to him. What if he had gone back to Virginia? To his parents or to the Tidewater plantation that he complained about so much in his letters, but clearly loved?

He hadn't walked to the front of the church, played one of his amazing songs, or his barely tolerable duets with Dovie. He had left.

She hadn't had a chance to ask about his family, or to express sympathy for his loss. They had only exchanged a few words, and hers had been so … so …, Charlotte's lips trembled, but she refused to cry. It was the day before Christmas. The Watkins would expect her for dinner tonight. Surely they would invite Delmar. There would be an opportunity to talk on the way to their house, or on the way back to her cabin.

CHAPTER FORTY-FIVE

When he saw the giant ahead of him, he hollered. "Wait up there, Davis, I need to talk to you."

The tall, bearded man turned and stared at him, a grin on his face. "Come to tussle with me, like you did Jasper? Seems to me you ain't growed that much while you were gone."

Delmar stopped beside him, stood so they were nearly eye to eye, shook his head, and waved a hand, "Nothing like that. I kind of need your advice." He looked around, then asked. "Where are Ivey and the boys?"

Davis looked like maybe he wouldn't, but then started talking. "I hated to do it, I purely did, but after that trouble at school, and the way they were after the schoolmarm, I started thinking about it. Too, they just kept deviling Ivey, and well, enough was enough. I've sent Eb and Ned down to spend some time with my brother. He's in the same line of work as me, down on the Tennessee/Georgia border. Ivey had me write him a letter back when we were in Knoxville, and well, he agreed he could use some help."

Delmar felt even more surprised. "Well, they're about the age my father sent me off to college. It will be good for them, no doubt about it."

Davis pulled the cork on his flask, offered it to Delmar. Delmar took a gulp, watched the bigger man swallow most of the rest. "Is Ivey shopping at the store?"

"No," his eyes sharpened as he stared at Delmar. "Why are you asking?"

Delmar grinned, but backed up a couple of steps. "No, nothing like that, I only know how she likes going places with you."

"Yeah, she does. But now she's got that little girl to take care of, I can't hardly get her to budge from the place."

Delmar waited, not speaking when Davis continued. "You heard about the Meany's. First Otis, then his missus passed from the lung fever. Little girl got it, but seems better. She was staying with the Sykes, but when Ivey saw her, her heart just filled up with needing that child. I told Jasper I'd do anything he liked, if he'd let Ivey have Kitty."

Delmar was surprised to hear the choked sound of the man, the way he swallowed and spit away his tears. "It was that little Widow Mouse of his, convinced Jasper we were fit to do it. For a little gal, she's got a big heart."

Both men stood in silence, thinking of how hard but sweet life could be.

"Any way's, Ivey didn't want to take Kitty out in the cold, so they's decorating a Christmas tree when I left. I found a pine, hell of a lot prettier than the one at the store or over at the church. They's talking about all kinds of things to make for Christmas and cooking dinner. You know, girl talk."

Delmar stopped in surprise, and looked around. They were already half-way up the ridge to the Daniel's place.

"Don't worry, come on home with me. They'll both be glad to see you. You know how fond of your music Ivey is?" then he squinted harder at Delmar.

Off the trail they heard a gobble, and Delmar pointed to the flock of turkeys disappearing around the bluff. "Think I'll have to go home to get my fiddle and rifle, before I come up your way." Then he stopped and stared up at the big man. It was now or never if he was going to plead his case.

It was late, and he wondered what Charlotte was thinking of his disappearance, but he'd talked to the Goins after leaving Davis.

The hardest would be the Watkins. This morning he had asked Dovie if Charlotte would be dining with them, and as he'd hoped, she had invited him to join them. Now, sitting at the table, staring at the older couple, he wondered if Charlotte was going to show up.

"Does she often come late?" Delmar asked.

Dovie extended a hand to join him and the reverend's. Annoyed, Delmar bowed his head, waiting for the long winded prayer to end.

"I saw her around noon at the store. She was buying a piece of cheese and an apple. Told me she still had bread and was so tired, she thought she might just eat and go on to bed," Dovie said.

"When was this?" he asked. Instantly, he knew the question had been asked too sharply.

"Maybe it was closer to one or so. You sound too disappointed Mr. Monroe, isn't our company good enough for you?"

Delmar had relaxed and raised his eyebrows. The teasing tone was all the opening he needed. He began to plead his case, and hopefully that of Charlotte's. Dovie had smiled, totally entranced by the idea of young love. Reverend Watkin had been vigorously opposed to altering a contract once signed. They agreed to honor his plea for silence. They would not reveal to anyone, even Charlotte, what he had proposed.

Whatever they had for supper, Delmar was glad when the evening finally came to an end. Walking home, he paused and stood shivering outside Charlotte's door. She was so close that he was tempted to knock on the door, to batter the solid wood to splinters. There had lingered all day the warmth of her lips on his when he had kissed her the second time. The thought of kissing her sleepy face, holding her close within his arms ended the same way such visions always ended. There was the torture of leaving her, and the fear that he would be unable to leave her alone.

This morning he had woken early enough to go hunting. Getting lucky, he had carried one of the big birds up to Davis. He was glad that he had gone. It was worth it to see Ivey in a high-topped blouse with her flame covered hair twisted into a tidy bun. She sat with a tiny, brown haired girl whose skin looked translucent.

When he had plopped the brightly colored Tom turkey on the porch, the little girl had rolled her eyes in astonishment. Delmar had asked for an introduction from Ivey to this beautiful creature, but it was the child who piped up and said. "You're the music man, and I'm Katie Meany, but my Pa in heaven called me Kitty."

"So do you want me to call you Miss Katie or Miss Kitty?"

"Well, my Ma in heaven called me Katie."

Delmar had purchased sweets at the store, although the jars were nearly empty this close to Christmas. He held up both empty hands, then folded them around a sweet before waving one fist and then the other. "Miss Katie, or Miss Kitty?"

The girl had given him a breathless giggle and tapped the right hand. He opened it and she took and put the candy in her mouth immediately. He still held the left hand out, she looked at Ivey before tapping his hand and taking the second piece of candy. This she put in her skirt pocket for later.

He smiled at her, noticed the child leaned back against Ivey's soft breasts, clearly weary from the little conversation. He reached out to place a hand on the neatly braided hair and bowed his head to say a simple prayer for the child and for the woman who cradled her so softly.

He stayed only long enough to play two songs, both soft, sweet ballads for Kitty and Ivey. The child was asleep as he walked down the trail with the smaller turkey hung over his shoulder beside the guitar case. He hoped it would give him a good opening to persuade Jasper Sykes to take his side. So far, all had agreed with his arguments, but none had given him a definitive answer. Who knew what the decision might be when it came to a vote.

Delmar walked past the teacher's cabin, whistling loudly and strumming his guitar. He felt relieved when Charlotte opened the door and stared out at him. She was already dressed for Christmas dinner at the Sykes. The dress was a cheerful red and green plaid wool with a tight green velvet jacket. She was beautiful, and he could tell she had on her stiff petticoat since the skirt swung forward like a bell where she stood anxiously on the steps.

He tried to clear his throat but couldn't. "Too much whistling," he joked.

Charlotte disappeared back inside and Delmar was putting away the guitar when she returned. She held out a glass of dark liquid to him. "I made a pitcher of sweet tea this morning, using Dovie's directions."

He rolled his eyes, seemed to accept the drink with trepidation, but stood still, his fingers touching hers on the side of the glass. Charlotte's hand actually trembled. He took a long, slow drink, aware of her eyes following the motion in his throat. As usual, her glance stirred him deeply.

This time when he spoke, his voice was deep and rumbly. "Maybe another, this time just water."

"Oh dear," Charlotte said and darted back inside to try to prime the cold pump to get him a drink. He moved so he could see inside the tiny cabin, the neatly made bed, the scattered clothes almost hiding it.

She looked behind her, blushed guiltily. "I couldn't decide," she padded over on bare feet.

Smiling Delmar brushed her hem to reveal her small pink toes and white, high arched feet. He drew in a strangled breath and Charlotte blushed scarlet.

Embarrassed, she forced the glass into his hands, then turned and passed out her single chair with instructions for him to sit and wait. She would be ready in a few minutes.

It took three tries, but he finally managed to set the chair so it wouldn't tilt over. Seated, he grunted, looked about before rearranging himself and then sat again. He pulled the watch from his pocket, winding the stem while he checked the time. If he hadn't let it run down, the watch said they had another two hours before Jeanne Sykes would be serving supper.

As much as Delmar liked the newlyweds, he knew they didn't need two strangers underfoot as Jeanne tried to complete her first Christmas dinner for company. Settled, Delmar closed his eyes against the bright, cold light. Inside, he heard Charlotte rushing about in the small space. He knew she was trying to hide the silk and cotton underthings that had been thrown about. He remembered how difficult it was for him, standing on the rope slung bed, to hang all her dresses on the line along the wall.

If Jasper hadn't teased him the other day about being a peeping Tom, he would have walked around and tried to watch her stretching and teetering on the precarious bed to hang them. Instead, just imagining her on tiptoe reaching for the rope above her head, he grinned.

When all the noise stopped, she still didn't come to open the door. He remembered her bare feet, and knew she was pulling on stockings and shoes. Again, he closed his eyes, imagined the bright rustling skirt and petticoats raised, while she threaded her foot and leg into a white stocking. He could feel how delightful it would be to help her push a garter up onto her small, shapely legs.

Delmar sighed, disgusted with himself. He would embarrass them both any minute. When had the sight of a woman's foot aroused him before? But all he could imagine was cupping her little foot in his hand, feeling the curve of it gripping his fingers, or brought around to press against his bare hip.

When he heard her hand on the latch, he stood up, jerkily grabbing the guitar case to hold in front of him. Charlotte opened the door. Delmar bowed to her and whispered.

"Darling, I'll be back in a few minutes. I have to go home to get something for you. Take your time, work on your hair and bonnet while I'm gone."

Charlotte stood still, a hand going instinctively to her hair as he walked stiffly off to his cabin. For the first time she noticed he had his rifle and the guitar case with him. Again, she wondered where he had been since the school party yesterday and until afternoon today.

CHAPTER FORTY-SIX

Charlotte fussed with her hair, then pulled on the green velvet bonnet, tying the bow until she was satisfied with the look. Finally, she lifted the guitar strap that she had spent so long making, thinking about him with every stitch. Fortunately, the knots in her embroidery were hidden when she'd sewn the red silk inside the woolen sash.

Although she had gone to the store twice to look, she had found nothing there nice enough to buy him for Christmas. Jasper Sykes carried tools, knives, and weapons, but she had no idea what Delmar had, would like that he didn't have, or that she could afford. Once again, she regretted the time she wasted with Mama when she could have been learning how to cook and sew.

She stood with the wrapped gift, the chalk drawing already a little smudged. She wondered if he would think her foolish for reusing the newspapers. He had graciously sent them when she complained about how hard it was to get mail or news in Kyles Ford. She had taken them to the store on Saturday mornings to read and share with the Sykes.

He'd researched the question about mail service for her and replied that the government would only open post offices in communities that connected to a major traffic road, railway, or river that had steam transports.

Delmar stood outside the cabin and knocked. Once again, Charlotte jumped to open the door.

She felt as nervous and excited as her students had yesterday. He raised a hand to assist her and she descended the two steps. This time he seated her in the chair, turned to dust the steps, and closed the door before sitting down across from her. Both were aware that anyone who wanted to look their way could see their every action. Charlotte tilted her head to hide shyly under the brim of her bonnet.

Delmar reached across, tilted her chin so he could see her eyes. "Please, let me look at you, my lovely," he whispered.

The words felt as soft and sweet as kisses. She blinked before staring upward into his clear blue eyes. She held out her present for him.

He took it, studying the drawing as he had watched her students look at theirs the day before. It was an image of a quartet of musicians playing music, although the faces were blurred, the proportions were good.

"I'm sorry, but I didn't have mother's remnant box to wrap it properly. I read every word before reusing the paper. Thank you for sending them, and for explaining about post offices. I must tell you though, because of our correspondence, we have a peddler who sorely peeves Mr. Sykes. He now makes the circuit up from the post-office in Sneedville to here, and on to Bristol, selling ribbons, combs, buttons, and pots and pans."

"Why would Jasper mind?"

"Jeanne always wants to purchase a new ribbon or trinket, but I'm not sure he minds that much. She has been sending letters home to her sisters too, although she has only received one in reply."

"Davis said he had received a couple of letters as well."

He saw how nervously she sat and casually raised the small instrument case to hand to her. "I didn't think a wrapper would make a difference on mine. I hope you like it."

Excitedly, she touched and stroked the outer shape of the case, surprised at the rough texture of the shiny gray hide.

"It was a shark, one of the boys killed. I know it is not the usual, but it is extremely durable. Go on, open it."

Charlotte unfastened the sides, opening it to stare at the curly maple top of a smaller version of Dovie's dulcimer. "I've never played an instrument."

His voice betrayed him as he said, "I know, that is part of the gift, my giving you lessons."

She dimpled as she said, "A gift for who?"

Delmar smiled wickedly at her as he watched her set the case aside and caress the smooth, beautifully finished instrument. "Let me show…"

"No, open your present first."

Delmar did, opening it so quickly that the paper tore. He remembered how slowly little Glory had opened her gift and wished he had made the effort. Carefully, he folded the paper, making sure to save the corner with the torn foot and base fiddle.

It took him a few minutes to finger the intricate pattern, turn the strap over and then decide he preferred the embroidered silk to face outward. He draped it over his shoulder, and took her dulcimer to pretend he had a guitar. "It's wonderful. I've never had one before."

"You don't like it."

He leaned over, taking both her hands, shocking both of them at his boldness.

"No, I love it. I just carried the guitar back to the cabin or I would put it on now. Here, let's give you your first lesson."

Charlotte squealed in alarm as he lifted the chair with her in it to turn and set on the uneven ground before him. In a minute, the instrument lay gleaming in her lap. His arms were around her, guiding her hands and fingers into position. The whispered words beside her neck set her body aglow.

When she turned her head, her lips almost met his. "Thank you, Delmar, this is lovely."

Dovie Watkins stood in front of them, her voice as scalding as though they were the Daniel boys, caught in mischief. "I've been watching you."

"Oh look, Dovie. Isn't it beautiful. Delmar was getting ready to show me how to play it."

"What I think is you two need to come on down to my house before the whole town starts talking. I can show you how to play it sitting at my table, without any improprieties."

Delmar laughed as he stood up. "A good idea Mizz Dovie. You two go on, I've got to run to my cabin for my guitar and fiddle. I've not figured out how to get fed in Kyles Ford without having to play for my dinner."

Charlotte turned and called to him, "Delmar, stop at my cabin. There's a box full of treats Mama and the girls sent, that I'd like to share with the Sykes."

While Charlotte and Dovie walked down to her house, the older woman informed Charlotte that it was unheard of for a woman to accept a present from a man she wasn't engaged or married to.

Charlotte stared at her in amazement. "Well, he has mentioned his intentions are honorable, but I hesitated to accept since I have the year's contract for teaching here. Although, when I reread the document yesterday, I noticed it forbade courting and marriage. It didn't say anything about betrothals."

Christmas Eve, Charlotte and Delmar arrived already happy. It seemed perfect when mid-meal Jeanne boldly announced that her gift to Jasper would be a baby next summer. Of course, the Watkins had seemed horrified, but Charlotte could not think of a couple who deserved the good news more.

Delmar explained that on his visit to Davis Daniel, he had learned Eb and Ned, the horrible duo, were headed south to torment the local ladies no more. Charlotte pointed out they had troubled her no more after she expelled them.

All were glad to hear Delmar describe how close Ivey and Kitty Meany had become and how much Ivey had changed. "I gave Davis the larger turkey, since all his children and four grandchildren will be there, except his oldest daughter, Alma."

Although Dovie complained about how much trouble babies seemed to be, Charlotte heard the wistfulness in her voice. They were sharing the special wine that the Bridger's had made and she leaned over to give the older woman a hug, startling her so much, she almost spilled her wine.

Hours later, stuffed full of turkey and the feast, the four walked home from the store in the clear night air. They stopped at the sound of shotgun blasts. "Tomorrow, my family will exchange their presents," Charlotte said.

"The same for my family," Delmar said. "My brother James has married fair Eleanor, and if I understood the dinner conversation when I was there, she will have a baby next summer as well. Oh, and my little sister, Debra, has a serious suitor."

"Fair Eleanor?" Charlotte asked.

"Father thought her dowry and my brilliance would make the perfect match. When I showed no interest, James did."

Charlotte giggled, "My Charles Newcomb is engaged to my eighteen-year-old sister, Rebecca."

"Your Charles Newcomb?" Delmar demanded.

"Well, he always wanted to be, but he never interested me at all."

Dovie motioned to her husband and the older couple moved in between the two young people, each taking one of Charlotte's arms.

"It was a long, but wonderful party," Dovie said.

"My favorite part was when Delmar and I sang the silly song, "There's a Hole in the Bucket," for baby Henry," Charlotte raised her hands to clap like the baby did every time he heard his name.

Delmar said, "My favorite was when Jeanne gave Jasper his hearing horn. His look of rapture at the music, I could have played all night."

Dovie laughed and the sound surprised them all.

"It was a miracle," the reverend said. "But if he's going to talk that much from now on, I don't know how the girl will stand it."

At her cabin all four stopped. Delmar insisted on taking her hand, opening the door, and handing her up into her home. Charlotte pointed up at the bright north star in the clear night. "Make a wish!"

Everyone turned to look at it and Charlotte reached out to cup Delmar's face and kiss him. Grinning, she closed the door on all three.

"It won't count," said Dovie. "It's not the first star, it has to be the first star of the evening."

"I don't know," the reverend said, "I think the poem says the first star I see tonight. It's the first time I've looked up."

Delmar was almost at his own house when he raised both instrument cases and called to the older couple. "Pretty cold out. Better go on home. Goodnight."

CHAPTER FORTY-SEVEN

Charlotte wore the same dress to church as she had to the Christmas Party at the Sykes, Delmar the same suit. When they arrived at church, they were both surprised to see the doors still locked. Everyone was gossiping and complaining about what was going on, but Dovie Watkin said she had no idea.

Charlotte stared at Dovie, not fooled at all. Yesterday, the woman had been at her house, far earlier than ever before. The woman had come on the silly pretense of bringing her some warm bread and jam. Charlotte wondered at what horrible hour Dovie woke to make the bread, but she brewed coffee, sat and listened to the woman go over the events of the last two days as though she hadn't been there and didn't know what had happened at all of them.

When Delmar knocked on her door, with the pretense of giving her another dulcimer lesson, he was invited inside to share the bread. She giggled, remembering the horrified look on his face when he'd seen Dovie seated at her desk.

When Delmar had sat on the rumpled bed, opening Charlotte's dulcimer for her lesson, Dovie had become agitated and insisted they move back to her kitchen for the lessons. After one song, the reverend walked into the kitchen to pour himself some coffee. He asked if Delmar had his carpentry tools with him this trip.

Delmar said he had the special ones he used to make his instruments, and some basic tools as well.

The reverend then came up with the amazing idea that they should visit people this Christmas day to see if they had any things they needed repaired. At their stares, he had bumbled on, explaining that many of his flock were too poor or untrained to make such repairs on their own.

Charlotte had volunteered as well, but Dovie had insisted that she needed her there to go through the church barrel. She needed to see if there were any dresses they could make over for that poor little orphan, Katie Meany.

Charlotte had pointed out that now Ivey Daniel was taking her in to raise, she would have more than enough money to buy the girl new dresses.

"You mean, Ivey Boggs?" Dovie said

"Well according to rumor, she and Davis were married when they were in Knoxville," Charlotte answered.

"I don't believe in rumors. Besides, such a woman, well no man, even a moonshiner, would marry a harlot."

"I've heard she has a wedding certificate."

"From a justice of the peace. It means nothing."

Charlotte had given up, since Dovie's answer meant she had probably already seen the proof of the wedding.

As she suspected, whenever it looked like they might speak or be alone together, someone would intervene.

Now, standing together in the courtyard of the church, Charlotte stared hungrily at Delmar. She walked over and said to him. "You are a good-looking man, even when you're playing and singing music."

He laughed and everyone turned to stare at the couple. "When did you decide that?"

Behind them the church doors swung open and the reverend motioned for everyone to enter.

Charlotte continued, "Jeanne told me that, but I was only beginning to decide it was true." She moved even closer and Delmar looked around, wondering where the bakers and people needing carpentry help had disappeared to.

"I guess I was wrong to want to be educated. Maybe what they say about women and learning is true," she said, staring up at him, daring him to resist. "Maybe it will interfere with my ability to be a wife and mother."

Delmar snorted, "That's the second ignorant statement I've heard you make.

"What was the first?" she asked.

"That maybe you weren't cut-out to be a teacher," he said. "I've never seen a better, or prettier teacher in my life."

"Even though I've paddled my students when they wouldn't obey."

He captured her hands and held them, aware of the winter silence. "Especially then," he stepped closer to her. "Did you get the news that my Great Uncle William died?"

Charlotte reached out to touch his arm. "Yes, I'm so sorry darling, I know how much you loved him."

"I guess I didn't mention I inherited his small plantation. It's kind of run-down, but I left some of Sparrow Walk's people fixing up the interior while I'm away. We put the new roof on and painted the outside when I was there the last two months."

"What do you plan to do with it?" Charlotte asked.

"Depends on what the woman I marry wants to do."

"You're planning on getting married?" In the background they heard the church bells ring three times. Everyone laughed as they looked out at the couple standing so close together.

"If the girl I love says yes," he said.

"But there is the contract, and I promised to teach all year, I can't leave until school is out in the spring."

"You're assuming we're talking about you," Delmar said.

"Yes, I'm...," but then he was kissing her and nothing else mattered.

Dovie hollered from the porch, "You better get in here before the board meets again and fires you for inappropriate conduct."

Charlotte turned to stare at the bossy woman who was still hollering. "I was married the ten years I taught school. Jasper and Davis finally got the others to see sense."

Charlotte stepped back from him, tilted her head coyly and said. "I haven't been properly asked."

Delmar grimaced, but sank on one knee on the muddy ground, "Charlotte, will you marry me, and teach me all the days of your life?"

"Yes, Delmar I will." She said as she tugged him to his feet. Together they walked through the front doors and didn't stop before they were standing in front of Reverend Watkin.

As soon as the words were spoken before God, the preacher, and the congregation, Charlotte leaned in to kiss the man she loved.

Davis Daniel shouted from the back of the congregation. "Dagnabbit, he done hit her with that mistletoe again."

CHAPTER FORTY-EIGHT

The wedding lunch was brief, the music and dancing cut short by the threat of a fresh snow.

Charlotte and Delmar walked toward their cabins with the whole town cheering and promising a pounding the next meeting. When she stared at Delmar, she realized his face was even redder than her own. They stopped at her cabin first and she thought it was to get her nightgown.

With the whole town watching, he kissed her again, grinned, and swept her into his arms. When he ordered her to open the door, Charlotte did, wishing the air blowing up her skirt didn't feel so cold. Delmar quickly carried her inside and locked the door. They both heard a few hoots and shouts behind them. Charlotte hung there, one arm around his shoulder. Delmar leaned closer and she kissed him, loving the wet warmth of his mouth on her cold one.

When he set her on the end of the counter, Charlotte opened her eyes in surprise. She watched him add firewood to the stove. He quickly stepped back, removing his hat to place on top of her hatbox.

Charlotte swallowed in alarm. "It's broad daylight, anyone might come by."

Delmar removed and hung his jacket on the hook beside the door, then began to unbutton his vest.

"But your cabin is farther from town, and so much bigger than this one," she said.

Delmar shook his head, "harder to keep warm." He sat in the small chair to remove one boot, then the other.

Charlotte had trouble swallowing. Slowly she tugged at the plush bow to untie her bonnet. Delmar tutted, and she stopped as the man removed his shirt. "I want to open my own Christmas present."

She blushed even redder and looked up at the ceiling as he removed his pants.

She was shaking, more with excitement than fear as she felt his warm breath on her face, his trembling hands pulling the bonnet free. She opened her eyes to stare at him, amazed at the naked man standing so closely beside her. Without asking permission, she ran a gloved hand over his shoulder. Delmar shivered, captured her hand and unbuttoned and removed, first one glove than the other.

She leaned her head forward to kiss his shoulder, let her free hand touch the warm skin on his chest, feeling the silky hair there. Delmar moaned, trying to stay focused on his task as he fumbled at the buttons on her little green vest. Charlotte purred and he knew he was in trouble as she wiggled to free herself from it, twisting so he could reach the long row of buttons on the back of the dress.

Like the wrapping on his guitar strap, he wanted to rip all her clothes from her body. Groaning, he carefully worked the small buttons through the fabric. This time when she offered help, he stood back to watch as she pulled the sleeves down, wiggled to push the dress down at her waist. She extended a hand and he helped her jump down from the counter to shake the dress down into a puddle at her feet, untie both petticoats, and wiggle them down as well.

Delmar sat, bare bottomed on the cold seat of the chair to ogle her in her white cotton pantalets and chemise. In wonder he watched her untie her corset, loosening the strings to pull it off over her head. Her eyes were glowing with mischief as she looked downward at him. He saw her blush even redder and freeze.

Delmar stood up, moved to pull her into his arms, aware of her warm softness pressed against him. Hurriedly, he lifted her again and sat her on the counter. This time, he took her little half booted foot firmly, unhooked and pulled the laces free, then removed it. He felt and found the little garter bunched beneath the ruffles and worried it and the sock down her leg. The smooth flesh was shapelier than he'd imagined, and when he'd freed her foot, he did stroke her bare insole, just to watch her eyes darken in reaction.

While he was tending her other foot, Charlotte released and shook out her hair then boldly pulled her chemise over her head so that she could press her own flesh against his. The reward was Delmar freezing in motion, his eyes rolling back in the pleasure of the moment.

He held her like that, stepped around the pile of discarded clothing and moved to open the covers of her bed.

"Darling, they say it's painful for a woman the first time."

She placed her mouth over his and then ended the kiss to whisper in his ear. "Better get this first time over, then."

He fell forward with her in his arms.

They both lay there, spent from all the anticipation of the moment to come. Delmar rolled so that all his weight wasn't on her, and she wrapped her arms around him to keep him from moving farther from her.

Delmar stared at her, helpless to do more for a few minutes, and to be gentle.

"Are we dreaming?" she whispered. "It feels so real, but I know there's no way it can be, that we're actually married."

Delmar raised a hand, pushed the cloud of silky black curls away from her face until he could see her. He kissed her, then when she took a deep breath, he slipped his tongue into her mouth, waited when she gasped, then tried it again.

This time when they stopped to breathe, he wasn't sure if it was him or her who was trembling. "I went and talked to each of the board members. Told them that I loved you desperately. That you had written me, telling me you felt the same."

"You weren't punishing me, leaving me because of what I said on the day of the school party."

He shook his head and it was her turn to run her fingers through his hair, push it back from his eyes so she could read the truth.

"No, I just feared I might do this if we were ever alone again."

She let him kiss her, felt his hands running over her skin, stroking her breasts, then pushing at the waist of her pantalettes. She felt a moment of panic, pushed against his chest as he dipped his head toward her breasts.

"You told them you were going to do this, if what, if they didn't permit us to marry?"

He caught her hand, raised her arms above her head as he bent to suckle one, then the other breast. Her moan vibrated between them. Without releasing her, he removed her last scrap of clothing.

"Why do you think they were so eager to chaperone us, find work to keep us busy?" He raised up so the covers formed a tent above them and he could look at her.

Charlotte pursed her mouth, thought about arguing some more, than his hand began to move, working its way down her body and she closed her eyes and whispered a prayer of thanks.

CHAPTER FORTY-NINE

It was the end of March, when Charlotte realized she was pregnant. She was visiting Jeanne Sykes in the store. The little woman complained of her breasts aching, then laughed, saying, "of course, it's all part of carrying a baby." Charlotte realized what the aching in her own breasts meant. All evening she worried about whether she should tell Delmar, but later, after they lay spooned together in the small bed he had asked how she was feeling.

Charlotte rolled her head toward him and waited. "I'm fine." But he had leaned forward, kissed her bare shoulder and cupped her breasts in his hands. "You seem to be growing, darling."

Charlotte blushed, managed to remove his hands so she could turn and look directly into his laughing blue eyes. Her reward was his hand caressing her stomach as he whispered. "It makes me very happy, to know that we'll have a child to show for all our loving."

"I know, but I'm not sure what will happen when Dovie and the school board members find out. Before, I didn't have to argue. I could show them that being married didn't affect my ability to teach. But being with child is even farther from the spinster schoolmarm they hired. And you heard Jasper Sykes say, 'he thought they should hire a man all along.'"

"You've changed his mind. You should hear him brag about what a great job you do. We'll just wait until they can tell about the baby for themselves. Now that you travel and play music with me nearly every weekend, they can't accuse you of not mingling with the parents and your students enough." He kissed her, taking his time to distract her.

As she was falling asleep, she wondered if it might be nice to have an excuse not to go along to every picnic or dance, to play music. Although she expected he would, Delmar never lost patience with trying to teach her to play music with him. The first time they had gone together to play for people, the men had all wanted to dance with her.

So he had given her a tambourine and the men had stopped asking. She had stood smiling at her new husband, keeping time beside him.

She had learned to play one instrument, the dulcimer, enough to use on her own. She played it sitting down, with it lying flat on her table or lap, another thing that made her like it. With the tambourine, she'd had to stand all evening. Charlotte appreciated being able to play it at school at the end of the class to carry the tune for the songs. It gave her an excuse not to sing, and after Philomena dropped out, she had needed one.

For the faster songs, the ones the mountain people all seemed to love the best, he had tried to talk her into playing the guitar or violin. She hadn't mastered the violin, but at least when he played the fast runs, she could play harmony to fill in the sound around him. The guitar just felt too large in her hands and against her breasts. They had both given up on her playing it.

<><><>

It was Jasper Sykes, who noticed her secret first. Of course with his loud voice and lack of tact, he had announced it in the store one day when she was standing beside his wife. Although Jeanne was two months further along, Charlotte was showing almost as much.

The school board meeting was called for the next Thursday and everyone came, not just the board members. Charlotte hoped some of the people might be there to support her, but there was no way to predict what any of them might say. Surprisingly, Charlotte wasn't afraid this time, with Delmar seated beside her to offer his support.

Living here, they had her small teaching salary, Delmar had his small fees to play and sing. Instead of cash, it was usually food, or another tree that would keep him busy working all week. Charlotte knew if she lost this job, they would still be fine. Delmar wasn't just hard working and gifted, he was one of the smartest men alive. She knew he would be able to provide for them both, then, she smiled and rested a hand over her stomach. Provide for all three of them.

As though he could hear what she was thinking, he whispered. "You know my father wants me to join the

Monroe law offices in Richmond. You did know you married a lawyer?" She shook her head, made a face at him as people continued to arrive behind them to fill the empty benches. "You'd never have to want for anything, it's a busy practice."

Charlotte sat there, imagining being married to a rich lawyer. Her eyes widened as she whispered. "Your father, is James Monroe the new Virginia Senator. I read some of his campaign speeches?"

"William Delmar Monroe, at your service, Mrs. Monroe."

Her eyes grew even wider and Delmar tried not to laugh. He merely nodded as she made the connection to his famous relative. "No, my grandfather was a brother to him, not the President."

The room was crowded and the few who lived in town were trying to talk to their neighbors. It took several minutes for Reverend Watkin to get the crowd quiet. Charlotte's ears grew pink when she heard the preacher inform everyone gathered there, that they had called the meeting to see what they should do about the Schoolmarm's delicate condition.

When Daniel heard the reason he hooted loudly. "I done warned them about that mistletoe." The crowd laughed again and it took several minutes for the reverend to restore order.

"We'll listen to Mizz Charlotte first," he announced, disgusted with trying to talk over the crowd.

Charlotte looked at her husband, let him squeeze her hand. "Do you need me to stand up with you?" he asked.

Charlotte shook her head, her eyes sparkling as she walked up to replace the reverend at her desk. She meant to start with an angry speech about the unfairness of the world, treating a woman so differently than a man, the same arguments she had used on her father before. Sighing, she looked around at all the familiar faces, the friends who had become like family to her.

"Yes, I am a woman, and yes, we have been blessed with the promise of a child." There was a mixed reaction among the crowd and she wished that more of the parents of her students were here, fewer of the other town members. "I don't see why any of this should matter. You've all had mothers or are mothers. My brain and education will not disappear because I am in the family way. Once our son or daughter is born, I should be able to resume teaching with only the shortest of delays."

There was so much spirited discussion that Charlotte raised her own bookend and began tapping with it to gain their silence. Looking very sad she looked from face to face. "I love Kyles Ford, this school, my children, and teaching here. This beautiful place, with its quiet beauty, the big forests and tall mountains, is all that I could ever wish for in a home, for a place to build and raise a family." This time there were no loud voices, only hushed silence as she stood there with tears glistening in her eyes. "I think Delmar feels the same way," she held a hand out to him and he rose and took it.

"This feels like home to me. You've welcomed us both with open arms, let us settle in to become mountain people like yourself. We hope you'll consider that, before you make your decision," Delmar said.

Charlotte didn't turn into his arms to hide. Instead she brushed her tears away and cleared her throat before stepping in front of him to say. "Whatever you decide, I want to thank you for giving me this opportunity. I will respect your decision."

She tugged at Delmar's hand and he let her lead him out of the school, leaving the noisy crowd inside arguing with each other.

Standing outside in the cold night air, she finally let him pull her into his arms to wrap her inside his coat. He whispered, "I'm also a man of property. Sparrow Walk isn't a prosperous plantation, but it does have over four hundred acres of arable land."

She pushed at him, to get enough room to lean back and stare up at him in annoyance. "You let me think you were an impoverished musician and I would have to work to support you, when you're the son of a Senator, a lawyer, and a Virginia Plantation owner."

"And a distant relative of a president. If our child is a son, like every other male in America, he could someday be President."

She rolled her eyes at him and he brought his mouth down over hers. When the kiss ended, she merely leaned into his warm embrace. "Is that what you want, to practice law and run a plantation?"

Delmar shook his head, then moved so his cheek was pressed against the top of her head. "What I want, is what

I've had this year with you. I want to make instruments and play them. Running a plantation requires labor, slave labor." He shuddered. "My Great Uncle had all that land, but he wouldn't keep a slave. I was thinking when everything is repaired, I will sell it. This summer, while you're not teaching, I thought we could go to Sparrow Walk and see about selling it."

"But slavery was abolished," she protested.

"The import of slaves was abolished. They were freed in five states up north, but none in the south. Tennessee, in particular, is already talking about impressing blacks, returning them to their rightful slave owners. You said you read Father's speeches, you know where he stands on the issue. The Tidewater land is all in plantations. I don't believe in profiting from another man's sweat."

The door opened on the little school and the light revealed them in tight embrace. Mizz Goins held the door, but didn't tease the couple as they were invited back inside.

Later, on the long quiet walk home, Charlotte was surprised when she didn't cry. All five board members had stood at the front of the room, but Jasper Sykes had made the announcement. "The Board has decided that you may finish out the school year. We will let you know our final decision after the graduation ceremony."

Charlotte hadn't needed him to say that there was almost no chance. It wasn't as though she was to blame. She had learned how to manage her class and it had been a good school year for her and her students. These fools were going to lose a good teacher.

CHAPTER FIFTY

June 1st, 1852

Delmar joined her and all the parents for the graduation celebration at the church. Only ten students remained of her original thirteen, all to be promoted to the next grade. Philomena was gone, after the girl had given Charlotte more trouble than both the Daniel boys. She had started to complain at all the rules, and declared "she was too old for all this school nonsense."

Charlotte was unwilling to paddle a girl, but had no intention of allowing one student to disrupt learning for everyone else. Philly had been sent home, with a note for her mother. Instead, the girl walked up the ridge to capture Zeke Tate's attention.

When Charlotte discussed the problems the girl had given her earlier in the week with her mother at church, the parents had learned exactly what the girl and the boy had been doing.

Although, it was Charlotte's first official shotgun wedding, she had laughed with Delmar about how close they had come to having one of their own.

As the school term came closer to an end, she spent alternate evenings arguing with herself, then explaining to Delmar why she wanted to return to teach next year, and then why she did not.

Delmar had written home, explaining his decision to sell Sparrow Walk. He had insisted that Delmar allow him to try to find the right owner and get him a better price. His father had also written to remind him there was a position open for him in the Monroe Law Offices in Richmond. Now that he was a United States Senator, James would need his brother's help.

Delmar and Charlotte both knew it was a chance to never know, want or hunger, a secure and respected job by virtue of his name alone. But Delmar wasn't sure he could hold his tongue, if he had to work with James and Father, who had both cast their fate with the Plantation owners who wanted slavery.

Even though Charlotte said the decision didn't matter, when the school board met and didn't offer her a contract she had been livid. Jasper Sykes and Davis Daniel both thought a married woman didn't belong in the classroom after all. The others, particularly the Watkins, thought a married teacher was fine, but not a new mother. What on earth would she do with the child during school hours? All the board members had finally agreed.

Worse, the school board had ordered a new school teacher from the honorable Reverend Benjamin Stewart, no less. After all, the mission was offering another to provide a supplement again next year, and they had already met the other requirements.

The learned professor agreed, that teaching in a one-room school was not the position for a wife and mother. He had recommended someone, and they had the young man under contract already when they met to tell Charlotte she would not be rehired.

After Charlotte had finally calmed down enough, she wrote her father a scathing letter for his betrayal. He had written her a loving letter in return, urging her to return to Boston. Because of her, the Seminary had met and agreed to accept female students to train as elementary school teachers. He had recommended that Charlotte would be excellent as an assistant professor to help with the difficulties a co-ed campus might pose, and the rest had readily concurred. Like Delmar's father, he was offering her a job.

Mama had scribbled a note. "If and when she had a family, living in Boston, her Mama and sisters could help with the baby while she worked."

Delmar pointed out that there were law offices there, and both their fathers had contacts that could help him get an opening. Also, there were many venues where he could play his music, and not for potatoes or trees.

With the wagon loaded, and the old ox cart as well, with all the wood, her belongings, his instruments, and the many gifts from parents and students, they were finally on their way back. Although she wondered if life would ever seem as simple or any place as beautiful as Tennessee.

On moving day, they were sure of only two things. They were moving to Sparrow Walk for the summer, before making a decision on keeping or getting rid of the plantation. More importantly, they planned to go by way of Sneedville and up to Big Haley's place to visit Cicely. Charlotte wanted to take her home with them if she was willing. Delmar's fears had become her own, and she didn't want to leave the girl where her freedom might be in jeopardy.

Traveling out of the beautiful mountains was a sweet sadness The world seemed unsettled outside this peaceful little place. Facing an uncertain future could not dampen either of their enthusiasm. They had each other. In a few months, they would have a child. Life could hardly seem more beautiful as they faced whatever awaited them, together.

THE END

ABOUT THE AUTHOR

J. R. Biery is a retired high school teacher of math and science. She has written for many years and is now publishing some of her recent work on Amazon.

Love to hear from readers at biery35@gmail.com

To learn about new writing projects and more about the author, you can follow her at:

Silver Dreamer blog at www.jrbiery.wordpress.com,

Twitter https://twitter.com/BieryjJanet

Pinterest at www.pinterest.com/bieryj, and on

Facebook at https://www.facebook.com/JRBiery-books-910322069020654/

DEAR READER

I hope you enjoy reading this book as much as I enjoyed writing it. If you find errors or things that I should change, please send me suggestions at biery35@gmail.com

If you like it and are so inclined, I would appreciate a kind review at http://amzn.to/2ci1n7L

CURRENT WORK ON AMAZON

Western Wives Series

The Milch Bride,

http://www.amazon.com/dp/B00JC6DOLK

From Darkness to Glory,

http://www.amazon.com/dp/B00LG1ZPMK

Valley of Shadows,

http://www.amazon.com/dp/B00RPTXMU4

Bright Morning Star,

http://www.amazon.com/dp/B0122DD7LQ

Mountain Wives Series

Wildwood Flowers,

http://www.amazon.com/dp/B01AE3AM3W

Widow Mouse,

http://www.amazon.com/dp/B01FP5TUF0

Wild Violets,

http://www.amazon.com/dp/B01LW6CDA1

Myths Retold Series

Glitter of Magic,

http://www.amazon.com/dp/B00TE9P6DO

The Mermaid's Gift,

http://www.amazon.com/dp/B00W6FCTME

The First Christmas Elf,

http://www.amazon.com/dp/B0193G42XC

Mysteries

Potter's Field,

http://www.amazon.com/dp/B00KH7Q8C0

Killing the Darlings,

http://www.amazon.com/dp/B00IRRMO2A

Edge of Night,

http://www.amazon.com/dp/B00J0LLQC6

Other Novels

He's My Baby Now,

http://www.amazon.com/dp/B00N1X6ZFW

Will Henry,

http://www.amazon.com/dp/B00K5POM0O

Chimera Pass,

http://www.amazon.com/dp/B00KALJYRY

Short Stories and Novellas

Ghost Warrior I,

http://www.amazon.com/dp/B013XHSZX0

Ghost Warrior II,

http://www.amazon.com/dp/B013Y12PCC

Happy Girl,

http://www.amazon.com/dp/B00MHHXMEA

The Revenooer,

http://www.amazon.com/dp/B00U25K5BW

High Desert Danger,

http://www.amazon.com/dp/B0137R82PW

Voodoo-I Do; Bride of a Zombie,

http://www.amazon.com/dp/B014OJVCKY

Made in the USA
Las Vegas, NV
06 March 2023

68653913R00262